John Keats was born in October 1795, [...] stable keeper. He was educated privately at the Reverend John Clarke's school in Enfield. His father died in 1804, his mother six years later, and her death affected Keats greatly. In that same year, 1810, he became a medical student, although he had no particular enthusiasm for the profession. Not long after this, Keats was introduced to the work of Spenser and discovered an awareness not only of the poetry of others but also of the poetry in himself. His early efforts at writing were shyly conceived, but in 1816 he announced to his guardian that he intended to devote his life to literature, and he was taken under the wing of the poet and journalist Henry Leigh Hunt.

In 1817 his first volume of poetry was published, which included 'Sleep and Beauty', and in 1818 'Endymion' appeared, which was attacked by the Tory *Blackwood's Magazine* and the *Quarterly Review*. At this time another personal tragedy struck, the death of his brother Tom. Towards the end of 1818 Keats fell in love with Fanny Brawne, whom he was never to marry. Under the emotional strain of this unhappy and tormenting love affair he produced some of his greatest works – 'Isabella; or the Pot of Basil', 'The Eve of Saint Agnes' and 'La Belle Dame Sans Merci', which were all written in 1820. However, it has been said that his odes represent the peak of his achievement, and they include 'Ode to a Nightingale', 'Ode on a Grecian Urn' and 'Ode to Autumn'. His final work was a rewritten version of an earlier poem, 'Hyperion'.

By 1820 the tuberculosis that had already killed his mother and brother was unmistakable, and Keats died in Rome a year later.

Keats

Poems

Selected by J.E. Morpurgo

PENGUIN BOOKS

Penguin Books Ltd, Harmondsworth, Middlesex, England
Viking Penguin Inc., 40 West 23rd Street, New York, New York 10010, U.S.A.
Penguin Books Australia Ltd, Ringwood, Victoria, Australia
Penguin Books Canada Ltd, 2801 John Street, Markham, Ontario, Canada L3R 1B4
Penguin Books (N.Z.) Ltd, 182–190 Wairau Road, Auckland 10, New Zealand

This selection first published 1953
Reprinted 1985

Made and printed in Great Britain by
Cox and Wyman Ltd, Reading

Typeset in Monotype Fournier
Introduction reset by Merrion Letters, London

CONTENTS

Selections from *Lamia, Isabella, The Eve of St Agnes, and Other Poems*

Selections from *Posthumous and Fugitive Poems*

CONTENTS

7

CONTENTS

INTRODUCTION

JOHN KEATS was born in London in October 1795, the eldest son of the head ostler of a London livery stable, who had the good fortune to marry his employer's daughter. His early childhood was passed comfortably enough; his father and mother were happy, sensible people, devoted to each other and to their children and affluent enough to provide John Keats with a sound education at the Reverend John Clarke's school in Enfield. Even his father's death in 1804 and his mother's unfortunate choice of one William Rawlings as successor to her first husband in both his marital and business capacity does not appear to have strained unduly the ease of the Keats family life, and it was not until his mother was taken ill with chronic rheumatism that Keats, who was to experience so much misery in his short life, first sensed the meaning of tragedy. 'He sat up whole nights with her in a great chair, would suffer nobody to give her medicine, or even cook her food, but himself, and read novels to her in her intervals of ease.' His mother's rheumatism turned to consumption, and her death in February 1810 affected her eldest son violently. 'He gave way to such impassioned and prolonged grief (hiding himself in a nook under the master's desk) as awakened the liveliest pity and sympathy in all who saw him.'

In that same year John Keats became a medical student. He was apprenticed to an Edmonton surgeon and began studies which would eventually take him into the practice of medicine; studies which seem to have aroused in him neither great enthusiasm nor great antipathy, but which were later to have considerable influence on his own career in that they sharpened in him the knowledge of inescapable doom.

9

Not long after, and with far more enthusiasm, he settled to other studies. The Reverend John Clarke's son, Cowden Clarke, introduced him to Spenser, reading him the 'Epithalamion' in the afternoon and lending him *The Fairie Queene* the same evening; Spenser introduced him to the excitements of poetry. And the boy, who had hitherto been famous among his school-fellows principally for his cheerfulness and pugnacity, became conscious not only of poetry in others, but of poetry in himself. His early efforts at creation were shyly conceived, and it was not until 1815 that he first showed any of his neophyte attempts to his friends, even to Cowden Clarke. As yet he had not thought of accepting poetry as a vocation, and in 1816 he passed his examination as a licentiate at Apothecary Hall, in the same year becoming a dresser at Guy's Hospital. But in the winter of 1816 Keats announced to his guardian that he intended to devote his life to literature.

The inspiration of Keats's early work was Elizabethan, but the model eighteenth-century, and Romantic energies released in an Augustan voice carry no great power, yet Keats's immature efforts brought him first to the notice and then to the acquaintance of the leaders of the Romantic revolution, and above all into touch with the editor-in-chief to the later Romantics, James Henry Leigh Hunt.

Hunt was worse than Gray as a model for a young man's attempts at poetry, but he was the finest literary patron in an age that had found a new manner of patronage. He had no money for himself and certainly none for the encouragement of young genius; most of his life he sought without success for some sinecure that could help him keep his own large family; but though neither wealth nor comfort were his to give, he had some control over the public eye and over the friendship of authors. In his time 'he "discovered" Shelley and Keats, encouraged

Byron (until Byron offended him and he grew distasteful to Byron), gave Lamb his first major opportunities in criticism, won recognition for Morley and befriended Carlyle. It was in Hunt's *Examiner* that Keats made his first public appearance as a poet – on 5 May 1816, with the sonnet, 'O Solitude! if I must with thee dwell' (p.46) – and it was in Hunt's *Examiner* in an essay by the editor that Keats first received critical attention – on 1 December 1816 in the essay on 'Young Poets'.

Through Hunt and through Hunt's essay Keats soon became the companion in literary conversation of Hunt himself and of the two other poets, Shelley and J. H. Reynolds, who had been joined with Keats in Hunt's essay as 'these young aspirants . . . who promise to help the new school to revive Nature and to put a spirit of youth in everything'.

Small wonder, then, that when Keats published, in March 1817, his first collection of poems with the publishing house of Charles and James Ollier he dedicated the work to Leigh Hunt.

The *Poems* of 1817 made but small impression, even on a public which was more receptive to poetry than is ours today. It cannot be argued that here genius was allowed to shout into the wind of disregard, for only the omniscience of after-know-ledge can pick from these pages of immature, confused, and hyper-sensitive poetical expressions the signs of growing genius and the few poems of genius already come to maturity – 'On First Looking into Chapman's Homer' (p.48), 'Keen fitful gusts are whisp'ring here and there . . .' (p.47), and 'To one who has been long in city pent' (p.47). But with this publication Keats became a poet dedicated – and soon a professional writer. Most men of imagination and ability dream of writing a book, a few work out their dream, and fewer still persuade a publisher to give it printed reality, but no man is a professional writer until he has thought up a second book; and given it substance.

This Keats proceeded to do during 1817. The Olliers had soon tired of their generosity to the young poet and agreed too easily with the customary complaint of authors, their relatives and friends, that the publishers were not really behind his work, but another publisher, John Taylor, of Taylor and Hessey, was ready to state that 'I cannot think he will fail to become a great Poet', and was ready to back his confidence with advice, encouragement, and even money.

So Keats went off to the Isle of Wight, to Margate, to Canterbury, and eventually back to Hampstead; and all the while he worked on 'Endymion'. Poetry had become the centre of his existence. He had other worries: his brother Tom was seriously ill, his brother George was thinking of emigrating to America, their family fortune had been dissipated by a careless guardian; but above all trials stood his care for poetry.

'I find I cannot do without poetry,' he wrote to Reynolds— 'without eternal poetry; half the day will not do—the whole of it. I began with a little, but habit has made me a leviathan . . .'

And after a year in which he produced many other short poems Keats finished the four books of 'Endymion'.

All that should be said to the poem's discredit was said by the poet in his preface:

Knowing within myself the manner in which this Poem has been produced, it is not without a feeling of regret that I make it public.

What manner I mean, will be quite clear to the reader, who must soon perceive great inexperience, immaturity, and every error denoting a feverish attempt, rather than a deed accomplished. The first two books, and indeed the last two, I feel sensible are not of such completion as to warrant their passing the press; nor should they if I thought a year's castigation would do them any good;—it will not: the foundations are too sandy. It is just that this youngster should die away: a sad thought for me, if I had not some hope that while it is dwindling I may be plotting, and fitting myself for verses fit to live.

This may be speaking too presumptiously, and may deserve a punishment: but no feeling man will be forward to inflict it: he will leave me alone, with the conviction that there is not a fiercer hell than the failure in a great object. This is not written with the least atom of purpose to forestall criticisms of course, but from the desire I have to conciliate men who are competent to look, and who do look with a zealous eye, to the honour of English literature.

The imagination of a boy is healthy, and the mature imagination of a man is healthy; but there is a space of life between, in which the soul is in a ferment, the character undecided, the way of life uncertain, the ambition thick-sighted: thence proceeds mawkishness, and all the thousand bitters which those men I speak of must necessarily taste in going over the following pages.

Both intellectually and technically, 'Endymion' is a young man's poem. Only youth could be so arrogant as to attempt to rewrite Greek myth (in which the author was completely unschooled) with the aid of two Elizabethan mentors (Fletcher and Drayton), a dictionary of mythology, and a roving sense of beauty. But, unlike Keats's earlier work ,'Endymion' is also a poet's poem. Over-emphasis, lack of emphasis, reiteration, rhythmic and even grammatical flaws cannot alter the fact that here is a generous offering of the gifts of poetry – lyricism, narrative, allegory, quotability – almost everything except discipline. It is, as Keats himself describes it, 'a little region to wander in' in which 'the reader may pick and choose'.

And this time there was no doubt that the public was roused to take notice of the poem and of the poet, though the manner of their attention was hardly what Keats would have wanted. Wiser than Keats to the meanness of journalism, both Hunt and Shelley had advised against publication, for both realized that jealous reviewers could easily hide the felicities of 'Endymion' behind much abuse of the infelicities. But not even Hunt and Shelley expected the violence that was poured out against Keats by *Blackwood's* and the *Quarterly Review*. History turned the laugh against his enemies; their judgements, not only about Keats, but also about Shelley, Lamb, Bryon, and Hazlitt, have proved so ludicrously wrong; and it was the laugh of history which the Cockney-hating *Quarterly* could never forgive. As late as 1848 it was still snarling resentfully – this time at Keats's biographer Monckton Milnes for his 'worship of such baby-idols as Mr John Keats and Mr Alfred Tennyson'. But in 1818 all Keats's friends were excited by the unscrupulousness and the cruelty of the attack, for even in that age of literary bitterness it was rare for one writer to descend so low as to write of another 'go back to the shop, Mr John, stick to plasters, pills, ointment boxes, &c'.

For a moment even Keats was convinced that if such was the treatment meted out by critic to poet he would never again attempt poetry, but, contrary to the accepted myth, Keats was not broken by the blows. While his friends still raged on his behalf, Keats shrugged his shoulders: 'He does not seem to care at all about Blackwood, he thinks it so poorly done', wrote Hessey, and Keats, with superb confidence in his own future, hardly bothered to thank his champions; instead he reiterated his conviction, 'I think I shall be among the English poets after my death.'

Far greater troubles than the vindictiveness of critics were pressing upon Keats. Left lonely when his brother George finally emigrated to America, he was now left desolate at the end of 1818 by the death of his brother Tom. Yet even his misery preserved him and seemed to drive him on to complete certainty in his vocation: 'I am obliged to write and plunge into abstract images to ease myself of his countenance, his voice and his feebleness ...'

In this mood he wrote 'only a little now and then: but nothing to speak of–being discontented and as it were moulting', but that little shows so much progress over his earlier work that it would appear as if, in his loneliness, he had finally achieved poetic independence. It was at this time that he shook off the limping influences that he had once accepted as his guide, and rose above his juvenile lack of virtuosity and the comparative weakness of his intellectual training. Before this Keats was ready to acknowledge and accept any mould for the work he longed to produce: Spenser, Byron, Chatterton, Leigh Hunt, the good and the bad, were all equally his masters; now he had learnt that to follow is not to imitate and his own fiercely original mind was ready to take on the task of leadership. John Keats, Apprentice to Poetry, had become John Keats, Poet.

'Hyperion' was his next work, a poem which was never completed, and which perhaps is most complete in its unfinished state. Eventually Keats surrendered to the difficulty of finishing the poem saying that 'there were too many Miltonic inversions in it' and that he wished to give himself up to other sensations, but long before this he had found a consolation that took him away from his grief and from the hard discipline of poetry. Towards the end of 1818 he met and fell in love with Fanny Brawne, whom he was never able to marry.

The history of the relationship between Keats and Fanny has been much handled by historians, most of whom have come back to agreeing with his own first impression that Fanny was 'beautiful and elegant, graceful, silly, fashionable and strange'. Certainly Fanny was not wise to the genius that courted her, but such failure can hardly be marked to her eternal discredit. He loved her intemperately, and had it not been that financial difficulties were plaguing him and that his own health was breaking down, Fanny's warmth and gaiety might have found response in the cheerfulness which was still part of the character of Keats. (His humorous verse is very much part of Keats's contribution to English poetry, and very much the product of his lightheartedness.)

Whatever his relations with Fanny, the power of his poetry was now full-grown; the first and second versions of 'Hyperion', 'The Eve of St Agnes', 'La Belle Dame Sans Merci', and 'Lamia', among the finest products of his or any other pen, all belong to this period of frustration, financial despair, and increasing sickness.

But his struggle with calamity was the cause of calamity more final than anything acquiescence in his troubles might have wrought: his body collapsed under the pressures on his mind and his spirit. Charles Brown, his most intimate friend, described, in terms that are pathetic even in their detailed practicality, the scene which was in reality the last in the true life of Keats:

One night February 3, 1820 at eleven o'clock, he came into the house in a state that looked like fierce intoxication. Such a state in him, I knew, was impossible; it therefore was the more fearful. I asked hurriedly, 'What is the matter? you are fevered?' 'Yes, yes,' he answered, 'I was on the outside of the stage this bitter day till I was severely chilled,—but now I don't feel it. Fevered! —of course, a little.' He mildly and instantly yielded, a property in his nature towards any friend, to my request that he should go to bed. I followed with the best immediate remedy in my power. I entered his chamber as he leapt into bed. On entering the cold sheets, before his head was on the pillow, he slightly coughed, and I heard him say, – 'That is blood from my mouth.' I went towards him; he was examining a single drop of blood upon the sheet. 'Bring me the candle, Brown, and let me see this blood.' After regarding it steadfastly, he looked up in my face, with a calmness of countenance that I can never forget, and said, – 'I know the colour of that blood;–it is arterial blood;–I cannot be deceived in that colour;–that drop of blood is my death-warrant; – I must die.'

In the time that was left to him he was as a man acting the part of his own executor, living what he described bitterly as 'a post-humous life'. His third book *Lamia, Isabella, The Eve of St Agnes and Other Poems* – the second from Taylor and Hessey – appeared in the summer of 1820 and had 'good success among literary people'. Here, with the longer poems are gathered 'Ode to a Nightingale', 'To Fancy', 'Ode on a Grecian Urn', 'To Autumn', 'Lines on the Mermaid Tavern' and an ode which begins 'Bards of Passion and of Mirth'. This collection contained much of Keats's greatest work. Chronologically, 'Isabella' follows 'Endymion', and its bright but stark balladic language and tone pave the way for the mature achievement of 'The Eve of St Agnes', a poem which brilliantly displays the more con-ventional characteristics of Romanticism that automatically associate Keats with the Romantic movement. In Spenserian stanzas it binds together sparkling heraldic symbols of love and cold threatening symbols of hostility to form a rich and clear-cut version of medievalism. 'La Belle Dame Sans Merci' is nightmarish in its apparent simplicity and chilling suggestiveness and 'Lamia' contains passages of immense power. But it is Keats's odes that represent the peak of his achievement. In these the impression of his senses responding to experience with a painful intensity is at its most powerful, and provides the root of his contradictory feelings and aspirations. In 'Ode to a Night-ingale' and 'Ode on a Grecian Urn' Keats explores the relation-ship between the static but immortal lifelessness of art and the vital but condemned experiences of life. Keats himself longs for death as an escape from decay, but embraces life with all his senses. The everlasting beauty of the figures on the urn is compelling, but experience is reduced to a cold, unfulfilled instant. 'To Autumn' is a less complex poem, creating a more optimistic mood out of a sympathetic identification with season and landscape. In these odes Keats's closely woven sensuous imagery, the deeply felt, precise and suggestive language and the flowing but measured rhythms combine to produce unforgettable poetry with great impact.

But the comparative success of the 1820 collection could no longer stir the poet. Even when Francis Jeffrey came out in the *Edinburgh Review* with a kindly if patronizing notice of both the 'Endymion' and the 'Lamia' volume, Keats had no strength left with which to resent the patronage or with which to appreciate the kindliness.

They manifestly require [wrote Jeffrey of the two books] all the indulgence that can be claimed for a first attempt; but we think it no less plain that they deserve it: for they are flushed all over with the rich lights of fancy . . . Mr Keats has unquestionably a very beautiful imagination, a perfect ear for harmony, and a great familiarity with the finest diction of English poetry; but he must learn not to misuse or misapply these advantages; and neither to waste the good gifts of Nature and study on intractable themes, nor to luxuriate too recklessly on such as are more suitable.

In charity to Jeffrey it must be assumed that much of his adverse criticism was levelled at 'Endymion', and was occasioned in part by the suspicion with which one generation inevitably regards the enthusiasms and rebellions of the next, for in the *Poems of 1820* Keats had already turned from the temptation to luxuriate and had outstripped by far the necessity to accept the indulgence due to a novice, but the irony of Jeffrey's comments was at least unintentional: he did not know that of the 'good gifts of Nature', only the kindliness of friends was left to Keats.

The Hunts, the Brawnes, his publishers John Taylor and James Hessey, all tried to help him. Shelley offered him hospitality in Italy, and though Keats refused the offer (he seems to have been strangely intractable to Shelley's charm), he was eventually persuaded to exchange the English winter for Italy's more kindly climate, and in September 1820, with the painter Joseph Severn as his companion, he left for Rome.

On 23 February 1821, John Keats died, and a few days later was buried in the English Cemetery in Rome.

J. E. MORPURGO

SELECTIONS FROM

Poems

PUBLISHED IN

1817

Dedication

TO LEIGH HUNT, ESQ.

GLORY and Loveliness have pass'd away;
   For if we wander out in early morn,
      No wreathed incense do we see upborne
Into the east to meet the smiling day:
No crowd of nymphs soft voic'd and young, and gay,
      In woven baskets bringing ears of corn,
      Roses, and pinks, and violets, to adorn
The shrine of Flora in her early May.
But there are left delights as high as these,
      And I shall ever bless my destiny,
That in a time, when under pleasant trees
      Pan is no longer sought, I feel a free,
A leafy luxury, seeing I could please,
      With these poor offerings, a man like thee.

Places of nestling green for poets made.
Story of Rimini.

I STOOD tip-toe upon a little hill,
The air was cooling, and so very still,
That the sweet buds which with a modest pride
Pull droopingly, in slanting curve aside,
Their scantly-leav'd, and finely tapering stems,
Had not yet lost their starry diadems
Caught from the early sobbing of the morn.
The clouds were pure and white as flocks new shorn,
And fresh from the clear brook; sweetly they slept
On the blue fields of heaven, and then there crept
A little noiseless noise among the leaves,
Born of the very sigh that silence heaves:
For not the faintest motion could be seen
Of all the shades that slanted o'er the green.
There was wide wand'ring for the greediest eye,
To peer about upon variety;
Far round the horizon's crystal air to skim,
And trace the dwindled edgings of its brim;
To picture out the quaint and curious bending
Of a fresh woodland alley, never-ending:
Or by the bowery clefts, and leafy shelves,
Guess where the jaunty streams refresh themselves.
I gazed awhile, and felt as light, and free
As though the fanning wings of Mercury
Had play'd upon my heels: I was light-hearted,
And many pleasures to my vision started;
So I straightway began to pluck a posey
Of luxuries bright, milky, soft and rosy.

A bush of May flowers with the bees about them;
Ah, sure no tasteful nook could be without them;

24

And let a lush laburnum oversweep them,
And let long grass grow round the roots to keep them
Moist, cool, and green; and shade the violets,
That they may bind the moss in leafy nets.

A filbert hedge with wildbriar overtwined,
And clumps of woodbine taking the soft wind
Upon their summer thrones; there too should be
The frequent chequer of a youngling tree,
That with a score of light green brethren shoots
From the quaint mossiness of aged roots:
Round which is heard a spring-head of clear waters
Babbling so wildly of its lovely daughters,
The spreading blue-bells: it may haply mourn
That such fair clusters should be rudely torn
From their fresh beds, and scattered thoughtlessly
By infant hands, left on the path to die.

Open afresh your round of starry folds,
Ye ardent marigolds!
Dry up the moisture from your golden lids,
For great Apollo bids
That in these days your praises should be sung
On many harps, which he has lately strung;
And when again your dewiness he kisses,
Tell him, I have you in my world of blisses:
So haply when I rove in some far vale,
His mighty voice may come upon the gale.

Here are sweet peas, on tiptoe for a flight:
With wings of gentle flush o'er delicate white,
And taper fingers catching at all things,
To bind them all about with tiny rings.

Linger awhile upon some bending planks
That lean against a streamlet's rushy banks,
And watch intently Nature's gentle doings:
They will be found softer than ring-doves' cooings.
How silent comes the water round that bend;
Not the minutest whisper does it send
To the o'erhanging sallows: blades of grass
Slowly across the chequer'd shadows pass.
Why, you might read two sonnets, ere they reach
To where the hurrying freshnesses aye preach
A natural sermon o'er their pebbly beds;
Where swarms of minnows show their little heads,
Staying their wavy bodies 'gainst the streams,
To taste the luxury of sunny beams
Temper'd with coolness. How they ever wrestle
With their own sweet delight, and ever nestle
Their silver bellies on the pebbly sand!
If you but scantily hold out the hand,
That very instant not one will remain;
But turn your eye, and they are there again.
The ripples seem right glad to reach those cresses,
And cool themselves among the em'rald tresses;
The while they cool themselves, they freshness give,
And moisture, that the bowery green may live:
So keeping up an interchange of favours,
Like good men in the truth of their behaviours.
Sometimes goldfinches one by one will drop
From low-hung branches; little space they stop;
But sip, and twitter, and their feathers sleek;
Then off at once, as in a wanton freak:
Or perhaps, to show their black and golden wings,
Pausing upon their yellow flutterings.
Were I in such a place, I sure should pray
That naught less sweet might call my thoughts away,

Than the soft rustle of a maiden's gown
Fanning away the dandelion's down;
Than the light music of her nimble toes
Patting against the sorrel as she goes.
How she would start, and blush, thus to be caught
Playing in all her innocence of thought.
O let me lead her gently o'er the brook,
Watch her half-smiling lips and downward look;
O let me for one moment touch her wrist;
Let me one moment to her breathing list;
And as she leaves me, may she often turn
Her fair eyes looking through her locks auburne.
What next? A tuft of evening primroses,
O'er which the mind may hover till it dozes;
O'er which it well might take a pleasant sleep,
But that 'tis ever startled by the leap
Of buds into ripe flowers; or by the flitting
Of divers moths, that aye their rest are quitting;
Or by the moon lifting her silver rim
Above a cloud, and with a gradual swim
Coming into the blue with all her light.
O Maker of sweet poets, dear delight
Of this fair world and all its gentle livers;
Spangler of clouds, halo of crystal rivers,
Mingler with leaves, and dew and tumbling streams,
Closer of lovely eyes to lovely dreams,
Lover of loneliness, and wandering,
Of upcast eye, and tender pondering!
Thee must I praise above all other glories
That smile us on to tell delightful stories.
For what has made the sage or poet write
But the fair paradise of Nature's light?
In the calm grandeur of a sober line,
We see the waving of the mountain pine;

And when a tale is beautifully staid,
We feel the safety of a hawthorn glade:
When it is moving on luxurious wings,
The soul is lost in pleasant smotherings:
Fair dewy roses brush against our faces,
And flowering laurels spring from diamond vases;
O'erhead we see the jasmine and sweetbriar,
And bloomy grapes laughing from green attire;
While at our feet, the voice of crystal bubbles
Charms us at once away from all our troubles:
So that we feel uplifted from the world,
Walking upon the white clouds wreath'd and curl'd.
So felt he, who first told how Psyche went
On the smooth wind to realms of wonderment;
What Psyche felt, and Love, when their full lips
First touch'd; what amorous and fondling nips
They gave each other's cheeks; with all their sighs,
And how they kist each other's tremulous eyes:
The silver lamp, – the ravishment, – the wonder –
The darkness, – loneliness, – the fearful thunder;
Their woes gone by, and both to heaven up-flown,
To bow for gratitude before Jove's throne.
So did he feel, who pull'd the boughs aside,
That we might look into a forest wide,
To catch a glimpse of Fauns, and Dryades
Coming with softest rustle through the trees;
And garlands woven of flowers wild, and sweet,
Upheld on ivory wrists, or sporting feet:
Telling us how fair trembling Syrinx fled
Arcadian Pan, with such a fearful dread.
Poor Nymph, – poor Pan, – how did he weep to find
Nought but a lovely sighing of the wind
Along the reedy stream; a half-heard strain,
Full of sweet desolation – balmy pain.

What first inspired a bard of old to sing
Narcissus pining o'er the untainted spring?
In some delicious ramble, he had found
A little space, with boughs all woven round;
And in the midst of all, a clearer pool
Than e'er reflected in its pleasant cool,
The blue sky here, and there, serenely peeping
Through tendril wreaths fantastically creeping.
And on the bank a lonely flower he spied,
A meek and forlorn flower, with naught of pride,
Drooping its beauty o'er the watery clearness,
To woo its own sad image into nearness:
Deaf to light Zephyrus it would not move;
But still would seem to droop, to pine, to love.
So while the poet stood in this sweet spot,
Some fainter gleamings o'er his fancy shot;
Nor was it long ere he had told the tale
Of young Narcissus, and sad Echo's bale.

Where had he been, from whose warm head out-flew
That sweetest of all songs, that ever new,
That aye refreshing, pure deliciousness,
Coming ever to bless
The wanderer by moonlight? to him bringing
Shapes from the invisible world, unearthly singing
From out the middle air, from flowery nests,
And from the pillowy silkiness that rests
Full in the speculation of the stars.
Ah! surely he had burst our mortal bars;
Into some wond'rous region he had gone,
To search for thee, divine Endymion!

He was a Poet, sure a lover too,
Who stood on Latmus' top, what time there blew

Soft breezes from the myrtle vale below;
And brought, in faintness solemn, sweet, and slow
A hymn from Dian's temple; while upswelling,
The incense went to her own starry dwelling.
But though her face was clear as infants' eyes,
Though she stood smiling o'er the sacrifice,
The Poet wept at her so piteous fate,
Wept that such beauty should be desolate:
So in fine wrath some golden sounds he won,
And gave meek Cynthia her Endymion.

Queen of the wide air; thou most lovely queen
Of all the brightness that mine eyes have seen!
As thou exceedest all things in thy shine,
So every tale, does this sweet tale of thine.
O for three words of honey, that I might
Tell but one wonder of thy bridal night!

Where distant ships do seem to show their keels,
Phoebus awhile delay'd his mighty wheels,
And turn'd to smile upon thy bashful eyes,
Ere he his unseen pomp would solemnise.
The evening weather was so bright, and clear,
That men of health were of unusual cheer;
Stepping like Homer at the trumpet's call,
Or young Apollo on the pedestal:
And lovely women were as fair and warm
As Venus looking sideways in alarm.
The breezes were ethereal, and pure,
And crept through half-closed lattices to cure
The languid sick; it cool'd their fever'd sleep,
And soothed them into slumbers full and deep.
Soon they awoke clear-eyed: nor burnt with thirsting,
Nor with hot fingers, nor with temples bursting,

And springing up, they met the wond'ring sight
Of their dear friends, nigh foolish with delight;
Who feel their arms, and breasts, and kiss and stare,
And on their placid foreheads part the hair.
Young men, and maidens at each other gaz'd
With hands held back, and motionless, amaz'd
To see the brightness in each other's eyes;
And so they stood, fill'd with a sweet surprise,
Until their tongues were loos'd in poesy.
Therefore no lover did of anguish die:
But the soft numbers, in that moment spoken,
Made silken ties, that never may be broken.
Cynthia! I cannot tell the greater blisses
That follow'd thine, and thy dear shepherd's kisses:
Was there a poet born? — But now no more,
My wand'ring spirit must no further soar. —

To Hope

WHEN by my solitary hearth I sit,
   And hateful thoughts enwrap my soul in gloom;
When no fair dreams before my 'mind's eye' flit,
   And the bare heath of life presents no bloom;
Sweet Hope! ethereal balm upon me shed,
And wave thy silver pinions o'er my head.

Whene'er I wander, at the fall of night,
   Where woven boughs shut out the moon's bright ray,
Should sad Despondency my musings fright,
   And frown, to drive fair Cheerfulness away,
Peep with the moonbeams through the leafy roof,
And keep that fiend Despondence far aloof.

Should Disappointment, parent of Despair,
   Strive for her son to seize my careless heart;
When, like a cloud, he sits upon the air,
   Preparing on his spell-bound prey to dart:
Chase him away, sweet Hope, with visage bright,
And fright him, as the morning frightens night.

Whene'er the fate of those I hold most dear
   Tells to my fearful breast a tale of sorrow,
O bright-eyed Hope, my morbid fancy cheer;
   Let me awhile thy sweetest comforts borrow:
Thy heaven-born radiance around me shed,
And wave thy silver pinions o'er my head!

Should e'er unhappy love my bosom pain,
   From cruel parents, or relentless fair;
O let me think it is not quite in vain
   To sigh out sonnets to the midnight air!
Sweet Hope! ethereal balm upon me shed,
And wave thy silver pinions o'er my head!

In the long vista of the years to roll,
    Let me not see our country's honour fade:
O let me see our land retain her soul!
    Her pride, her freedom; and not freedom's shade.
From thy bright eyes unusual brightness shed –
Beneath thy pinions canopy my head!

Let me not see the patriot's high bequest,
    Great liberty! how great in plain attire!
With the base purple of a court oppress'd,
    Bowing her head, and ready to expire:
But let me see thee stoop from Heaven on wings
That fill the skies with silver glitterings!

And as, in sparkling majesty, a star
    Gilds the bright summit of some gloomy cloud;
Brightening the half-veil'd face of heaven afar:
    So, when dark thoughts my boding spirit shroud,
Sweet Hope, celestial influence round me shed,
Waving thy silver pinions o'er my head.

Epistle to My Brother George

FULL many a dreary hour have I past,
My brain bewilder'd, and my mind o'ercast
With heaviness; in seasons when I've thought
No sphery strains by me could e'er be caught
From the blue dome, though I to dimness gaze
On the far depth where sheeted lightning plays;
Or, on the wavy grass outstretch'd supinely,
Pry 'mong the stars, to strive to think divinely:
That I should never hear Apollo's song,
Though feathery clouds were floating all along
The purple west, and, two bright streaks between,
The golden lyre itself were dimly seen:
That the still murmur of the honey bee
Would never teach a rural song to me:
That the bright glance from beauty's eyelids slanting
Would never make a lay of mine enchanting,
Or warm my breast with ardour to unfold
Some tale of love and arms in time of old.

But there are times, when those that love the bay,
Fly from all sorrowing far, far away;
A sudden glow comes on them, nought they see
In water, earth, or air, but poesy.
It has been said, dear George, and true I hold it,
(For knightly Spenser to Libertas told it,)
That when a Poet is in such a trance,
In air he sees white coursers paw, and prance,
Bestridden of gay knights, in gay apparel,
Who at each other tilt in playful quarrel,
And what we, ignorantly, sheet-lightning call,
Is the swift opening of their wide portal,
When the bright warder blows his trumpet clear,
Whose tones reach naught on earth but Poet's ear.

34

When these enchanted portals open wide,
And through the light the horsemen swiftly glide,
The Poet's eye can reach those golden halls,
And view the glory of their festivals:
Their ladies fair, that in the distance seem
Fit for the silv'ring of a seraph's dream;
Their rich brimm'd goblets, that incessant run
Like the bright spots that move about the sun;
And, when upheld, the wine from each bright jar
Pours with the lustre of a falling star.
Yet further off, are dimly seen their bowers,
Of which, no mortal eye can reach the flowers;
And 'tis right just, for well Apollo knows
'Twould make the Poet quarrel with the rose.
All that's reveal'd from that far seat of blisses,
Is, the clear fountains' interchanging kisses,
As gracefully descending, light and thin,
Like silver streaks across a dolphin's fin,
When he upswimmeth from the coral caves,
And sports with half his tail above the waves.

These wonders strange he sees, and many more,
Whose head is pregnant with poetic lore.
Should he upon an evening ramble fare
With forehead to the soothing breezes bare,
Would he naught see but the dark, silent blue,
With all its diamonds trembling through and through?
Or the coy moon, when in the waviness
Of whitest clouds she does her beauty dress,
And staidly paces higher up, and higher,
Like a sweet nun in holy-day attire?
Ah, yes! much more would start into his sight –
The revelries, and mysteries of night:

And should I ever see them, I will tell you
Such tales as needs must with amazement spell you.

    These are the living pleasures of the bard:
But richer far posterity's award.
What does he murmur with his latest breath,
While his proud eye looks through the film of death?
'What though I leave this dull and earthly mould,
Yet shall my spirit lofty converse hold
With after times. – The patriot shall feel
My stern alarum, and unsheath his steel;
Or in the senate thunder out my numbers,
To startle princes from their easy slumbers.
The sage will mingle with each moral theme
My happy thoughts sententious; he will teem
With lofty periods when my verses fire him,
And then I'll stoop from heaven to inspire him.
Lays have I left of such a dear delight
That maids will sing them on their bridal night.
Gay villagers, upon a morn of May,
When they have tired their gentle limbs with play,
And form'd a snowy circle on the grass,
And plac'd in midst of all that lovely lass
Who chosen is their queen, – with her fine head
Crowned with flowers purple, white, and red:
For there the lily and the musk-rose, sighing,
Are emblems true of hapless lovers dying:
Between her breasts, that never yet felt trouble,
A bunch of violets full blown, and double,
Serenely sleep: – she from a casket takes
A little book, – and then a joy awakes
About each youthful heart, – with stifled cries,
And rubbing of white hands, and sparkling eyes:

For she's to read a tale of hopes, and fears;
One that I foster'd in my youthful years:
The pearls, that on each glist'ning circlet sleep,
Gush ever and anon with silent creep,
Lured by the innocent dimples. To sweet rest
Shall the dear babe, upon its mother's breast,
Be lull'd with songs of mine. Fair world, adieu!
Thy dales, and hills, are fading from my view:
Swiftly I mount, upon wide spreading pinions,
Far from the narrow bounds of thy dominions.
Full joy I feel, while thus I cleave the air,
That my soft verse will charm thy daughters fair,
And warm thy sons!' Ah, my dear friend and brother,
Could I, at once, my mad ambition smother,
For tasting joys like these, sure I should be
Happier, and dearer to society.
At times, 'tis true, I've felt relief from pain
When some bright thought has darted through my brain:
Through all that day I've felt a greater pleasure
Than if I'd brought to light a hidden treasure.
As to my sonnets, though none else should heed them,
I feel delighted, still, that you should read them.
Of late, too, I have had much calm enjoyment,
Stretch'd on the grass at my best lov'd employment
Of scribbling lines for you. These things I thought
While, in my face, the freshest breeze I caught.
E'en now I'm pillow'd on a bed of flowers
That crowns a lofty clift, which proudly towers
Above the ocean waves. The stalks, and blades,
Chequer my tablet with their quivering shades.
On one side is a field of drooping oats,
Through which the poppies show their scarlet coats;
So pert and useless, that they bring to mind
The scarlet-coats that pester humankind.

And on the other side, outspread, is seen
Ocean's blue mantle streak'd with purple, and green.
Now, 'tis I see a canvass'd ship, and now
Mark the bright silver curling round her prow.
I see the lark down-dropping to his nest,
And the broad wing'd sea-gull never at rest;
For when no more he spreads his feathers free,
His breast is dancing on the restless sea.
Now I direct my eyes into the west,
Which at this moment is in sun-beams drest:
Why westward turn? 'Twas but to say adieu!
'Twas but to kiss my hand, dear George, to you!

Epistle to Charles Cowden Clarke

OFT have you seen a swan superbly frowning,
And with proud breast his own white shadow crowning;
He slants his neck beneath the waters bright
So silently, it seems a beam of light
Come from the galaxy: anon he sports, —
With outspread wings the Naiad Zephyr courts,
Or ruffles all the surface of the lake
In striving from its crystal face to take
Some diamond water drops, and them to treasure
In milky nest, and sip them off at leisure.
But not a moment can he there ensure them,
Nor to such downy rest can he allure them;
For down they rush as though they would be free,
And drop like hours into eternity.
Just like that bird am I in loss of time,
Whene'er I venture on the stream of rhyme;
With shatter'd boat, oar snapt, and canvas rent,
I slowly sail, scarce knowing my intent;
Still scooping up the water with my fingers,
In which a trembling diamond never lingers.
By this, friend Charles, you may full plainly see
Why I have never penn'd a line to thee:
Because my thoughts were never free, and clear,
And little fit to please a classic ear;
Because my wine was of too poor a savour
For one whose palate gladdens in the flavour
Of sparkling Helicon: — small good it were
To take him to a desert rude and bare,
Who had on Baiae's shore reclined at ease,
While Tasso's page was floating in a breeze
That gave soft music from Armida's bowers,
Mingled with fragrance from her rarest flowers:

Small good to one who had by Mulla's stream
Fondled the maidens with the breasts of cream;
Who had beheld Belphoebe in a brook,
And lovely Una in a leafy nook,
And Archimago leaning o'er his book:
Who had of all that's sweet tasted, and seen,
From silv'ry ripple, up to beauty's queen;
From the sequester'd haunts of gay Titania,
To the blue dwelling of divine Urania:
One who of late had ta'en sweet forest walks
With him who elegantly chats and talks –
The wrong'd Libertas, – who has told your stories
Of laurel chaplets, and Apollo's glories;
Of troops chivalrous prancing through a city,
And tearful ladies made for love and pity:
With many else which I have never known.
Thus have I thought; and days on days have flown
Slowly, or rapidly – unwilling still
For you to try my dull, unlearned quill.
Nor should I now, but that I've known you long;
That you first taught me all the sweets of song:
The grand, the sweet, the terse, the free, the fine;
What swell'd with pathos, and what right divine:
Spenserian vowels that elope with ease,
And float along like birds o'er summer seas;
Miltonian storms, and more, Miltonian tenderness;
Michael in arms, and more, meek Eve's fair slenderness.
Who read for me the sonnet swelling loudly
Up to its climax, and then dying proudly?
Who found for me the grandeur of the ode,
Growing, like Atlas, stronger from its load?
Who let me taste that more than cordial dram,
The sharp, the rapier-pointed epigram?
Show'd me that epic was of all the king,

Round, vast, and spanning all, like Saturn's ring?
You too upheld the veil from Clio's beauty,
And pointed out the patriot's stern duty;
The might of Alfred, and the shaft of Tell;
The hand of Brutus, that so grandly fell
Upon a tyrant's head. Ah! had I never seen,
Or known your kindness, what might I have been?
What my enjoyments in my youthful years,
Bereft of all that now my life endears?
And can I e'er these benefits forget?
And can I e'er repay the friendly debt?
No, doubly no; – yet should these rhymings please,
I shall roll on the grass with two-fold ease:
For I have long time been my fancy feeding
With hopes that you would one day think the reading
Of my rough verses not an hour misspent;
Should it e'er be so, what a rich content!
Some weeks have pass'd since last I saw the spires
In lucent Thames reflected: – warm desires
To see the sun o'er-peep the eastern dimness,
And morning shadows streaking into slimness
Across the lawny fields, and pebbly water;
To mark the time as they grow broad and shorter;
To feel the air that plays about the hills,
And sips its freshness from the little rills;
To see high, golden corn wave in the light
When Cynthia smiles upon a summer's night,
And peers among the cloudlets jet and white,
As though she were reclining in a bed
Of bean blossoms, in heaven freshly shed.
No sooner had I stepp'd into these pleasures,
Than I began to think of rhymes and measures:
The air that floated by me seem'd to say
'Write! thou wilt never have a better day.'

And so I did. When many lines I'd written,
Though with their grace I was not oversmitten,
Yet, as my hand was warm, I thought I'd better
Trust to my feelings, and write you a letter.
Such an attempt required an inspiration
Of a peculiar sort, – a consummation; –
Which, had I felt, these scribblings might have been
Verses from which the soul would never wean:
But many days have past since last my heart
Was warm'd luxuriously by divine Mozart;
By Arne delighted, or by Handel madden'd;
Or by the song of Erin pierc'd and sadden'd:
What time you were before the music sitting,
And the rich notes to each sensation fitting.
Since I have walk'd with you through shady lanes
That freshly terminate in open plains,
And revell'd in a chat that ceased not
When at night-fall, among your books we got:
No, nor when supper came, nor after that, –
Nor when reluctantly I took my hat;
No, nor till cordially you shook my hand
Mid-way between our homes: – your accents bland
Still sounded in my ears, when I no more
Could hear your footsteps touch the grav'lly floor.
Sometimes I lost them, and then found again;
You chang'd the footpath for the grassy plain.
In those still moments I have wish'd you joys
That well you know to honour: – 'Life's very toys,
With him,' said I, 'will take a pleasant charm;
It cannot be that aught will work him harm'.
These thoughts now come o'er me with all their might: –
Again I shake your hand, – friend Charles, good night.

A GROUP OF SONNETS

To My Brother George

MANY the wonders I this day have seen:
   The sun, when first he kist away the tears
   That fill'd the eyes of morn; – the laurell'd peers
Who from the feathery gold of evening lean; –
The ocean with its vastness, its blue green,
   Its ships, its rocks, its caves, its hopes, its fears, –
   Its voice mysterious, which whoso hears
Must think on what will be, and what has been.
E'en now, dear George, while this for you I write,
   Cynthia is from her silken curtains peeping
So scantly, that it seems her bridal night,
   And she her half-discover'd revels keeping.
But what, without the social thought of thee,
Would be the wonders of the sky and sea?

To ——

HAD I a man's fair form, then might my sighs
   Be echoed swiftly through that ivory shell
   Thine ear, and find thy gentle heart; so well
Would passion arm me for the enterprise:
But ah! I am no knight whose foeman dies;
   No cuirass glistens on my bosom's swell;
   I am no happy shepherd of the dell
Whose lips have trembled with a maiden's eyes.
Yet must I dote upon thee, – call thee sweet,
   Sweeter by far than Hybla's honied roses
   When steep'd in dew rich to intoxication.
Ah! I will taste that dew, for me 'tis meet,
   And when the moon her pallid face discloses,
   I'll gather some by spells, and incantation.

Written on the day that Mr Leigh Hunt left Prison

WHAT though, for showing truth to flatter'd state,
  Kind Hunt was shut in prison, yet has he,
  In his immortal spirit, been as free
As the sky-searching lark, and as elate.
Minion of grandeur! think you he did wait?
  Think you he naught but prison walls did see,
  Till, so unwilling, thou unturn'dst the key?
Ah, no! far happier, nobler was his fate!
In Spenser's halls he stray'd, and bowers fair,
  Culling enchanted flowers; and he flew
With daring Milton through the fields of air:
  To regions of his own his genius true
Took happy flights. Who shall his fame impair
  When thou art dead, and all thy wretched crew?

*

HOW many bards gild the lapses of time!
  A few of them have ever been the food
  Of my delighted fancy, – I could brood
Over their beauties, earthly, or sublime:
And often, when I sit me down to rhyme,
  These will in throngs before my mind intrude:
  But no confusion, no disturbance rude
Do they occasion; 'tis a pleasing chime.
So the unnumber'd sounds that evening store;
  The songs of birds – the whisp'ring of the leaves –
The voice of waters — the great bell that heaves
  With solemn sound, – and thousand others more,
That distance of recognizance bereaves,
  Make pleasing music, and not wild uproar.

To a Friend who sent me some Roses

As late I rambled in the happy fields,
    What time the skylark shakes the tremulous dew
    From his lush clover covert; – when anew
Adventurous knights take up their dinted shields:
I saw the sweetest flower wild nature yields,
    A fresh-blown musk-rose; 'twas the first that threw
    Its sweets upon the summer: graceful it grew
As is the wand that queen Titania wields.
And, as I feasted on its fragrancy,
    I thought the garden-rose it far excell'd:
But when, O Wells! thy roses came to me
    My sense with their deliciousness was spell'd:
Soft voices had they, that with tender plea
    Whisper'd of peace, and truth, and friendliness unquell'd.

To G. A. W.

[Georgiana Augusta Wylie]

Nymph of the downward smile and sidelong glance,
    In what diviner moments of the day
    Art thou most lovely? – when gone far astray
Into the labyrinths of sweet utterance,
Or when serenely wand'ring in a trance
    Of sober thought? – Or when starting away
    With careless robe to meet the morning ray
Thou spar'st the flowers in thy mazy dance?
Haply 'tis when thy ruby lips part sweetly,
    And so remain, because thou listenest:
But thou to please wert nurtured so completely
    That I can never tell what mood is best.
I shall as soon pronounce which Grace more neatly
    Trips it before Apollo than the rest.

O SOLITUDE! if I must with thee dwell,
   Let it not be among the jumbled heap
   Of murky buildings; climb with me the steep, –
Nature's observatory – whence the dell,
Its flowery slopes, its river's crystal swell,
   May seem a span; let me thy vigils keep
   'Mongst boughs pavilion'd, where the deer's swift leap
Startles the wild bee from the foxglove bell.
   But though I'll gladly trace these scenes with thee,
   Yet the sweet converse of an innocent mind,
Whose words are images of thoughts refin'd,
   Is my soul's pleasure; and it sure must be
Almost the highest bliss of human-kind,
   When to thy haunts two kindred spirits flee.

To My Brothers

SMALL, busy flames play through the fresh laid coals,
   And their faint cracklings o'er our silence creep
   Like whispers of the household gods that keep
A gentle empire o'er fraternal souls.
And while, for rhymes, I search around the poles,
   Your eyes are fix'd, as in poetic sleep,
   Upon the lore so voluble and deep,
That aye at fall of night our care condoles.
This is your birth-day Tom, and I rejoice
   That thus it passes smoothly, quietly.
Many such eves of gently whisp'ring noise
   May we together pass, and calmly try
What are this world's true joys, – ere the great voice
   From its fair face, shall bid our spirits fly.

KEEN, fitful gusts are whisp'ring here and there
   Among the bushes half leafless, and dry;
   The stars look very cold about the sky,
And I have many miles on foot to fare.
Yet feel I little of the cool bleak air,
   Or of the dead leaves rustling drearily,
   Or of those silver lamps that burn on high,
Or of the distance from home's pleasant lair:
For I am brimful of the friendliness
   That in a little cottage I have found;
Of fair-hair'd Milton's eloquent distress,
   And all his love for gentle Lycid drown'd,
Of lovely Laura in her light green dress,
   And faithful Petrarch gloriously crown'd.

*

To one who has been long in city pent,
   'Tis very sweet to look into the fair
   And open face of heaven, – to breathe a prayer
Full in the smile of the blue firmament.
Who is more happy, when, with heart's content,
   Fatigued he sinks into some pleasant lair
   Of wavy grass, and reads a debonair
And gentle tale of love and languishment?
Returning home at evening, with an ear
   Catching the notes of Philomel, – an eye
Watching the sailing cloudlet's bright career,
   He mourns that day so soon has glided by:
E'en like the passage of an angel's tear
   That falls through the clear ether silently.

On First Looking into Chapman's Homer

MUCH have I travell'd in the realms of gold,
    And many goodly states and kingdoms seen;
    Round many western islands have I been
Which bards in fealty to Apollo hold.
Oft of one wide expanse had I been told
    That deep-brow'd Homer ruled as his demesne:
    Yet did I never breathe its pure serene
Till I heard Chapman speak out loud and bold:
Then felt I like some watcher of the skies
    When a new planet swims into his ken;
Or like stout Cortez when with eagle eyes
    He star'd at the Pacific – and all his men
Look'd at each other with a wild surmise –
    Silent, upon a peak in Darien.

On Leaving some Friends at an Early Hour

GIVE me a golden pen, and let me lean
    On heap'd up flowers, in regions clear, and far;
    Bring me a tablet whiter than a star,
Or hand of hymning angel, when 'tis seen
The silver strings of heavenly harp atween:
    And let there glide by many a pearly car,
    Pink robes, and wavy hair, and diamond jar,
And half discovered wings, and glances keen.
The while let music wander round my ears,
    And as it reaches each delicious ending,
      Let me write down a line of glorious tone,
And full of many wonders of the spheres:
    For what a height my spirit is contending!
      'Tis not content so soon to be alone.

Addressed to Haydon

HIGHMINDEDNESS, a jealousy for good,
   A loving-kindness for the great man's fame,
   Dwells here and there with people of no name,
In noisome alley, and in pathless wood:
And where we think the truth least understood,
   Oft may be found a 'singleness of aim',
   That ought to frighten into hooded shame
A money-mong'ring, pitiable brood.
How glorious this affection for the cause
   Of stedfast genius, toiling gallantly!
What when a stout unbending champion awes
   Envy and Malice to their native sty?
Unnumber'd souls breathe out a still applause,
   Proud to behold him in his country's eye.

Addressed to the Same

GREAT spirits now on earth are sojourning:
   He of the cloud, the cataract, the lake,
   Who on Helvellyn's summit, wide awake,
Catches his freshness from Archangel's wing:
He of the rose, the violet, the spring,
   The social smile, the chain for Freedom's sake:
   And lo! – whose stedfastness would never take
A meaner sound than Raphael's whispering.
And other spirits there are standing apart
   Upon the forehead of the age to come;
These, these will give the world another heart,
   And other pulses. Hear ye not the hum
Of mighty workings? –
   Listen awhile, ye nations, and be dumb.

On the Grasshopper and Cricket

THE poetry of earth is never dead:
  When all the birds are faint with the hot sun,
  And hide in cooling trees, a voice will run
From hedge to hedge about the new-mown mead;
That is the Grasshopper's – he takes the lead
  In summer luxury, – he has never done
  With his delights; for when tired out with fun
He rests at ease beneath some pleasant weed.
The poetry of earth is ceasing never:
  On a lone winter evening, when the frost
    Has wrought a silence, from the stove there shrills
The Cricket's song, in warmth increasing ever,
  And seems to one in drowsiness half lost,
    The Grasshopper's among some grassy hills.

To Kosciusko

GOOD Kosciusko, thy great name alone
  Is a full harvest whence to reap high feeling;
  It comes upon us like the glorious pealing
Of the wide spheres – an everlasting tone.
And now it tells me, that in worlds unknown,
  The names of heroes, burst from clouds concealing,
  And changed to harmonies, for ever stealing
Through cloudless blue, and round each silver throne.
It tells me too, that on a happy day,
  When some good spirit walks upon the earth,
    Thy name with Alfred's, and the great of yore
Gently commingling, gives tremendous birth
  To a loud hymn, that sounds far, far away
    To where the great God lives for evermore.

HAPPY is England! I could be content
  To see no other verdure than its own;
  To feel no other breezes than are blown
Through its tall woods with high romances blent:
Yet do I sometimes feel a languishment
  For skies Italian, and an inward groan
  To sit upon an Alp as on a throne,
And half forget what world or worldling meant.
Happy is England, sweet her artless daughters;
  Enough their simple loveliness for me,
    Enough their whitest arms in silence clinging:
Yet do I often warmly burn to see
    Beauties of deeper glance, and hear their singing,
      And float with them about the summer waters.

Sleep and Poetry

As I lay in my bed slepe full unmete
Was unto me, but why that I ne might
Rest I ne wist, for there n' as erthly wight
(As I suppose) had more of hertis ese
Than I, for I n' ad sicknesse nor disese.

CHAUCER

WHAT is more gentle than a wind in summer?
What is more soothing than the pretty hummer
That stays one moment in an open flower,
And buzzes cheerily from bower to bower?
What is more tranquil than a musk-rose blowing
In a green island, far from all men's knowing?
More healthful than the leafiness of dales?
More secret than a nest of nightingales?
More serene than Cordelia's countenance?
More full of visions than a high romance?
What, but thee Sleep? Soft closer of our eyes!
Low murmurer of tender lullabies!
Light hoverer around our happy pillows!
Wreather of poppy buds, and weeping willows!
Silent entangler of a beauty's tresses!
Most happy listener! when the morning blesses
Thee for enlivening all the cheerful eyes
That glance so brightly at the new sun-rise.

But what is higher beyond thought than thee?
Fresher than berries of a mountain-tree?
More strange, more beautiful, more smooth, more regal,
Than wings of swans, than doves, than dim-seen eagle?
What is it? And to what shall I compare it?
It has a glory, and naught else can share it:

The thought thereof is awful, sweet, and holy,
Chasing away all worldliness and folly;
Coming sometimes like fearful claps of thunder,
Or the low rumblings earth's regions under;
And sometimes like a gentle whispering
Of all the secrets of some wondrous thing
That breathes about us in the vacant air;
So that we look around with prying stare,
Perhaps to see shapes of light, aerial limning,
And catch soft floatings from a faint-heard hymning;
To see the laurel wreath, on high suspended,
That is to crown our name when life is ended.
Sometimes it gives a glory to the voice,
And from the heart up-springs, rejoice! rejoice!
Sounds which will reach the Framer of all things,
And die away in ardent mutterings.

No one who once the glorious sun has seen,
And all the clouds, and felt his bosom clean
For his great Maker's presence, but must know
What 'tis I mean, and feel his being glow:
Therefore no insult will I give his spirit,
By telling what he sees from native merit.

O Poesy! for thee I hold my pen
That am not yet a glorious denizen
Of thy wide heaven – Should I rather kneel
Upon some mountain-top until I feel
A glowing splendour round about me hung,
And echo back the voice of thine own tongue?
O Poesy! for thee I grasp my pen
That am not yet a glorious denizen

Of thy wide heaven; yet, to my ardent prayer,
Yield from thy sanctuary some clear air,
Smoothed for intoxication by the breath
Of flowering bays, that I may die a death
Of luxury, and my young spirit follow
The morning sun-beams to the great Apollo,
Like a fresh sacrifice; or, if I can bear
The o'erwhelming sweets, 'twill bring me to the fair
Visions of all places: a bowery nook
Will be elysium – an eternal book
Whence I may copy many a lovely saying
About the leaves, and flowers – about the playing
Of nymphs in woods and fountains; and the shade
Keeping a silence round a sleeping maid;
And many a verse from so strange influence
That we must ever wonder how, and whence
It came. Also imaginings will hover
Round my fire-side, and haply there discover
Vistas of solemn beauty, where I'd wander
In happy silence, like the clear Meander
Through its lone vales; and where I found a spot
Of awfuller shade, or an enchanted grot,
Or a green hill o'erspread with chequer'd dress
Of flowers, and fearful from its loveliness,
Write on my tablets all that was permitted,
All that was for our human senses fitted.
Then the events of this wide world I'd seize
Like a strong giant, and my spirit tease
Till at its shoulders it should proudly see
Wings to find out an immortality.

Stop and consider! life is but a day;
A fragile dewdrop on its perilous way

From a tree's summit; a poor Indian's sleep
While his boat hastens to the monstrous steep
Of Montmorenci. Why so sad a moan?
Life is the rose's hope while yet unblown;
The reading of an ever-changing tale;
The light uplifting of a maiden's veil;
A pigeon tumbling in clear summer air;
A laughing schoolboy, without grief or care,
Riding the springy branches of an elm.

O for ten years, that I may overwhelm
Myself in poesy! so I may do the deed
That my own soul has to itself decreed.
Then I will pass the countries that I see
In long perspective, and continually
Taste their pure fountains. First the realm I'll pass
Of Flora, and old Pan, sleep in the grass,
Feed upon apples red, and strawberries,
And choose each pleasure that my fancy sees;
Catch the white-handed nymphs in shady places,
To woo sweet kisses from averted faces, —
Play with their fingers, touch their shoulders white
Into a pretty shrinking with a bite
As hard as lips can make it; till agreed,
A lovely tale of human life we'll read.
And one will teach a tame dove how it best
May fan the cool air gently o'er my rest;
Another, bending o'er her nimble tread,
Will set a green robe floating round her head,
And still will dance with ever-varied ease,
Smiling upon the flowers and the trees;
Another will entice me on, and on,
Through almond blossoms and rich cinnamon;

Till in the bosom of a leafy world
We rest in silence, like two gems upcurl'd
In the recesses of a pearly shell.

    And can I ever bid these joys farewell?
Yes, I must pass them for a nobler life,
Where I may find the agonies, the strife
Of human hearts: for lo! I see afar,
O'er-sailing the blue cragginess, a car
And steeds with streamy manes – the charioteer
Looks out upon the winds with glorious fear;
And now the numerous tramplings quiver lightly
Along a huge cloud's ridge; and now with sprightly
Wheel downward come they into fresher skies,
Tipt round with silver from the sun's bright eyes.
Still downward with capacious whirl they glide;
And now I see them on a green-hill side
In breezy rest among the nodding stalks.
The charioteer with wondrous gesture talks
To the trees and mountains; and there soon appear
Shapes of delight, of mystery, and fear,
Passing along before a dusky space
Made by some mighty oaks; as they would chase
Some ever-fleeting music, on they sweep.
Lo! how they murmur, laugh, and smile, and weep:
Some with upholden hand and mouth severe;
Some with their faces muffled to the ear
Between their arms; some clear in youthful bloom,
Go glad and smilingly athwart the gloom;
Some looking back, and some with upward gaze;
Yes, thousands in a thousand different ways
Flit onward – now a lovely wreath of girls
Dancing their sleek hair into tangled curls;

And now broad wings. Most awfully intent
The driver of those steeds is forward bent,
And seems to listen: O that I might know
All that he writes with such a hurrying glow.

    The visions all are fled – the car is fled
Into the light of heaven, and in their stead
A sense of real things comes doubly strong,
And, like a muddy stream, would bear along
My soul to nothingness: but I will strive
Against all doubtings, and will keep alive
The thought of that same chariot, and the strange
Journey it went.

                Is there so small a range
In the present strength of manhood, that the high
Imagination cannot freely fly
As she was wont of old? prepare her steeds,
Paw up against the light, and do strange deeds
Upon the clouds? Has she not shown us all?
From the clear space of ether, to the small
Breath of new buds unfolding? From the meaning
Of Jove's large eyebrow, to the tender greening
Of April meadows? Here her altar shone,
E'en in this isle; and who could paragon
The fervid choir that lifted up a noise
Of harmony, to where it aye will poise
Its mighty self of convoluting sound,
Huge as a planet, and like that roll round,
Eternally around a dizzy void?
Ay, in those days the Muses were nigh cloy'd
With honours; nor had any other care
Than to sing out and soothe their wavy hair.

Could all this be forgotten? Yes, a schism
Nurtured by foppery and barbarism
Made great Apollo blush for this his land.
Men were thought wise who could not understand
His glories; with a puling infant's force
They sway'd about upon a rocking-horse,
And thought it Pegasus. Ah, dismal-soul'd!
The winds of heaven blew, the ocean roll'd
Its gathering waves — ye felt it not. The blue
Bared its eternal bosom, and the dew
Of summer night collected still to make
The morning precious: Beauty was awake!
Why were ye not awake? But ye were dead
To things ye knew not of, — were closely wed
To musty laws lined out with wretched rule
And compass vile; so that ye taught a school
Of dolts to smooth, inlay, and clip, and fit,
Till, like the certain wands of Jacob's wit,
Their verses tallied. Easy was the task:
A thousand handicraftsmen wore the mask
Of Poesy. Ill-fated, impious race!
That blasphemed the bright Lyrist to his face,
And did not know it, — no, they went about,
Holding a poor, decrepit standard out,
Mark'd with most flimsy mottoes, and in large
The name of one Boileau!

                   O ye whose charge
It is to hover round our pleasant hills!
Whose congregated majesty so fills
My boundly reverence, that I cannot trace
Your hallow'd names, in this unholy place,
So near those common folk; did not their shames
Affright you? Did our old lamenting Thames

Delight you? did ye never cluster round
Delicious Avon, with a mournful sound,
And weep? Or did ye wholly bid adieu
To regions where no more the laurel grew?
Or did ye stay to give a welcoming
To some lone spirits who could proudly sing
Their youth away, and die? 'Twas even so:
But let me think away those times of woe:
Now 'tis a fairer season; ye have breathed
Rich benedictions o'er us; ye have wreathed
Fresh garlands: for sweet music has been heard
In many places; some has been upstirr'd
From out its crystal dwelling in a lake,
By a swan's ebon bill; from a thick brake,
Nested and quiet in a valley mild,
Bubbles a pipe; fine sounds are floating wild
About the earth: happy are ye and glad.
These things are, doubtless; yet in truth we've had
Strange thunders from the potency of song;
Mingled indeed with what is sweet and strong,
From majesty: but in clear truth the themes
Are ugly clubs, the Poets' Polyphemes
Disturbing the grand sea. A drainless shower
Of light is poesy; 'tis the supreme of power;
'Tis might half slumb'ring on its own right arm:
The very archings of her eyelids charm
A thousand willing agents to obey,
And still she governs with the mildest sway:
But strength alone, though of the Muses born,
Is like a fallen angel: trees uptorn,
Darkness, and worms, and shrouds, and sepulchres
Delight it; for it feeds upon the burrs,
And thorns of life; forgetting the great end
Of poesy, that it should be a friend

To soothe the cares, and lift the thoughts of man.

Yet I rejoice: a myrtle fairer than
E'er grew in Paphos, from the bitter weeds
Lifts its sweet head into the air, and feeds
A silent space with ever-sprouting green.
All tenderest birds there find a pleasant screen,
Creep through the shade with jaunty fluttering,
Nibble the little cupped flowers and sing.
Then let us clear away the choking thorns
From round its gentle stem; let the young fawns,
Yeaned in after-times, when we are flown,
Find a fresh sward beneath it, overgrown
With simple flowers: let there nothing be
More boisterous than a lover's bended knee;
Naught more ungentle than the placid look
Of one who leans upon a closed book;
Naught more untranquil than the grassy slopes
Between two hills. All hail delightful hopes!
As she was wont, th' imagination
Into most lovely labyrinths will be gone,
And they shall be accounted poet kings
Who simply tell the most heart-easing things.
O may these joys be ripe before I die!

Will not some say that I presumptuously
Have spoken? that from hastening disgrace
'Twere better far to hide my foolish face?
That whining boyhood should with reverence bow
Ere the dread thunderbolt could reach? How!
If I do hide myself, it sure shall be
In the very fane, the light of Poesy:
If I do fall, at least I will be laid
Beneath the silence of a poplar shade;

And over me the grass shall be smooth shaven;
And there shall be a kind memorial graven.
But off, Despondence! miserable bane!
They should not know thee, who athirst to gain
A noble end, are thirsty every hour.
What though I am not wealthy in the dower
Of spanning wisdom; though I do not know
The shiftings of the mighty winds that blow
Hither and thither all the changing thoughts
Of man: though no great minist'ring reason sorts
Out the dark mysteries of human souls
To clear conceiving: yet there ever rolls
A vast idea before me, and I glean
Therefrom my liberty; thence too I've seen
The end and aim of Poesy. 'Tis clear
As anything most true; as that the year
Is made of the four seasons – manifest
As a large cross, some old cathedral's crest,
Lifted to the white clouds. Therefore should I
Be but the essence of deformity,
A coward, did my very eyelids wink
At speaking out what I have dared to think.
Ah! rather let me like a madman run
Over some precipice; let the hot sun
Melt my Dedalian wings, and drive me down
Convulsed and headlong! Stay! an inward frown
Of conscience bids me be more calm awhile.
An ocean dim, sprinkled with many an isle,
Spreads awfully before me. How much toil!
How many days! what desperate turmoil!
Ere I can have explored its widenesses.
Ah, what a task! upon my bended knees,
I could unsay those – no, impossible;
Impossible!

For sweet relief I'll dwell
On humbler thoughts, and let this strange assay
Begun in gentleness die so away.
E'en now all tumult from my bosom fades:
I turn full-hearted to the friendly aids
That smooth the path of honour; brotherhood,
And friendliness, the nurse of mutual good.
The hearty grasp that sends a pleasant sonnet
Into the brain ere one can think upon it;
The silence when some rhymes are coming out;
And when they're come, the very pleasant rout:
The message certain to be done to-morrow.
'Tis perhaps as well that it should be to borrow
Some precious book from out its snug retreat,
To cluster round it when we next shall meet.
Scarce can I scribble on; for lovely airs
Are fluttering round the room like doves in pairs;
Many delights of the glad day recalling,
When first my senses caught their tender falling.
And with these airs come forms of elegance
Stooping their shoulders o'er a horse's prance,
Careless, and grand – fingers soft and round
Parting luxuriant curls; and the swift bound
Of Bacchus from his chariot, when his eye
Made Ariadne's cheek look blushingly.
Thus I remember all the pleasant flow
Of words at opening a portfolio.

Things such as these are ever harbingers
To trains of peaceful images: the stirs
Of a swan's neck unseen among the rushes:
A linnet starting all about the bushes:
A butterfly, with golden wings broad-parted,
Nestling a rose, convuls'd as though it smarted

With over-pleasure – many, many more,
Might I indulge at large in all my store
Of luxuries: yet I must not forget
Sleep, quiet with his poppy coronet:
For what there may be worthy in these rhymes
I partly owe to him: and thus, the chimes
Of friendly voices had just given place
To as sweet a silence, when I 'gan retrace
The pleasant day, upon a couch at ease.
It was a poet's house who keeps the keys
Of Pleasure's temple – round about were hung
The glorious features of the bards who sung
In other ages – cold and sacred busts
Smiled at each other. Happy he who trusts
To clear Futurity his darling fame!
Then there were fauns and satyrs taking aim
At swelling apples with a frisky leap
And reaching fingers 'mid a luscious heap
Of vine-leaves. Then there rose to view a fane
Of liney marble, and thereto a train
Of nymphs approaching fairly o'er the sward:
One, loveliest, holding her white hand toward
The dazzling sun-rise; two sisters sweet
Bending their graceful figures till they meet
Over the trippings of a little child:
And some are hearing, eagerly, the wild
Thrilling liquidity of dewy piping.
See, in another picture, nymphs are wiping
Cherishingly Diana's timorous limbs;
A fold of lawny mantle dabbling swims
At the bath's edge, and keeps a gentle motion
With the subsiding crystal: as when ocean
Heaves calmly its broad swelling smoothness o'er
Its rocky marge, and balances once more

The patient weeds; that now unshent by foam
Feel all about their undulating home.

Sappho's meek head was there half smiling down
At nothing; just as though the earnest frown
Of over-thinking had that moment gone
From off her brow, and left her all alone.

Great Alfred's too, with anxious, pitying eyes,
As if he always listen'd to the sighs
Of the goaded world; and Kosciusko's, worn
By horrid suffrance – mightily forlorn.

Petrarch, outstepping from the shady green,
Starts at the sight of Laura; nor can wean
His eyes from her sweet face. Most happy they!
For over them was seen a free display
Of outspread wings, and from between them shone
The face of Poesy: from off her throne
She overlook'd things that I scarce could tell.
The very sense of where I was might well
Keep Sleep aloof : but more than that there came
Thought after thought to nourish up the flame
Within my breast; so that the morning light
Surprised me even from a sleepless night;
And up I rose refresh'd, and glad, and gay,
Resolving to begin that very day
These lines; and howsoever they be done,
I leave them as a father does his son.

SELECTIONS FROM

Endymion

ORIGINALLY PUBLISHED

IN 1818

Book I

A THING of beauty is a joy for ever:
Its loveliness increases; it will never
Pass into nothingness; but still will keep
A bower quiet for us, and a sleep
Full of sweet dreams, and health, and quiet breathing.
Therefore, on every morrow, are we wreathing
A flowery band to bind us to the earth,
Spite of despondence, of the inhuman dearth
Of noble natures, of the gloomy days,
Of all the unhealthy and o'er-darkened ways
Made for our searching: yes, in spite of all,
Some shape of beauty moves away the pall
From our dark spirits. Such the sun, the moon,
Trees old and young, sprouting a shady boon
For simple sheep; and such are daffodils
With the green world they live in; and clear rills
That for themselves a cooling covert make
'Gainst the hot season; the mid-forest brake,
Rich with a sprinkling of fair musk-rose blooms:
And such too is the grandeur of the dooms
We have imagined for the mighty dead;
All lovely tales that we have heard or read:
An endless fountain of immortal drink,
Pouring unto us from the heaven's brink.

Nor do we merely feel these essences
For one short hour; no, even as the trees
That whisper round a temple become soon
Dear as the temple's self, so does the moon,
The passion poesy, glories infinite,
Haunt us till they become a cheering light

Unto our souls, and bound to us so fast,
That, whether there be shine, or gloom o'ercast,
They always must be with us, or we die.

Therefore, 'tis with full happiness that I
Will trace the story of Endymion.
The very music of the name has gone
Into my being, and each pleasant scene
Is growing fresh before me as the green
Of our own vallies: so I will begin
Now while I cannot hear the city's din;
Now while the early budders are just new,
And run in mazes of the youngest hue
About old forests; while the willow trails
Its delicate amber; and the dairy pails
Bring home increase of milk. And, as the year
Grows lush in juicy stalks, I'll smoothly steer
My little boat, for many quiet hours,
With streams that deepen freshly into bowers.
Many and many a verse I hope to write,
Before the daisies, vermeil rimm'd and white,
Hide in deep herbage; and ere yet the bees
Hum about globes of clover and sweet peas,
I must be near the middle of my story.
O may no wintry season, bare and hoary,
See it half-finish'd: but let Autumn bold,
With universal tinge of sober gold,
Be all about me when I make an end.
And now at once, adventuresome, I send
My herald thought into a wilderness:
There let its trumpet blow, and quickly dress
My uncertain path with green, that I may speed
Easily onward, thorough flowers and weed.

Upon the sides of Latmos was outspread
A mighty forest; for the moist earth fed
So plenteously all weed-hidden roots
Into o'erhanging boughs, and precious fruits.
And it had gloomy shades, sequestered deep,
Where no man went; and if from shepherd's keep
A lamb stray'd far a-down those inmost glens,
Never again saw he the happy pens
Whither his brethren, bleating with content,
Over the hills at every nightfall went.
Among the shepherds 'twas believed ever,
That not one fleecy lamb which thus did sever
From the white flock, but pass'd unworried
By angry wolf, or pard with prying head,
Until it came to some unfooted plains
Where fed the herds of Pan: ay great his gains
Who thus one lamb did lose. Paths there were many,
Winding through palmy fern, and rushes fenny,
And ivy banks; all leading pleasantly
To a wide lawn, whence one could only see
Stems thronging all around between the swell
Of tuft and slanting branches: who could tell
The freshness of the space of heaven above,
Edg'd round with dark tree-tops? through which a dove
Would often beat its wings, and often too
A little cloud would move across the blue.

Full in the middle of this pleasantness
There stood a marble altar, with a tress
Of flowers budded newly; and the dew
Had taken fairy phantasies to strew
Daisies upon the sacred sward last eve,
And so the dawned light in pomp receive.

69

For 'twas the morn: Apollo's upward fire
Made every eastern cloud a silvery pyre
Of brightness so unsullied, that therein
A melancholy spirit well might win
Oblivion, and melt out his essence fine
Into the winds: rain-scented eglantine
Gave temperate sweets to that well-wooing sun;
The lark was lost in him; cold springs had run
To warm their chilliest bubbles in the grass;
Man's voice was on the mountains; and the mass
Of nature's lives and wonders pulsed tenfold,
To feel this sun-rise and its glories old.

Now while the silent workings of the dawn
Were busiest, into that self-same lawn
All suddenly, with joyful cries, there sped
A troop of little children garlanded;
Who gathering round the altar, seem'd to pry
Earnestly round as wishing to espy
Some folk of holiday: nor had they waited
For many moments, ere their ears were sated
With a faint breath of music, which even then
Fill'd out its voice, and died away again.
Within a little space again it gave
Its airy swellings, with a gentle wave,
To light-hung leaves, in smoothest echoes breaking
Through copse-clad valleys, – ere their death, o'ertaking
The surgy murmurs of the lonely sea.

And now, as deep into the wood as we
Might mark a lynx's eye, there glimmered light
Fair faces and a rush of garments white,

Plainer and plainer showing, till at last
Into the widest alley they all past,
Making directly for the woodland altar.
O kindly muse! let not my weak tongue falter
In telling of this goodly company,
Of their old piety, and of their glee:
But let a portion of ethereal dew
Fall on my head, and presently unmew
My soul; that I may dare, in wayfaring,
To stammer where old Chaucer used to sing.

   Leading the way, young damsels danced along,
Bearing the burden of a shepherd's song;
Each having a white wicker, overbrimm'd
With April's tender younglings: next, well trimm'd,
A crowd of shepherds with as sunburnt looks
As may be read of in Arcadian books;
Such as sat listening round Apollo's pipe,
When the great deity, for earth too ripe,
Let his divinity o'erflowing die
In music, through the vales of Thessaly:
Some idly trail'd their sheep-hooks on the ground,
And some kept up a shrilly mellow sound
With ebon-tipped flutes: close after these,
Now coming from beneath the forest trees,
A venerable priest full soberly,
Begirt with ministring looks: alway his eye
Stedfast upon the matted turf he kept,
And after him his sacred vestments swept.
From his right hand there swung a vase, milk-white,
Of mingled wine, out-sparkling generous light;
And in his left he held a basket full
Of all sweet herbs that searching eye could cull:

Wild thyme, and valley-lilies whiter still
Than Leda's love, and cresses from the rill.
His aged head, crowned with beechen wreath,
Seem'd like a poll of ivy in the teeth
Of winter hoar. Then came another crowd
Of shepherds, lifting in due time aloud
Their share of the ditty. After them appear'd,
Up-followed by a multitude that rear'd
Their voices to the clouds, a fair-wrought car,
Easily rolling, so as scarce to mar
The freedom of three steeds of dapple brown:
Who stood therein did seem of great renown
Among the throng. His youth was fully blown,
Showing like Ganymede to manhood grown;
And, for those simple times, his garments were
A chieftain king's: beneath his breast, half bare,
Was hung a silver bugle, and between
His nervy knees there lay a boar-spear keen.
A smile was on his countenance; he seem'd
To common lookers-on, like one who dream'd
Of idleness in groves Elysian:
But there were some who feelingly could scan
A lurking trouble in his nether lip,
And see that oftentimes the reins would slip
Through his forgotten hands: then would they sigh
And think of yellow leaves, of owlets' cry,
Of logs piled solemnly. – Ah, well-a-day,
Why should our young Endymion pine away!

Soon the assembly, in a circle ranged,
Stood silent round the shrine: each look was changed
To sudden veneration: women meek
Beckon'd their sons to silence; while each cheek

Of virgin bloom paled gently for slight fear.
Endymion too, without a forest peer,
Stood, wan, and pale, and with an awed face,
Among his brothers of the mountain chace.
In midst of all, the venerable priest
Eyed them with joy from greatest to the least,
And, after lifting up his aged hands,
Thus spake he: 'Men of Latmos! shepherd bands
Whose care it is to guard a thousand flocks:
Whether descended from beneath the rocks
That overtop your mountains; whether come
From valleys where the pipe is never dumb;
Or from your swelling downs, where sweet air stirs
Blue hare-bells lightly, and where prickly furze
Buds lavish gold; or ye, whose precious charge
Nibble their fill at ocean's very marge,
Whose mellow reeds are touch'd with sounds forlorn
By the dim echoes of old Triton's horn:
Mothers and wives! who day by day prepare
The scrip, with needments, for the mountain air;
And all ye gentle girls who foster up
Udderless lambs, and in a little cup
Will put choice honey for a favoured youth:
Yea, every one attend! for in good truth
Our vows are wanting to our great god Pan.
Are not our lowing heifers sleeker than
Night-swollen mushrooms? Are not our wide plains
Speckled with countless fleeces? Have not rains
Green'd over April's lap? No howling sad
Sickens our fearful ewes; and we have had
Great bounty from Endymion our lord.
The earth is glad: the merry lark has pour'd
His early song against yon breezy sky,
That spreads so clear o'er our solemnity.'

Thus ending, on the shrine he heap'd a spire
Of teeming sweets, enkindling sacred fire;
Anon he stain'd the thick and spongy sod
With wine, in honour of the shepherd-god.
Now while the earth was drinking it, and while
Bay leaves were crackling in the fragrant pile,
And gummy frankincense was sparkling bright
'Neath smothering parsley, and a hazy light
Spread greyly eastward, thus a chorus sang:

'O thou, whose mighty palace roof doth hang
From jagged trunks, and overshadoweth
Eternal whispers, glooms, the birth, life, death
Of unseen flowers in heavy peacefulness;
Who lov'st to see the hamadryads dress
Their ruffled locks where meeting hazels darken;
And through whole solemn hours dost sit, and hearken
The dreary melody of bedded reeds –
In desolate places, where dank moisture breeds
The pipy hemlock to strange overgrowth,
Bethinking thee, how melancholy loth
Thou wast to lose fair Syrinx – do thou now,
By thy love's milky brow!
By all the trembling mazes that she ran,
Hear us, great Pan!

'O thou, for whose soul-soothing quiet, turtles
Passion their voices cooingly 'mong myrtles,
What time thou wanderest at eventide
Through sunny meadows, that outskirt the side
Of thine enmossed realms: O thou, to whom
Broad-leaved fig-trees even now foredoom
Their ripen'd fruitage; yellow-girted bees
Their golden honeycombs; our village leas

74

Their fairest-blossom'd beans and poppied corn;
The chuckling linnet its five young unborn,
To sing for thee; low-creeping strawberries
Their summer coolness; pent-up butterflies
Their freckled wings; yea, the fresh-budding year
All its completions – be quickly near,
By every wind that nods the mountain pine,
O forester divine!

  'Thou, to whom every faun and satyr flies
For willing service; whether to surprise
The squatted hare while in half-sleeping fit;
Or upward ragged precipices flit
To save poor lambkins from the eagle's maw;
Or by mysterious enticement draw
Bewilder'd shepherds to their path again;
Or to tread breathless round the frothy main,
And gather up all fancifullest shells
For thee to tumble into Naiads' cells,
And, being hidden, laugh at their outpeeping;
Or to delight thee with fantastic leaping,
The while they pelt each other on the crown
With silvery oak-apples, and fir-cones brown –
By all the echoes that about thee ring,
Hear us, O satyr king!

  'O Hearkener to the loud-clapping shears,
While ever and anon to his shorn peers
A ram goes bleating: Winder of the horn,
When snouted wild-boars routing tender corn
Anger our huntsmen: Breather round our farms,
To keep off mildews, and all weather harms:
Strange ministrant of undescribed sounds,
That come a-swooning over hollow grounds,

And wither drearily on barren moors:
Dread opener of the mysterious doors
Leading to universal knowledge – see,
Great son of Dryope,
The many that are come to pay their vows
With leaves about their brows!

    'Be still the unimaginable lodge
For solitary thinkings; such as dodge
Conception to the very bourne of heaven,
Then leave the naked brain: be still the leaven
That spreading in this dull and clodded earth,
Gives it a touch ethereal – a new birth:
Be still a symbol of immensity;
A firmament reflected in a sea;
An element filling the space between;
An unknown – but no more: we humbly screen
With uplift hands our foreheads, lowly bending,
And giving out a shout most heaven-rending,
Conjure thee to receive our humble Paean,
Upon thy Mount Lycean!'

                    *   *   *

    Who whispers him so pantingly and close?
Peona, his sweet sister: of all those,
His friends, the dearest. Hushing signs she made,
And breath'd a sister's sorrow to persuade
A yielding up, a cradling on her care.
Her eloquence did breathe away the curse.
She led him, like some midnight spirit nurse
Of happy changes in emphatic dreams,
Along a path between two little streams, –
Guarding his forehead, with her round elbow,
From low-grown branches, and his footsteps slow

From stumbling over stumps and hillocks small;
Until they came to where these streamlets fall,
With mingled bubblings and a gentle rush,
Into a river, clear, brimful, and flush
With crystal mocking of the trees and sky.
A little shallop, floating there hard by,
Pointed its beak over the fringed bank;
And soon it lightly dipt, and rose, and sank,
And dipt again, with the young couple's weight, –
Peona guiding, through the water straight,
Towards a bowery island opposite;
Which gaining presently, she steered light
Into a shady, fresh, and ripply cove,
Where nested was an arbour, overwove
By many a summer's silent fingering;
To whose cool bosom she was used to bring
Her playmates, with their needle broidery,
And minstrel memories of times gone by.

So she was gently glad to see him laid
Under her favourite bower's quiet shade,
On her own couch, new made of flower leaves,
Dried carefully on the cooler side of sheaves
When last the sun his autumn tresses shook,
And the tann'd harvesters rich armfuls took.
Soon was he quieted to slumbrous rest:
But, ere it crept upon him, he had prest
Peona's busy hand against his lips,
And still, a-sleeping, held her finger-tips
In tender pressure. And as a willow keeps
A patient watch over the stream that creeps
Windingly by it, so the quiet maid
Held her in peace: so that a whispering blade

Of grass, a wailful gnat, a bee bustling
Down in the blue-bells, or a wren light rustling
Among sere leaves and twigs, might all be heard.

O magic sleep! O comfortable bird,
That broodest o'er the troubled sea of the mind
Till it is hush'd and smooth! O unconfin'd
Restraint! imprisoned liberty! great key
To golden palaces, strange minstrelsy,
Fountains grotesque, new trees, bespangled caves,
Echoing grottoes, full of tumbling waves
And moonlight; aye, to all the mazy world
Of silvery enchantment! — who, upfurl'd
Beneath thy drowsy wing a triple hour,
But renovates and lives? — Thus, in the bower,
Endymion was calm'd to life again.
Opening his eyelids with a healthier brain,
He said: 'I feel this thine endearing love
All through my bosom: thou art as a dove
Trembling its closed eyes and sleeked wings
About me; and the pearliest dew not brings
Such morning incense from the fields of May,
As do those brighter drops that twinkling stray
From those kind eyes, — the very home and haunt
Of sisterly affection. Can I want
Aught else, aught nearer heaven, than such tears?
Yet dry them up, in bidding hence all fears
That, any longer, I will pass my days
Alone and sad. No, I will once more raise
My voice upon the mountain-heights; once more
Make my horn parley from their foreheads hoar:
Again my trooping hounds their tongues shall loll
Around the breathed boar: again I'll poll

The fair-grown yew tree, for a chosen bow:
And, when the pleasant sun is getting low,
Again I'll linger in a sloping mead
To hear the speckled thrushes, and see feed
Our idle sheep. So be thou cheered, sweet!
And, if thy lute is here, softly entreat
My soul to keep in its resolved course.'

* * *

Endymion look'd at her, and press'd her hand,
And said, 'Art thou so pale, who wast so bland
And merry in our meadows? How is this?
Tell me thine ailment: tell me all amiss!
Ah! thou hast been unhappy at the change
Wrought suddenly in me. What indeed more strange?
Or more complete to overwhelm surmise?
Ambition is no sluggard: 'tis no prize,
That toiling years would put within my grasp,
That I have sighed for: with so deadly gasp
No man e'er panted for a mortal love.
So all have set my heavier grief above
These things which happen. Rightly have they done:
I, who still saw the horizontal sun
Heave his broad shoulder o'er the edge of the world,
Out-facing Lucifer, and then had hurl'd
My spear aloft, as signal for the chace –
I, who, for very sport of heart, would race
With my own steed from Araby; pluck down
A vulture from his towery perching; frown
A lion into growling, loth retire –
To lose, at once, all my toil-breeding fire,
And sink thus low! but I will ease my breast
Of secret grief, here in this bowery nest.

'This river does not see the naked sky,
Till it begins to progress silverly
Around the western border of the wood,
Whence, from a certain spot, its winding flood
Seems at the distance like a crescent moon:
And in that nook, the very pride of June,
Had I been used to pass my weary eves;
The rather for the sun unwilling leaves
So dear a picture of his sovereign power,
And I could witness his most kingly hour,
When he doth tighten up the golden reins,
And paces leisurely down amber plains
His snorting four. Now when his chariot last
Its beams against the zodiac-lion cast,
There blossom'd suddenly a magic bed
Of sacred dittany, and poppies red:
At which I wonder'd greatly, knowing well
That but one night had wrought this flowery spell;
And, sitting down close by, began to muse
What it might mean. Perhaps, thought I, Morpheus,
In passing here, his owlet pinions shook;
Or, it may be, ere matron Night uptook
Her ebon urn, young Mercury, by stealth,
Had dipt his rod in it: such garland wealth
Came not by common growth. Thus on I thought,
Until my head was dizzy and distraught.
Moreover, through the dancing poppies stole
A breeze most softly lulling to my soul;
And shaping visions all about my sight
Of colours, wings, and bursts of spangly light:
The which became more strange, and strange, and dim,
And then were gulf'd in a tumultuous swim:
And then I fell asleep. Ah, can I tell
The enchantment that afterwards befel?

Yet it was but a dream: yet such a dream
That never tongue, although it overteem
With mellow utterance, like a cavern spring,
Could figure out and to conception bring
All I beheld and felt. Methought I lay
Watching the zenith, where the milky way
Among the stars in virgin splendour pours;
And travelling my eye, until the doors
Of heaven appear'd to open for my flight,
I became loth and fearful to alight
From such high soaring by a downward glance;
So kept me stedfast in that airy trance,
Spreading imaginary pinions wide.
When, presently, the stars began to glide,
And faint away, before my eager view:
At which I sigh'd that I could not pursue,
And dropt my vision to the horizon's verge;
And lo! from opening clouds, I saw emerge
The loveliest moon, that ever silver'd o'er
A shell for Neptune's goblet; she did soar
So passionately bright, my dazzled soul
Commingling with her argent spheres did roll
Through clear and cloudy, even when she went
At last into a dark and vapoury tent –
Whereat, methought, the lidless-eyed train
Of planets all were in the blue again.
To commune with those orbs, once more I raised
My sight right upward: but it was quite dazed
By a bright something, sailing down apace,
Making me quickly veil my eyes and face:
Again I look'd, and, O ye deities,
Who from Olympus watch our destinies!
Whence that completed form of all completeness?
Whence came that high perfection of all sweetness?

Speak, stubborn earth, and tell me where, O where
Hast thou a symbol of her golden hair?
Not oat-sheaves drooping in the western sun;
Not – thy soft hand, fair sister! let me shun
Such follying before thee – yet she had,
Indeed, locks bright enough to make me mad;
And they were simply gordian'd up and braided,
Leaving, in naked comeliness, unshaded,
Her pearl round ears, white neck, and orbed brow:
The which were blended in, I know not how,
With such a paradise of lips and eyes,
Blush-tinted cheeks, half smiles, and faintest sighs,
That, when I think thereon, my spirit clings
And plays about its fancy, till the stings
Of human neighbourhood envenom all.
Unto what awful power shall I call?
To what high fane? – Ah! see her hovering feet,
More bluely vein'd, more soft, more whitely sweet
Than those of sea-born Venus, when she rose
From out her cradle shell. The wind outblows
Her scarf into a fluttering pavilion;
'Tis blue, and over-spangled with a million
Of little eyes, as though thou wert to shed,
Over the darkest, lushest blue-bell bed,
Handfuls of daisies.' – 'Endymion, how strange!
Dream within dream!' – 'She took an airy range,
And then, towards me, like a very maid,
Came blushing, waning, willing, and afraid,
And press'd me by the hand: Ah! 'twas too much;
Methought I fainted at the charmed touch,
Yet held my recollection, even as one
Who dives three fathoms where the waters run
Gurgling in beds of coral: for anon,
I felt upmounted in that region

Where falling stars dart their artillery forth,
And eagles struggle with the buffeting north
That ballances the heavy meteor-stone; –
Felt too, I was not fearful, nor alone,
But lapp'd and lull'd along the dangerous sky.
Soon, as it seem'd, we left our journeying high,
And straightway into frightful eddies swoop'd;
Such as aye muster where grey Time has scoop'd
Huge dens and caverns in a mountain's side:
There hollow sounds aroused me, and I sigh'd
To faint once more by looking on my bliss –
I was distracted; madly did I kiss
The wooing arms which held me, and did give
My eyes at once to death: but 'twas to live,
To take in draughts of life from the gold fount
Of kind and passionate looks; to count, and count
The moments, by some greedy help that seem'd
A second self, that each might be redeem'd
And plunder'd of its load of blessedness.
Ah, desperate mortal! I even dared to press
Her very cheek against my crowned lip,
And, at that moment, felt my body dip
Into a warmer air: a moment more,
Our feet were soft in flowers. There was store
Of newest joys upon that alp. Sometimes
A scent of violets, and blossoming limes,
Loiter'd around us; then of honey cells,
Made delicate from all white-flower bells, –
And once, above the edges of our nest,
An arch face peep'd, – an Oread as I guess'd.

'Why did I dream that sleep o'erpower'd me
In midst of all this heaven? Why not see,

Far off, the shadows of his pinions dark,
And stare them from me? But no, like a spark
That needs must die, although its little beam
Reflects upon a diamond, my sweet dream
Fell into nothing – into stupid sleep.
And so it was, until a gentle creep,
A careful moving caught my waking ears,
And up I started: Ah! my sighs, my tears,
My clenched hands; – for lo! the poppies hung
Dew-dabbled on their stalks, the ouzel sung
A heavy ditty, and the sullen day
Had chidden herald Hesperus away,
With leaden looks: the solitary breeze
Bluster'd, and slept, and its wild self did teaze
With wayward melancholy; and I thought,
Mark me, Peona! that sometimes it brought
Faint fare-thee-wells, and sigh-shrilled adieus! –
Away I wander'd – all the pleasant hues
Of heaven and earth had faded: deepest shades
Were deepest dungeons; heaths and sunny glades
Were full of pestilent light; our taintless rills
Seem'd sooty, and o'erspread with upturn'd gills
Of dying fish; the vermeil rose had blown
In frightful scarlet, and its thorns outgrown
Like spiked aloe. If an innocent bird
Before my heedless footsteps stirr'd, and stirr'd
In little journeys, I beheld in it
A disguis'd demon, missioned to knit
My soul with under darkness; to entice
My stumblings down some monstrous precipice:
Therefore I eager follow'd, and did curse
The disappointment. Time, that aged nurse,
Rock'd me to patience. Now, thank gentle heaven!
These things, with all their comfortings, are given

To my down-sunken hours, and with thee,
Sweet sister, help to stem the ebbing sea
Of weary life.'

      *   *   *

  'Peona! ever have I long'd to slake
My thirst for the world's praises: nothing base,
No merely slumberous phantasm, could unlace
The stubborn canvas for my voyage prepared –
Though now 'tis tatter'd; leaving my bark bared
And sullenly drifting: yet my higher hope
Is of too wide, too rainbow-large a scope,
To fret at myriads of earthly wrecks.
Wherein lies happiness? In that which becks
Our ready minds to fellowship divine,
A fellowship with essence; till we shine,
Full alchemized, and free of space. Behold
The clear religion of heaven! Fold
A rose-leaf round thy finger's taperness,
And soothe thy lips: hist! when the airy stress
Of music's kiss impregnates the free winds,
And with a sympathetic touch unbinds
Aeolian magic from their lucid wombs:
Then old songs waken from enclouded tombs,
Old ditties sigh above their father's grave;
Ghosts of melodious prophesyings rave
Round every spot where trod Apollo's foot;
Bronze clarions awake, and faintly bruit,
Where long ago a giant battle was;
And, from the turf, a lullaby doth pass
In every place where infant Orpheus slept.
Feel we these things? – that moment have we stept
Into a sort of oneness, and our state
Is like a floating spirit's. But there are
Richer entanglements, enthralments far

POEMS OF JOHN KEATS

More self-destroying, leading, by degrees,
To the chief intensity: the crown of these
Is made of love and friendship, and sits high
Upon the forehead of humanity.
All its more ponderous and bulky worth
Is friendship, whence there ever issues forth
A steady splendour; but at the tip-top,
There hangs by unseen film, an orbed drop
Of light, and that is love: its influence
Thrown in our eyes genders a novel sense,
At which we start and fret; till in the end,
Melting into its radiance, we blend,
Mingle, and so become a part of it, –
Nor with aught else can our souls interknit
So wingedly: when we combine therewith,
Life's self is nourish'd by its proper pith,
And we are nurtured like a pelican brood.
Aye, so delicious is the unsating food,
That men, who might have tower'd in the van
Of all the congregated world, to fan
And winnow from the coming step of time
All chaff of custom, wipe away all slime
Left by men-slugs and human serpentry,
Have been content to let occasion die,
Whilst they did sleep in love's elysium.
And, truly, I would rather be struck dumb
Than speak against this ardent listlessness:
For I have ever thought that it might bless
The world with benefits unknowingly;
As does the nightingale, upperched high,
And cloister'd among cool and bunched leaves –
She sings but to her love, nor e'er conceives
How tiptoe Night holds back her dark-grey hood.
Just so may love, although 'tis understood

86

The mere commingling of passionate breath,
Produce more than our searching witnesseth:
What I know not: but who, of men, can tell
That flowers would bloom, or that green fruit would swell
To melting pulp, that fish would have bright mail,
The earth its dower of river, wood, and vale,
The meadows runnels, runnels pebble-stones,
The seed its harvest, or the lute its tones,
Tones ravishment, or ravishment its sweet,
If human souls did never kiss and greet?

'Now, if this earthly love has power to make
Men's being mortal, immortal; to shake
Ambition from their memories, and brim
Their measure of content: what merest whim,
Seems all this poor endeavour after fame,
To one, who keeps within his stedfast aim
A love immortal, an immortal too.
Look not so wilder'd; for these things are true,
And never can be born of atomies
That buzz about our slumbers, like brain-flies,
Leaving us fancy-sick. No, no, I'm sure,
My restless spirit never could endure
To brood so long upon one luxury,
Unless it did, though fearfully, espy
A hope beyond the shadow of a dream.
My sayings will the less obscured seem
When I have told thee how my waking sight
Has made me scruple whether that same night
Was pass'd in dreaming. Hearken, sweet Peona!
Beyond the matron-temple of Latona,
Which we should see but for these darkening boughs
Lies a deep hollow, from whose ragged brows

Bushes and trees do lean all round athwart,
And meet so nearly, that with wings outraught,
And spreaded tail, a vulture could not glide
Past them, but he must brush on every side.
Some moulder'd steps lead into this cool cell,
Far as the slabbed margin of a well,
Whose patient level peeps its crystal eye
Right upward, through the bushes, to the sky.
Oft have I brought thee flowers, on their stalks set
Like vestal primroses, but dark velvet
Edges them round, and they have golden pits:
'Twas there I got them, from the gaps and slits
In a mossy stone, that sometimes was my seat,
When all above was faint with mid-day heat.
And there in strife no burning thoughts to heed,
I'd bubble up the water through a reed;
So reaching back to boyhood: make me ships
Of moulted feathers, touchwood, alder chips,
With leaves stuck in them; and the Neptune be
Of their petty ocean. Oftener, heavily,
When lovelorn hours had left me less a child,
I sat contemplating the figures wild
Of o'erhead clouds melting the mirror through.
Upon a day, while thus I watch'd, by flew
A cloudy Cupid, with his bow and quiver;
So plainly character'd, no breeze would shiver
The happy chance: so happy, I was fain
To follow it upon the open plain,
And, therefore, was just going; when, behold!
A wonder, fair as any I have told –
The same bright face I tasted in my sleep,
Smiling in the clear well. My heart did leap
Through the cool depth. – It moved as if to flee –
I started up, when lo! refreshfully,

There came upon my face, in plenteous showers,
Dew-drops, and dewy buds, and leaves, and flowers,
Wrapping all objects from my smothered sight,
Bathing my spirit in a new delight.
Aye, such a breathless honey-feel of bliss
Alone preserved me from the drear abyss
Of death, for the fair form had gone again.
Pleasure is oft a visitant; but pain
Clings cruelly to us, like the gnawing sloth
On the deer's tender haunches: late, and loth,
'Tis scared away by slow-returning pleasure.
How sickening, how dark the dreadful leisure
Of weary days, made deeper exquisite,
By a foreknowledge of unslumbrous night!
Like sorrow came upon me, heavier still,
Than when I wander'd from the poppy hill
And a whole age of lingering moments crept
Sluggishly by, ere more contentment swept
Away at once the deadly yellow spleen.
Yes, thrice have I this fair enchantment seen;
Once more been tortured with renewed life.
When last the wintry gusts gave over strife
With the conquering sun of spring, and left the skies
Warm and serene, but yet with moisten'd eyes
In pity of the shatter'd infant buds, —
That time thou didst adorn, with amber studs,
My hunting cap, because I laugh'd and smiled,
Chatted with thee, and many days exiled
All torment from my breast; — 'twas even then,
Straying about, yet, coop'd up in the den
Of helpless discontent, — hurling my lance
From place to place, and following at chance,
At last, by hap, through some young trees it struck,
And, plashing among bedded pebbles, stuck

In the middle of a brook, – whose silver ramble
Down twenty little falls through reeds and bramble,
Tracing along, it brought me to a cave,
Whence it ran brightly forth, and white did lave
The nether sides of mossy stones and rock, –
'Mong which it gurgled blithe adieus, to mock
Its own sweet grief at parting. Overhead
Hung a lush screen of drooping weeds, and spread
Thick, as to curtain up some wood-nymph's home.
"Ah! impious mortal, whither do I roam!"
Said I, low-voiced: "Ah, whither! 'Tis the grot
Of Proserpine, when Hell, obscure and hot,
Doth her resign: and where her tender hands
She dabbles, on the cool and sluicy sands;
Or 'tis the cell of Echo, where she sits,
And babbles thorough silence, till her wits
Are gone in tender madness, and anon,
Faints into sleep, with many a dying tone
Of sadness. O that she would take my vows,
And breathe them sighingly among the boughs,
To sue her gentle ears for whose fair head,
Daily, I pluck sweet flowerets from their bed,
And weave them dyingly – send honey-whispers
Round every leaf, that all those gentle lispers
May sigh my love unto her pitying!
O charitable Echo! hear, and sing
This ditty to her! – tell her" – so I stay'd
My foolish tongue, and listening, half afraid,
Stood stupefied with my own empty folly,
And blushing for the freaks of melancholy.
Salt tears were coming, when I heard my name
Most fondly lipp'd, and then these accents came:
"Endymion! the cave is secreter
Than the isle of Delos. Echo hence shall stir

No sighs but sigh-warm kisses, or light noise
Of thy combing hand, the while it travelling cloys
And trembles through my labyrinthine hair."
At that oppress'd, I hurried in. — Ah! where
Are those swift moments? Whither are they fled?
I'll smile no more, Peona; nor will wed
Sorrow, the way to death; but patiently
Bear up against it: so farewell, sad sigh;
And come instead demurest meditation,
To occupy me wholly, and to fashion
My pilgrimage for the world's dusky brink.
No more will I count over, link by link,
My chain of grief: no longer strive to find
A half-forgetfulness in mountain wind
Blustering about my ears: aye, thou shalt see,
Dearest of sisters, what my life shall be;
What a calm round of hours shall make my days.
There is a paly flame of hope that plays
Where'er I look: but yet, I'll say 'tis naught –
And here I bid it die. Have not I caught,
Already, a more healthy countenance?
By this the sun is setting; we may chance
Meet some of our near-dwellers with my car.'

This said, he rose, faint-smiling like a star
Through autumn mists, and took Peona's hand:
They stept into the boat, and launch'd from land.

Book II

O SOVEREIGN power of love! O grief! O balm!
All records, saving thine, come cool, and calm,
And shadowy, through the mist of passed years:
For others, good or bad, hatred and tears
Have become indolent; but touching thine,
One sigh doth echo, one poor sob doth pine,
One kiss brings honey-dew from buried days.
The woes of Troy, towers smothering o'er their blaze,
Stiff-holden shields, far-piercing spears, keen blades,
Struggling, and blood, and shrieks – all dimly fades
Into some backward corner of the brain;
Yet, in our very souls, we feel amain
The close of Troïlus and Cressid sweet.
Hence, pageant history! hence, gilded cheat!
Swart planet in the universe of deeds!
Wide sea, that one continuous murmur breeds
Along the pebbled shore of memory!
Many old rotten-timber'd boats there be
Upon thy vaporous bosom, magnified
To goodly vessels; many a sail of pride,
And golden-keel'd, is left unlaunch'd and dry.
But wherefore this? What care, though owl did fly
About the great Athenian admiral's mast?
What care, though striding Alexander past
The Indus with his Macedonian numbers?
Though old Ulysses tortured from his slumbers
The glutted Cyclops, what care? – Juliet leaning
Amid her window-flowers, – sighing, – weaning
Tenderly her fancy from its maiden snow,
Doth more avail than these: the silver flow
Of Hero's tears, the swoon of Imogen,
Fair Pastorella in the bandit's den,

Are things to brood on with more ardency
Than the death-day of empires. Fearfully
Must such conviction come upon his head,
Who, thus far, discontent, has dared to tread,
Without one muse's smile, or kind behest,
The path of love and poesy. But rest,
In chafing restlessness, is yet more drear
Than to be crush'd, in striving to uprear
Love's standard on the battlements of song.
So once more days and nights aid me along,
Like legion'd soldiers.

*   *   *

After a thousand mazes overgone,
At last, with sudden step, he came upon
A chamber, myrtle wall'd, embowered high,
Full of light, incense, tender minstrelsy,
And more of beautiful and strange beside:
For on a silken couch of rosy pride,
In midst of all, there lay a sleeping youth
Of fondest beauty; fonder, in fair sooth,
Than sighs could fathom, or contentment reach:
And coverlids gold-tinted like the peach,
Or ripe October's faded marigolds,
Fell sleek about him in a thousand folds –
Not hiding up an Apollonian curve
Of neck and shoulder, nor the tenting swerve
Of knee from knee, nor ankles pointing light;
But rather, giving them to the fill'd sight
Officiously. Sideway his face reposed
On one white arm, and tenderly unclos'd,
By tenderest pressure, a faint damask mouth
To slumbery pout; just as the morning south
Disparts a dew-lipp'd rose. Above his head,
Four lily stalks did their white honours wed

To make a coronal; and round him grew
All tendrils green, of every bloom and hue,
Together intertwined and trammel'd fresh:
The vine of glossy sprout; the ivy mesh,
Shading its Ethiop berries; and woodbine,
Of velvet leaves and bugle-blooms divine;
Convolvulus in streaked vases flush;
The creeper, mellowing for an autumn blush;
And virgin's bower, trailing airily;
With others of the sisterhood. Hard by,
Stood serene Cupids watching silently.
One, kneeling to a lyre, touch'd the strings,
Muffling to death the pathos with his wings;
And, ever and anon, uprose to look
At the youth's slumber; while another took
A willow-bough, distilling odorous dew,
And shook it on his hair; another flew
In through the woven roof, and fluttering-wise
Rain'd violets upon his sleeping eyes.

* * *

                  Ye who have yearn'd
With too much passion, will here stay and pity,
For the mere sake of truth; as 'tis a ditty
Not of these days, but long ago 'twas told
By a cavern wind unto a forest old;
And then the forest told it in a dream
To a sleeping lake, whose cool and level gleam
A poet caught as he was journeying
To Phoebus' shrine; and in it he did fling
His weary limbs, bathing an hour's space,
And after, straight in that inspired place
He sang the story up into the air,
Giving it universal freedom. There

Has it been ever sounding for those ears
Whose tips are glowing hot. The legend cheers
Yon sentinel stars; and he who listens to it
Must surely be self-doom'd or he will rue it:
For quenchless burnings come upon the heart,
Made fiercer by a fear lest any part
Should be engulfed in the eddying wind.
As much as here is penn'd doth always find
A resting place, thus much comes clear and plain;
Anon the strange voice is upon the wane –
And 'tis but echoed from departing sound,
That the fair visitant at last unwound
Her gentle limbs, and left the youth asleep. –
Thus the tradition of the gusty deep.

Now turn we to our former chroniclers. –
Endymion awoke, that grief of hers
Sweet paining on his ear: he sickly guess'd
How lone he was once more, and sadly press'd
His empty arms together, hung his head,
And most forlorn upon that widow'd bed
Sat silently. Love's madness he had known:
Often with more than tortured lion's groan
Moanings had burst from him; but now that rage
Had pass'd away: no longer did he wage
A rough-voiced war against the dooming stars.
No, he had felt too much for such harsh jars:
The lyre of his soul Aeolian tuned
Forgot all violence, and but communed
With melancholy thought: O he had swoon'd
Drunken from pleasure's nipple! and his love
Henceforth was dove-like. – Loth was he to move
From the imprinted couch, and when he did,
'Twas with slow, languid paces, and face hid

In muffling hands. So temper'd, out he stray'd
Half seeing visions that might have dismay'd
Alecto's serpents; ravishments more keen
Than Hermes' pipe, when anxious he did lean
Over eclipsing eyes: and at the last
It was a sounding grotto, vaulted, vast,
O'er studded with a thousand, thousand pearls,
And crimson-mouthed shells with stubborn curls
Of every shape and size, even to the bulk
In which whales harbour close, to brood and sulk
Against an endless storm. Moreover too,
Fish-semblances, of green and azure hue,
Ready to snort their streams. In this cool wonder
Endymion sat down, and 'gan to ponder
On all his life: his youth, up to the day
When 'mid acclaim, and feasts, and garlands gay,
He stept upon his shepherd throne: the look
Of his white palace in wild forest nook,
And all the revels he had lorded there:
Each tender maiden whom he once thought fair,
With every friend and fellow-woodlander –
Pass'd like a dream before him. Then the spur
Of the old bards to mighty deeds: his plans
To nurse the golden age 'mong shepherd clans:
That wondrous night: the great Pan-festival:
His sister's sorrow; and his wanderings all,
Until into the earth's deep maw he rush'd:
Then all its buried magic, till it flush'd
High with excessive love. 'And now,' thought he,
'How long must I remain in jeopardy
Of blank amazements that amaze no more?
Now I have tasted her sweet soul to the core,
All other depths are shallow: essences,
Once spiritual, are like muddy lees,

Meant but to fertilize my earthly root,
And make my branches lift a golden fruit
Into the bloom of heaven: other light,
Though it be quick and sharp enough to blight
The Olympian eagle's vision, is dark,
Dark as the parentage of chaos. Hark!
My silent thoughts are echoing from these shells;
Or they are but the ghosts, the dying swells
Of noises far away? – list!' – Hereupon
He kept an anxious ear. The humming tone
Came louder, and behold, there as he lay,
On either side outgush'd, with misty spray,
A copious spring; and both together dash'd
Swift, mad, fantastic round the rocks, and lash'd
Among the conchs and shells of the lofty grot,
Leaving a trickling dew. At last they shot
Down from the ceiling's height, pouring a noise
As of some breathless racers whose hopes poise
Upon the last few steps, and with spent force
Along the ground they took a winding course.
Endymion follow'd – for it seem'd that one
Ever pursued, the other strove to shun –
Follow'd their languid mazes, till well-nigh
He had left thinking of the mystery, –
And was now rapt in tender hoverings
Over the vanish'd bliss. Ah! what is it sings
His dream away? What melodies are these?
They sound as through the whispering of trees,
Not native in such barren vaults. Give ear!

*   *   *

                                    'Dear maiden, steal
Blushing into my soul, and let us fly
These dreary caverns for the open sky.

I will delight thee all my winding course,
From the green sea up to my hidden source
About Arcadian forests; and will show
The channels where my coolest waters flow
Through mossy rocks; where 'mid exuberant green
I roam in pleasant darkness, more unseen
Than Saturn in his exile; where I brim
Round flowery islands, and take thence a skim
Of mealy sweets, which myriads of bees
Buzz from their honey'd wings: and thou shouldst please
Thyself to choose the richest, where we might
Be incense-pillow'd every summer night.
Doff all sad fears, thou white deliciousness,
And let us be thus comforted; unless
Thou couldst rejoice to see my hopeless stream
Hurry distracted from Sol's temperate beam,
And pour to death along some hungry sands.' –
'What can I do, Alpheus? Dian stands
Severe before me: persecuting fate!
Unhappy Arethusa! thou wast late
A huntress free in –' At this, sudden fell
Those two sad streams adown a fearful dell.
The Latmian listen'd, but he heard no more,
Save echo, faint repeating o'er and o'er
The name of Arethusa. On the verge
Of that dark gulf he wept, and said: 'I urge
Thee, gentle Goddess of my pilgrimage,
By our eternal hopes, to soothe, to assuage,
If thou art powerful, these lovers' pains;
And make them happy in some happy plains.'

He turn'd – there was a whelming sound – he stept,
There was a cooler light; and so he kept

Towards it by a sandy path, and lo!
More suddenly than doth a moment go,
The visions of the earth were gone and fled –
He saw the giant sea above his head.

Book III

THERE are who lord it o'er their fellow-men
With most prevailing tinsel: who unpen
Their baaing vanities, to browse away
The comfortable green and juicy hay
From human pastures; or, O torturing fact!
Who, through an idiot blink, will see unpack'd
Fire-branded foxes to sear up and singe
Our gold and ripe-ear'd hopes. With not one tinge
Of sanctuary splendour, not a sight
Able to face an owl's, they still are dight
By the blear-eyed nations in empurpled vests,
And crowns, and turbans. With unladen breasts,
Save of blown self-applause, they proudly mount
To their spirit's perch, their being's high account,
Their tip-top nothings, their dull skies, their thrones –
Amid the fierce intoxicating tones
Of trumpets, shoutings, and belabour'd drums,
And sudden cannon. Ah! how all this hums,
In wakeful ears, like uproar past and gone –
Like thunder-clouds that spake to Babylon,
And set those old Chaldeans to their tasks. –
Are then regalities all gilded masks?
No, there are throned seats unscalable
But by a patient wing, a constant spell,
Or by ethereal things that, unconfined,
Can make a ladder of the eternal wind,
And poise about in cloudy thunder-tents
To watch the abysm-birth of elements.
Aye, 'bove the withering of old-lipp'd Fate
A thousand Powers keep religious state,
In water, fiery realm, and airy bourne;
And, silent as a consecrated urn,

Hold sphery sessions for a season due.
Yet few of these far majesties, ah, few!
Have bared their operations to this globe –
Few, who with gorgeous pageantry enrobe
Our piece of heaven – whose benevolence
Shakes hand with our own Ceres; every sense
Filling with spiritual sweets to plenitude,
As bees gorge full their cells. And by the feud
'Twixt Nothing and Creation, I here swear,
Eterne Apollo! that thy Sister fair
Is of all these the gentlier-mightiest.
When thy gold breath is misting in the west,
She unobserved steals unto her throne,
And there she sits most meek and most alone;
As if she had not pomp subservient;
As if thine eye, high Poet! was not bent
Towards her with the Muses in thine heart;
As if the ministring stars kept not apart,
Waiting for silver-footed messages.
O Moon! the oldest shades 'mong oldest trees
Feel palpitations when thou lookest in.
O Moon! old boughs lisp forth a holier din
The while they feel thine airy fellowship.
Thou dost bless everywhere, with silver lip
Kissing dead things to life. The sleeping kine,
Couch'd in thy brightness, dream of fields divine:
Innumerable mountains rise, and rise,
Ambitious for the hallowing of thine eyes;
And yet thy benediction passeth not
One obscure hiding-place, one little spot
Where pleasure may be sent: the nested wren
Has thy fair face within its tranquil ken,
And from beneath a sheltering ivy leaf
Takes glimpses of thee; thou art a relief

To the poor patient oyster, where it sleeps,
Within its pearly house; – The mighty deeps,
The monstrous sea is thine – the myriad sea!
O Moon! far-spooming Ocean bows to thee,
And Tellus feels her forehead's cumbrous load.

*   *   *

'What is there in thee, Moon! that thou shouldst move
My heart so potently? When yet a child
I oft have dried my tears when thou hast smiled.
Thou seem'dst my sister: hand in hand we went
From eve to morn across the firmament.
No apples would I gather from the tree,
Till thou hadst cool'd their cheeks deliciously:
No tumbling water ever spake romance,
But when my eyes with thine thereon could dance:
No woods were green enough, no bower divine,
Until thou liftedst up thine eyelids fine:
In sowing-time ne'er would I dibble take,
Or drop a seed, till thou wast wide awake;
And, in the summer-tide of blossoming,
No one but thee hath heard me blithely sing
And mesh my dewy flowers all the night.
No melody was like a passing spright
If it went not to solemnise thy reign.
Yes, in my boyhood, every joy and pain
By thee were fashion'd to the self-same end;
And as I grew in years, still didst thou blend
With all my ardours: thou wast the deep glen –
Thou wast the mountain-top – the sage's pen –
The poet's harp – the voice of friends – the sun;
Thou wast the river – thou wast glory won;
Thou wast my clarion's blast – thou wast my steed –
My goblet full of wine – my topmost deed: –

Thou wast the charm of women, lovely Moon!
O what a wild and harmonized tune
My spirit struck from all the beautiful!
On some bright essence could I lean, and lull
Myself to immortality: I prest
Nature's soft pillow in a wakeful rest.
But gentle Orb! there came a nearer bliss –
My strange love came – Felicity's abyss!
She came, and thou didst fade, and fade away –
Yet not entirely; no, thy starry sway
Has been an under-passion to this hour.
Now I begin to feel thine orby power
Is coming fresh upon me: O be kind!
Keep back thine influence, and do not blind
My sovereign vision. – Dearest love, forgive
That I can think away from thee and live! –
Pardon me, airy planet, that I prize
One thought beyond thine argent luxuries!
How far beyond!'

* * *

Far as the mariner on highest mast
Can see all round upon the calmed vast,
So wide was Neptune's hall: and as the blue
Doth vault the waters, so the waters drew
Their doming curtains, high, magnificent,
Awed from the throne aloof; – and when storm-rent
Disclosed the thunder-gloomings in Jove's air;
But soothed as now, flash'd sudden everywhere,
Noiseless, sub-marine cloudlets, glittering
Death to a human eye: for there did spring
From natural west, and east, and south, and north,
A light as of four sunsets, blazing forth
A gold-green zenith 'bove the Sea-God's head.
Of lucid depth the floor, and far outspread

As breezeless lake, on which the slim canoe
Of feather'd Indian darts about, as through
The delicatest air: air verily,
But for the portraiture of clouds and sky:
This palace floor breath-air, – but for the amaze
Of deep-seen wonders motionless, – and blaze
Of the dome pomp, reflected in extremes,
Globing a golden sphere.

*   *   *

        O 'tis a very sin
For one so weak to venture his poor verse
In such a place as this. O do not curse,
High Muses! let him hurry to the ending.

  All suddenly were silent. A soft blending
Of dulcet instruments came charmingly;
And then a hymn.

        'King of the stormy sea!
Brother of Jove, and co-inheritor
Of elements! Eternally before
Thee the waves awful bow. Fast, stubborn rock,
At thy fear'd trident shrinking, doth unlock
Its deep foundations, hissing into foam.
All mountain-rivers lost, in the wide home
Of thy capacious bosom ever flow.
Thou frownest, and old Aeolus thy foe
Skulks to his cavern, 'mid the gruff complaint
Of all his rebel tempests. Dark clouds faint
When, from thy diadem, a silver gleam
Slants over blue dominion. Thy bright team
Gulfs in the morning light, and scuds along
To bring thee nearer to that golden song

Apollo singeth, while his chariot
Waits at the doors of heaven. Thou art not
For scenes like this: an empire stern hast thou;
And it hath furrow'd that large front: yet now,
As newly come of heaven, dost thou sit
    To blend and interknit
Subdued majesty with this glad time.
    O shell-born King sublime!
We lay our hearts before thee evermore –
We sing, and we adore!'

    * * *

Book IV

MUSE of my native land! loftiest Muse!
O first-born on the mountains! By the hues
Of heaven on the spiritual air begot:
Long didst thou sit alone in northern grot,
While yet our England was a wolfish den;
Before our forests heard the talk of men;
Before the first of Druids was a child; –
Long didst thou sit amid our regions wild,
Rapt in a deep prophetic solitude.
There came an eastern voice of solemn mood: –
Yet wast thou patient. Then sang forth the Nine,
Apollo's garland: – yet didst thou divine
Such home-bred glory, that they cried in vain,
'Come hither, Sister of the Island!' Plain
Spake fair Ausonia; and once more she spake
A higher summons: – still didst thou betake
Thee to thy native hopes. O thou hast won
A full accomplishment! The thing is done,
Which undone, these our latter days had risen
On barren souls. Great Muse, thou know'st what prison
Of flesh and bone, curbs, and confines, and frets
Our spirits' wings: despondency besets
Our pillows; and the fresh to-morrow morn
Seems to give forth its light in very scorn
Of our dull, uninspired, snail-paced lives.
Long have I said, how happy he who shrives
To thee! But then I thought on poets gone,
And could not pray: – nor can I now – so on
I move to the end in lowliness of heart. –

* * *

                                            Upon a bough
He leant, wretched. He surely cannot now
Thirst for another love: O impious,

That he can even dream upon it thus!
Thought he, 'Why am I not as are the dead,
Since to a woe like this I have been led
Through the dark earth, and through the wondrous sea?
Goddess! I love thee not the less: from thee,
By Juno's smile, I turn not – no, no, no –
While the great waters are at ebb and flow, –
I have a triple soul! O fond pretence –
For both, for both my love is so immense,
I feel my heart is cut in twain for them.'

    * * *

           – Then she,
Sitting beneath the midmost forest tree,
For pity sang this roundelay – –

   'O Sorrow,
    Why dost borrow
The natural hue of health, from vermeil lips? –
    To give maiden blushes
    To the white rose bushes?
Or is't thy dewy hand the daisy tips?

   'O Sorrow,
    Why dost borrow
The lustrous passion from a falcon-eye? –
    To give the glow-worm light?
    Or, on a moonless night,
To tinge, on syren shores, the salt sea-spry?

   'O Sorrow,
    Why dost borrow
The mellow ditties from a mourning tongue? –
    To give at evening pale
    Unto the nightingale,
That thou mayst listen the cold dews among?

'O Sorrow,
 Why dost borrow
Heart's lightness from the merriment of May?
 A lover would not tread
 A cowslip on the head,
Though he should dance from eve till peep of day –
 Nor any drooping flower
 Held sacred for thy bower,
Wherever he may sport himself and play.

 'To Sorrow,
 I bade good morrow,
And thought to leave her far away behind;
 But cheerly, cheerly,
 She loves me dearly;
She is so constant to me, and so kind:
 I would deceive her,
 And so leave her,
But ah! she is so constant and so kind.

'Beneath my palm-trees, by the river side,
I sat a-weeping: in the whole world wide
There was no one to ask me why I wept –
 And so I kept
Brimming the water-lily cups with tears
 Cold as my fears.

'Beneath my palm-trees, by the river side,
I sat a-weeping: what enamour'd bride,
Cheated by shadowy wooer from the clouds,
 But hides and shrouds
Beneath dark palm trees by a river side?'

* * *

He did not stir
His eyes from the dead leaves, or one small pulse
Of joy he might have felt. The spirit culls
Unfaded amaranth, when wild it strays
Through the old garden-ground of boyish days.
A little onward ran the very stream
By which he took his first soft poppy dream;
And on the very bark 'gainst which he leant
A crescent he had carved, and round it spent
His skill in little stars. The teeming tree
Had swollen and green'd the pious charactery,
But not ta'en out. Why, there was not a slope
Up which he had not fear'd the antelope;
And not a tree, beneath whose rooty shade
He had not with his tamed leopards play'd;
Nor could an arrow light, or javelin,
Fly in the air where his had never been –
And yet he knew it not.

O treachery!
Why does his lady smile, pleasing her eye
With all his sorrowing? He sees her not.
But who so stares on him? His sister sure!
Peona of the woods! – Can she endure? –
Impossible – how dearly they embrace!
His lady smiles; delight is in her face;
It is no treachery.

*   *   *

As feels a dreamer what doth most create
His own particular fright, so these three felt.
Or like one who, in after ages, knelt
To Lucifer or Baal, when he'd pine
After a little sleep: or when in mine

Far under-ground, a sleeper meets his friends
Who know him not. Each diligently bends
Towards common thoughts and things for very fear;
Striving their ghastly malady to cheer,
By thinking it a thing of yes and no,
That housewives talk of. But the spirit-blow
Was struck, and all were dreamers. At the last
Endymion said: 'Are not our fates all cast?
Why stand we here? Adieu, ye tender pair!
Adieu!' Whereat those maidens, with wild stare,
Walk'd dizzily away. Pained and hot
His eyes went after them, until they got
Near to a cypress grove, whose deadly maw,
In one swift moment, would what then he saw
Engulf for ever. 'Stay!' he cried, 'ah, stay!
Turn, damsels! hist! one word I have to say.
Sweet Indian, I would see thee once again.
It is a thing I dote on: so I'd fain,
Peona, ye should hand in hand repair,
Into those holy groves that silent are
Behind great Dian's temple. I'll be yon,
At vesper's earliest twinkle – they are gone –
But once, once, once again –' At this he press'd
His hands against his face, and then did rest
His head upon a mossy hillock green,
And so remain'd as he a corpse had been
All the long day; save when he scantly lifted
His eyes abroad, to see how shadows shifted
With the slow move of time, – sluggish and weary
Until the poplar tops, in journey dreary,
Had reach'd the river's brim. Then up he rose,
And, slowly as that very river flows,
Walk'd towards the temple-grove with this lament:
'Why such a golden eve? The breeze is sent

Careful and soft, that not a leaf may fall
Before the serene father of them all
Bows down his summer head below the west.
Now am I of breath, speech, and speed possest,
But at the setting I must bid adieu
To her for the last time. Night will strew
On the damp grass myriads of lingering leaves,
And with them shall I die; nor much it grieves
To die, when summer dies on the cold sward.
Why, I have been a butterfly, a lord
Of flowers, garlands, love-knots, silly posies,
Groves, meadows, melodies, and arbour-roses;
My kingdom's at its death, and just it is
That I should die with it: so in all this
We miscall grief, bale, sorrow, heart-break, woe,
What is there to plain of? By Titan's foe
I am but rightly served.' So saying, he
Tripp'd lightly on, in sort of deathful glee;
Laughing at the clear stream and setting sun,
As though they jests had been: nor had he done
His laugh at nature's holy countenance,
Until that grove appear'd, as if perchance,
And then his tongue with sober seemlihed
Gave utterance as he enter'd: 'Ha!' he said,
'King of the butterflies; but by this gloom,
And by old Rhadamanthus' tongue of doom,
This dusk religion, pomp of solitude,
And the Promethean clay by thief endued,
By old Saturnus' forelock, by his head
Shook with eternal palsy, I did wed
Myself to things of light from infancy;
And thus to be cast out, thus lorn to die,
Is sure enough to make a mortal man
Grow impious.' So he inwardly began

On things for which no wording can be found
Deeper and deeper sinking, until drown'd
Beyond the reach of music: for the choir
Of Cynthia he heard not, though rough brier
Nor muffling thicket interposed to dull
The vesper hymn, far swollen, soft and full,
Through the dark pillars of those sylvan aisles.
He saw not the two maidens, nor their smiles,
Wan as primroses gather'd at midnight
By chilly-finger'd spring. Unhappy wight!
'Endymion!' said Peona, 'we are here!
What wouldst thou ere we all are laid on bier?'
Then he embraced her, and his lady's hand
Press'd, saying: 'Sister, I would have command,
If it were heaven's will, on our sad fate.'
At which that dark-eyed stranger stood elate
And said, in a new voice, but sweet as love,
To Endymion's amaze: 'By Cupid's dove,
And so thou shalt! and by the lily truth
Of my own breast thou shalt, beloved youth!'
And as she spake, into her face there came
Light, as reflected from a silver flame:
Her long black hair swell'd ampler, in display
Full golden; in her eyes a brighter day
Dawn'd blue, and full of love. Ay, he beheld
Phoebe, his passion! joyous she upheld
Her lucid bow, continuing thus; 'Drear, drear
Has our delaying been; but foolish fear
Withheld me first; and then decrees of fate:
And then 'twas fit that from this mortal state
Thou shouldst, my love, by some unlook'd-for change
Be spiritualiz'd. Peona, we shall range
These forests, and to thee they safe shall be
As was thy cradle; hither shalt thou flee

To meet us many a time.' Next Cynthia bright
Peona kiss'd, and bless'd with fair good night:
Her brother kiss'd her too, and knelt adown
Before his goddess, in a blissful swoon.
She gave her fair hands to him, and behold,
Before three swiftest kisses he had told,
They vanish'd far away! – Peona went
Home through the gloomy wood in wonderment.

SELECTIONS FROM THE VOLUME

ENTITLED

Lamia, Isabella, The Eve of St Agnes,

and Other Poems

ORIGINALLY PUBLISHED

IN 1820

LAMIA

Part I

UPON a time, before the faery broods
Drove Nymph and Satyr from the prosperous woods,
Before King Oberon's bright diadem,
Sceptre, and mantle, clasp'd with dewy gem,
Frighted away the Dryads and the Fauns
From rushes green, and brakes, and cowslipp'd lawns,
The ever-smitten Hermes empty left
His golden throne, bent warm on amorous theft:
From high Olympus had he stolen light,
On this side of Jove's clouds, to escape the sight
Of his great summoner, and made retreat
Into a forest on the shores of Crete.
For somewhere in that sacred island dwelt
A nymph, to whom all hoofed Satyrs knelt;
At whose white feet the languid Tritons poured
Pearls, while on land they wither'd and adored.
Fast by the springs where she to bathe was wont,
And in those meads where sometimes she might haunt,
Were strewn rich gifts, unknown to any Muse,
Though Fancy's casket were unlock'd to choose.
Ah, what a world of love was at her feet!
So Hermes thought, and a celestial heat
Burnt from his winged heels to either ear,
That from a whiteness, as the lily clear,
Blush'd into roses 'mid his golden hair,
Fallen in jealous curls about his shoulders bare.
From vale to vale, from wood to wood, he flew,
Breathing upon the flowers his passion new,
And wound with many a river to its head,
To find where this sweet nymph prepared her secret bed:

In vain; the sweet nymph might nowhere be found,
And so he rested, on the lonely ground,
Pensive, and full of painful jealousies
Of the Wood-Gods, and even the very trees.
There as he stood he heard a mournful voice,
Such as, once heard, in gentle heart destroys
All pain but pity: thus the lone voice spake:
'When from this wreathed tomb shall I awake?
When move in a sweet body fit for life,
And love, and pleasure, and the ruddy strife
Of hearts and lips! Ah, miserable me!'
The God, dove-footed, glided silently
Round bush and tree, soft-brushing in his speed
The taller grasses and full-flowering weed,
Until he found a palpitating snake,
Bright and cirque-couchant in a dusky brake.

She was a gordian shape of dazzling hue,
Vermilion-spotted, golden, green, and blue;
Striped like a zebra, freckled like a pard,
Eyed like a peacock, and all crimson-barr'd;
And full of silver moons, that, as she breathed,
Dissolved, or brighter shone, or interwreathed
Their lustres with the gloomier tapestries —
So rainbow-sided, touch'd with miseries,
She seem'd at once, some penanced lady elf,
Some demon's mistress, or the demon's self.
Upon her crest she wore a wannish fire
Sprinkled with stars, like Ariadne's tiar:
Her head was serpent, but ah, bitter-sweet!
She had a woman's mouth with all its pearls complete:
And for her eyes — what could such eyes do there
But weep and weep, that they were born so fair?
As Proserpine still weeps for her Sicilian air.

Her throat was serpent, but the words she spake
Came, as through bubbling honey, for Love's sake,
And thus; while Hermes on his pinions lay,
Like a stoop'd falcon ere he takes his prey.

'Fair Hermes! crown'd with feathers, fluttering light,
I had a splendid dream of thee last night!
I saw thee sitting, on a throne of gold,
Among the Gods, upon Olympus old,
The only sad one; for thou didst not hear
The soft lute-finger'd Muses chanting clear,
Nor even Apollo when he sang alone,
Deaf to his throbbing throat's long, long melodious moan.
I dreamt I saw thee, robed in purple flakes,
Break amorous through the clouds, as morning breaks,
And swiftly as a bright Phoebean dart
Strike for the Cretan isle; and here thou art!
Too gentle Hermes, hast thou found the maid?'
Whereat the star of Lethe not delay'd
His rosy eloquence, and thus inquired:
'Thou smooth-lipp'd serpent, surely high-inspired!
Thou beauteous wreath, with melancholy eyes,
Possess whatever bliss thou canst devise,
Telling me only where my nymph is fled –
Where she doth breathe!' 'Bright planet, thou hast said,'
Return'd the snake, 'but seal with oaths, fair God!'
'I swear,' said Hermes, 'by my serpent rod,
And by thine eyes, and by thy starry crown!'
Light flew his earnest words, among the blossoms blown.
Then thus again the brilliance feminine:
'Too frail of heart! for this lost nymph of thine,
Free as the air, invisibly she strays
About these thornless wilds; her pleasant days

She tastes unseen; unseen her nimble feet
Leave traces in the grass and flowers sweet:
From weary tendrils and bow'd branches green
She plucks the fruit unseen, she bathes unseen:
And by my power is her beauty veil'd
To keep it unaffronted, unassail'd
By the love-glances of unlovely eyes,
Of Satyrs, Fauns, and blear'd Silenus' sighs.
Pale grew her immortality, for woe
Of all these lovers, and she grieved so
I took compassion on her, bade her steep
Her hair in weïrd syrops, that would keep
Her loveliness invisible, yet free
To wander as she loves, in liberty.
Thou shalt behold her, Hermes, thou alone,
If thou wilt, as thou swearest, grant my boon!'
Then, once again, the charmed God began
An oath, and through the serpent's ears it ran
Warm, tremulous, devout, psalterian.
Ravish'd she lifted her Circean head,
Blush'd a live damask, and swift-lisping said,
'I was a woman, let me have once more
A woman's shape, and charming as before.
I love a youth of Corinth — O the bliss!
Give me my woman's form, and place me where he is.
Stoop, Hermes, let me breathe upon thy brow,
And thou shalt see thy sweet nymph even now.'
The God on half-shut feathers sank serene,
She breathed upon his eyes, and swift was seen
Of both the guarded nymph near-smiling on the green.
It was no dream; or say a dream it was,
Real are the dreams of Gods, and smoothly pass
Their pleasures in a long immortal dream.
One warm, flush'd moment, hovering, it might seem,

Dash'd by the wood-nymph's beauty, so he burn'd;
Then, lighting on the printless verdure, turn'd
To the swoon'd serpent, and with languid arm,
Delicate, put to proof the lithe Caducean charm.
So done, upon the nymph his eyes he bent
Full of adoring tears and blandishment,
And towards her stept: she, like a moon in wane,
Faded before him, cower'd, nor could restrain
Her fearful sobs, self-folding like a flower
That faints into itself at evening hour:
But the God fostering her chilled hand,
She felt the warmth, her eyelids open'd bland,
And, like new flowers at morning song of bees,
Bloom'd, and gave up her honey to the lees.
Into the green-recessed woods they flew;
Nor grew they pale, as mortal lovers do.

Left to herself, the serpent now began
To change; her elfin blood in madness ran,
Her mouth foam'd, and the grass, therewith besprent,
Wither'd at dew so sweet and virulent;
Her eyes in torture fix'd and anguish drear,
Hot, glazed, and wide, with lid-lashes all sear,
Flash'd phosphor and sharp sparks, without one cooling tear.
The colours all inflamed throughout her train,
She writhed about, convulsed with scarlet pain:
A deep volcanian yellow took the place
Of all her milder-mooned body's grace;
And, as the lava ravishes the mead,
Spoilt all her silver mail, and golden brede:
Made gloom of all her frecklings, streaks and bars,
Eclipsed her crescents, and lick'd up her stars:
So that, in moments few, she was undrest
Of all her sapphires, greens, and amethyst,

And rubious-argent; of all these bereft,
Nothing but pain and ugliness were left.
Still shone her crown; that vanish'd, also she
Melted and disappear'd as suddenly;
And in the air, her new voice luting soft,
Cried, 'Lycius! gentle Lycius!' – borne aloft
With the bright mists about the mountains hoar
These words dissolved: Crete's forests heard no more.

Whither fled Lamia, now a lady bright,
A full-born beauty new and exquisite?
She fled into that valley they pass o'er
Who go to Corinth from Cenchreas' shore;
And rested at the foot of those wild hills,
The rugged founts of the Peraean rills,
And of that other ridge whose barren back
Stretches, with all its mist and cloudy rack,
South-westward to Cleone. There she stood
About a young bird's flutter from a wood,
Fair, on a sloping green of mossy tread,
By a clear pool, wherein she passioned
To see herself escap'd from so sore ills,
While her robes flaunted with the daffodils.

Ah, happy Lycius! – for she was a maid
More beautiful than ever twisted braid,
Or sigh'd, or blush'd, or on spring-flowered lea
Spread a green kirtle to the minstrelsy:
A virgin purest lipp'd, yet in the lore
Of love deep learned to the red heart's core:
Not one hour old, yet of sciential brain
To unperplex bliss from its neighbour pain;
Define their pettish limits, and estrange
Their points of contact, and swift counterchange;

Intrigue with the specious chaos, and dispart
Its most ambiguous atoms with sure art;
As though in Cupid's college she had spent
Sweet days a lovely graduate, still unshent,
And kept his rosy terms in idle languishment.

Why this fair creature chose so faerily
By the wayside to linger, we shall see;
But first 'tis fit to tell how she could muse
And dream, when in the serpent prison-house,
Of all she list, strange or magnificent:
How, ever, where she will'd her spirit went;
Whether to faint Elysium, or where
Down through tress-lifting waves the Nereids fair
Wind into Thetis' bower by many a pearly stair;
Or where God Bacchus drains his cups divine,
Stretch'd out, at ease, beneath a glutinous pine;
Or where in Pluto's gardens palatine
Mulciber's columns gleam in far piazzian line.
And sometimes into cities she would send
Her dream, with feast and rioting to blend;
And once, while among mortals dreaming thus,
She saw the young Corinthian Lycius
Charioting foremost in the envious race,
Like a young Jove with calm uneager face,
And fell into a swooning love of him.
Now on the moth-time of that evening dim
He would return that way, as well she knew,
To Corinth from the shore; for freshly blew
The eastern soft wind, and his galley now
Grated the quay-stones with her brazen prow
In port Cenchreas, from Egina isle
Fresh anchor'd; whither he had been awhile

To sacrifice to Jove, whose temple there
Waits with high marble doors for blood and incense rare.
Jove heard his vows, and better'd his desire;
For by some freakful chance he made retire
From his companions, and set forth to walk,
Perhaps grown wearied of their Corinth talk:
Over the solitary hills he fared,
Thoughtless, at first, but ere eve's star appear'd
His phantasy was lost, where reason fades,
In the calm'd twilight of Platonic shades.
Lamia beheld him coming, near, more near –
Close to her passing, in indifference drear,
His silent sandals swept the mossy green;
So neighbour'd to him, and yet so unseen,
She stood: he pass'd, shut up in mysteries,
His mind wrapp'd like his mantle, while her eyes
Follow'd his steps, and her neck regal white
Turn'd – syllabling thus: 'Ah, Lycius bright!
And will you leave me on the hills alone?
Lycius, look back! and be some pity shown.'
He did; not with cold wonder, fearingly,
But Orpheus-like at an Eurydice;
For so delicious were the words she sung,
It seem'd he had loved them a whole summer long.
And soon his eyes had drunk her beauty up,
Leaving no drop in the bewildering cup,
And still the cup was full, – while he, afraid
Lest she should vanish ere his lip had paid
Due adoration, thus began to adore;
Her soft look growing coy, she saw his chain so sure:
'Leave thee alone! Look back! Ah, Goddess, see
Whether my eyes can ever turn from thee!
For pity do not this sad heart belie –
Even as thou vanishest so I shall die.

Stay! though a Naiad of the rivers, stay!
To thy far wishes will thy streams obey:
Stay! though the greenest woods be thy domain,
Alone they can drink up the morning rain:
Though a descended Pleiad, will not one
Of thine harmonious sisters keep in tune
Thy spheres, and as thy silver proxy shine?
So sweetly to these ravish'd ears of mine
Came thy sweet greeting, that if thou shouldst fade,
Thy memory will waste me to a shade.
For pity do not melt!' 'If I should stay,'
Said Lamia, 'here, upon this floor of clay,
And pain my steps upon these flowers too rough,
What canst thou say or do of charm enough
To dull the nice remembrance of my home?
Thou canst not ask me with thee here to roam
Over these hills and vales, where no joy is, –
Empty of immortality and bliss!
Thou art a scholar, Lycius, and must know
That finer spirits cannot breathe below
In human climes, and live: Alas! poor youth,
What taste of purer air hast thou to soothe
My essence? What serener palaces,
Where I may all my many senses please
And by mysterious sleights a hundred thirsts appease?
It cannot be – Adieu!' So said, she rose
Tiptoe, with white arms spread. He, sick to lose
The amorous promise of her lone complain,
Swoon'd murmuring of love and pale with pain.
The cruel lady, without any show
Of sorrow for her tender favourite's woe,
But rather, if her eyes could brighter be,
With brighter eyes and slow amenity,
Put her new lips to his, and gave afresh

The life she had so tangled in her mesh:
And as he from one trance was wakening
Into another, she began to sing,
Happy in beauty, life, and love, and every thing, –
A song of love, too sweet for earthly lyres,
While, like held breath, the stars drew in their panting fires,
And then she whisper'd in such trembling tone
As those who, safe together met alone
For the first time through many anguish'd days,
Use other speech than looks; bidding him raise
His drooping head, and clear his soul of doubt,
For that she was a woman, and without
Any more subtle fluid in her veins
Than throbbing blood, and that the self-same pains
Inhabited her frail-strung heart as his.
And next she wonder'd how his eyes could miss
Her face so long in Corinth, where, she said,
She dwelt but half retired, and there had led
Days happy as the gold coin could invent
Without the aid of love; yet in content,
Till she saw him, as once she pass'd him by
Where 'gainst a column he leant thoughtfully
At Venus' temple porch, 'mid baskets heap'd
Of amorous herbs and flowers, newly reap'd
Late on that eve, as 'twas the night before
The Adonian feast; whereof she saw no more,
But wept alone those days, for why should she adore?
Lycius from death awoke into amaze
To see her still, and singing so sweet lays;
Then from amaze into delight he fell
To hear her whisper woman's lore so well;
And every word she spake enticed him on
To unperplex'd delight and pleasure known.
Let the mad poets say whate'er they please

Of the sweets of Fairies, Peris, Goddesses,
There is not such a treat among them all
Haunters of cavern, lake, and waterfall
As a real woman, lineal indeed
From Pyrrha's pebbles or old Adam's seed.
Thus gentle Lamia judg'd, and judg'd aright,
That Lycius could not love in half a fright,
So threw the goddess off, and won his heart
More pleasantly by playing woman's part,
With no more awe than what her beauty gave,
That, while it smote, still guaranteed to save.
Lycius to all made eloquent reply,
Marrying to every word a twin-born sigh;
And last, pointing to Corinth, ask'd her sweet,
If 'twas too far that night for her soft feet.
The way was short, for Lamia's eagerness
Made, by a spell, the triple league decrease
To a few paces; not at all surmised
By blinded Lycius. So, in her comprized,
They pass'd the city gates, he knew not how,
So noiseless, and he never thought to know.

As men talk in a dream, so Corinth all,
Throughout her palaces imperial,
And all her populous streets and temples lewd,
Mutter'd, like tempest in the distance brew'd,
To the wide-spreaded night above her towers.
Men, women, rich and poor, in the cool hours,
Shuffled their sandals o'er the pavement white,
Companion'd or alone; while many a light
Flared, here and there, from wealthy festivals,
And threw their moving shadows on the walls,
Or found them cluster'd in the corniced shade
Of some arch'd temple door, or dusky colonnade.

Muffling his face, of greeting friends in fear,
Her finger he press'd hard, as one came near
With curl'd gray beard, sharp eyes, and smooth bald crown,
Slow-stepp'd, and robed in philosophic gown:
Lycius shrank closer, as they met and past,
Into his mantle, adding wings to haste,
While hurried Lamia trembled: 'Ah,' said he,
'Why do you shudder, love, so ruefully?
Why does your tender palm dissolve in dew?' –
'I'm wearied,' said fair Lamia: 'tell me who
Is that old man? I cannot bring to mind
His features: – Lycius! wherefore did you blind
Yourself from his quick eyes?' Lycius replied
''Tis Apollonius sage, my trusty guide
And good instructor; but to-night he seems
The ghost of folly haunting my sweet dreams.'

While yet he spake they had arrived before
A pillar'd porch, with lofty portal door,
Where hung a silver lamp, whose phosphor glow
Reflected in the slabbed steps below,
Mild as a star in water; for so new
And so unsullied was the marble's hue,
So through the crystal polish, liquid fine,
Ran the dark veins, that none but feet divine
Could e'er have touch'd there. Sounds Aeolian
Breath'd from the hinges, as the ample span
Of the wide doors disclos'd a place unknown
Some time to any, but those two alone,
And a few Persian mutes, who that same year
Were seen about the markets: none knew where
They could inhabit; the most curious
Were foil'd, who watch'd to trace them to their house:

And but the flitter-winged verse must tell,
For truth's sake what woe afterwards befel,
'Twould humour many a heart to leave them thus
Shut from the busy world of more incredulous.

Part II

LOVE in a hut, with water and a crust,
Is – Love, forgive us! – cinders, ashes, dust;
Love in a palace is perhaps at last
More grievous torment than a hermit's fast: –
That is a doubtful tale from faery land,
Hard for the non-elect to understand.
Had Lycius liv'd to hand his story down,
He might have given the moral a fresh frown,
Or clench'd it quite: but too short was their bliss
To breed distrust and hate, that make the soft voice hiss.
Besides, there, nightly, with terrific glare,
Love, jealous grown of so complete a pair,
Hover'd and buzz'd his wings, with fearful roar,
Above the lintel of their chamber door,
And down the passage cast a glow upon the floor.

For all this came a ruin: side by side
They were enthroned, in the even tide,
Upon a couch, near to a curtaining
Whose airy texture, from a golden string,
Floated into the room, and let appear
Unveil'd the summer heaven, blue and clear,
Betwixt two marble shafts: – there they reposed,
Where use had made it sweet, with eyelids closed,
Saving a tïthe which love still open kept,
That they might see each other while they almost slept;
When from the slope side of a suburb hill,
Deafening the swallow's twitter, came a thrill
Of trumpets. Lycius started – the sounds fled,
But left a thought, a buzzing in his head.
For the first time, since first he harbour'd in
That purple-lined palace of sweet sin,

His spirit pass'd beyond its golden bourn
Into the noisy world almost forsworn.
The lady, ever watchful, penetrant,
Saw this with pain, so arguing a want
Of something more, more than her empery
Of joys; and she began to moan and sigh
Because he mused beyond her, knowing well,
That but a moment's thought is passion's passing bell.
'Why do you sigh, fair creature?' whisper'd he:
'Why do you think?' return'd she tenderly:
'You have deserted me; – where am I now?
Not in your heart while care weighs on your brow:
No, no, you have dismiss'd me; and I go,
From your breast houseless: aye, it must be so.'
He answer'd, bending to her open eyes,
Where he was mirror'd small in paradise, –
'My silver planet, both of eve and morn!
Why will you plead yourself so sad forlorn,
While I am striving how to fill my heart
With deeper crimson and a double smart?
How to entangle, trammel up, and snare
Your soul in mine, and labyrinth you there,
Like the hid scent in an unbudded rose?
Aye, a sweet kiss – you see your mighty woes.
My thoughts! shall I unveil them? Listen then.
What mortal hath a prize, that other men
May be confounded and abash'd withal,
But lets it sometimes pace abroad majestical,
And triumph, as in thee I should rejoice
Amid the hoarse alarm of Corinth's voice.
Let my foes choke, and my friends shout afar,
While through the thronged streets your bridal car
Wheels round its dazzling spokes.' – The lady's cheek
Trembled; she nothing said, but, pale and meek,

Arose and knelt before him, wept a rain
Of sorrows at his words; at last with pain
Beseeching him, the while his hand she wrung,
To change his purpose. He thereat was stung,
Perverse, with stronger fancy to reclaim
Her wild and timid nature to his aim:
Besides, for all his love, in self despite,
Against his better self, he took delight
Luxurious in her sorrows, soft and new.
His passion, cruel grown, took on a hue
Fierce and sanguineous as 'twas possible
In one whose brow had no dark veins to swell.
Fine was the mitigated fury, like
Apollo's presence when in act to strike
The serpent – Ha, the serpent! certes, she
Was none. She burnt, she lov'd the tyranny,
And, all subdued, consented to the hour
When to the bridal he should lead his paramour.
Whispering in midnight silence, said the youth,
'Sure some sweet name thou hast, though, by my truth,
I have not ask'd it, ever thinking thee
Not mortal, but of heavenly progeny,
As still I do. Hast any mortal name,
Fit appellation for this dazzling frame?
Or friends or kinsfolk on the citied earth,
To share our marriage feast and nuptial mirth?'
'I have no friends,' said Lamia, 'no, not one;
My presence in wide Corinth hardly known:
My parents' bones are in their dusty urns
Sepulchred, where no kindled incense burns,
Seeing all their luckless race are dead save me,
And I neglect the holy rite for thee.
Even as you list invite your many guests;
But if, as now it seems, your vision rests

With any pleasure on me, do not bid
Old Apollonius – from him keep me hid.'
Lycius, perplex'd at words so blind and blank,
Made close inquiry; from whose touch she shrank,
Feigning a sleep; and he to the dull shade
Of deep sleep in a moment was betray'd.

    It was the custom then to bring away
The bride from home at blushing shut of day,
Veil'd, in a chariot, heralded along
By strewn flowers, torches, and a marriage song,
With other pageants: but this fair unknown
Had not a friend. So being left alone
(Lycius was gone to summon all his kin),
And knowing surely she could never win
His foolish heart from its mad pompousness,
She set herself, high-thoughted, how to dress
The misery in fit magnificence.
She did so, but 'tis doubtful how and whence
Came and who were her subtle servitors.
About the halls, and to and from the doors,
There was a noise of wings, till in short space
The glowing banquet-room shone with wide-arched grace;
A haunting music, sole perhaps and lone
Supportress of the faery-roof, made moan
Throughout, as fearful the whole charm might fade.
Fresh carved cedar, mimicking a glade
Of palm and plantain, met from either side,
High in the midst, in honour of the bride:
Two palms and then two plantains, and so on,
From either side their stems branch'd one to one
All down the aisled place; and beneath all
There ran a stream of lamps straight on from wall to wall.

So canopied, lay an untasted feast
Teeming with odours. Lamia, regal drest,
Silently paced about, and as she went,
In pale contented sort of discontent,
Mission'd her viewless servants to enrich
The fretted splendour of each nook and niche.
Between the tree-stems, marbled plain at first,
Came jasper panels; then anon there burst
Forth creeping imagery of slighter trees,
And with the larger wove in small intricacies.
Approving all, she faded at self-will,
And shut the chamber up, close, hush'd and still,
Complete and ready for the revels rude,
When dreadful guests would come to spoil her solitude.

The day appear'd, and all the gossip rout.
O senseless Lycius! Madman! wherefore flout
The silent-blessing fate, warm cloister'd hours,
And show to common eyes these secret bowers?
The herd approach'd; each guest, with busy brain,
Arriving at the portal, gazed amain,
And enter'd marvelling: for they knew the street,
Remember'd it from childhood all complete
Without a gap, yet ne'er before had seen
That royal porch, that high-built fair demesne;
So in they hurried all, mazed, curious and keen:
Save one, who look'd thereon with eye severe,
And with calm-planted steps walk'd in austere;
'Twas Apollonius: something too he laugh'd,
As though some knotty problem, that had daft
His patient thought, had now begun to thaw
And solve and melt: — 'twas just as he foresaw.

He met within the murmurous vestibule
His young disciple. ''Tis no common rule,

Lycius,' said he, 'for uninvited guest
To force himself upon you, and infest
With an unbidden presence the bright throng
Of younger friends; yet must I do this wrong,
And you forgive me.' Lycius blush'd, and led
The old man through the inner doors broad-spread;
With reconciling words and courteous mien
Turning into sweet milk the sophist's spleen.

Of wealthy lustre was the banquet-room,
Fill'd with pervading brilliance and perfume:
Before each lucid panel fuming stood
A censer fed with myrrh and spiced wood,
Each by a sacred tripod held aloft,
Whose slender feet wide-swerved upon the soft
Wool-woofed carpets: fifty wreaths of smoke
From fifty censers their light voyage took
To the high roof, still mimick'd as they rose
Along the mirror'd walls by twin-clouds odorous.
Twelve sphered tables by silk seats insphered,
High as the level of a man's breast rear'd
On libbard's paws, upheld the heavy gold
Of cups and goblets, and the store thrice told
Of Ceres' horn, and, in huge vessels, wine
Came from the gloomy tun with merry shine.
Thus loaded with a feast the tables stood,
Each shrining in the midst the image of a God.

When in an antechamber every guest
Had felt the cold full sponge to pleasure press'd
By minist'ring slaves upon his hands and feet,
And fragrant oils with ceremony meet
Pour'd on his hair, they all mov'd to the feast
In white robes, and themselves in order placed

Around the silken couches, wondering
Whence all this mighty cost and blaze of wealth could spring.

Soft went the music the soft air along,
While fluent Greek a vowel'd under-song
Kept up among the guests, discoursing low
At first, for scarcely was the wine at flow;
But when the happy vintage touch'd their brains,
Louder they talk, and louder come the strains
Of powerful instruments: – the gorgeous dyes,
The space, the splendour of the draperies,
The roof of awful richness, nectarous cheer,
Beautiful slaves, and Lamia's self, appear,
Now, when the wine has done its rosy deed
And every soul from human trammels freed,
No more so strange; for merry wine, sweet wine,
Will make Elysian shades not too fair, too divine.
Soon was God Bacchus at meridian height;
Flush'd were their cheeks, and bright eyes double bright:
Garlands of every green and every scent
From vales deflower'd or forest-trees branch-rent,
In baskets of bright osier'd gold were brought,
High as the handles heap'd, to suit the thought
Of every guest; that each, as he did please,
Might fancy-fit his brows, silk-pillow'd at his ease.

What wreath for Lamia? What for Lycius?
What for the sage, old Apollonius?
Upon her aching forehead be there hung
The leaves of willow and of adder's tongue;
And for the youth, quick, let us strip for him
The thyrsus, that his watching eyes may swim
Into forgetfulness; and, for the sage,
Let spear-grass and the spiteful thistle wage

War on his temples. Do not all charms fly
At the mere touch of cold philosophy?
There was an awful rainbow once in heaven:
We know her woof, her texture; she is given
In the dull catalogue of common things.
Philosophy will clip an Angel's wings,
Conquer all mysteries by rule and line,
Empty the haunted air and gnomed mine –
Unweave a rainbow, as it erewhile made
The tender-person'd Lamia melt into a shade.

By her glad Lycius sitting, in chief place,
Scarce saw in all the room another face,
Till, checking his love trance, a cup he took
Full brimm'd, and opposite sent forth a look
'Cross the broad table, to beseech a glance
From his old teacher's wrinkled countenance,
And pledge him. The bald-head philosopher
Had fix'd his eye, without a twinkle or a stir,
Full on the alarmed beauty of the bride,
Brow-beating her fair form and troubling her sweet pride.
Lycius then press'd her hand, with devout touch,
As pale it lay upon the rosy couch:
'Twas icy, and the cold ran through his veins;
Then sudden it grew hot, and all the pains
Of an unnatural heat shot to his heart.
'Lamia, what means this? Wherefore dost thou start?
Know'st thou that man?' Poor Lamia answer'd not.
He gazed into her eyes, and not a jot
Own'd they the lovelorn piteous appeal:
More, more he gazed: his human senses reel:
Some hungry spell that loveliness absorbs;
There was no recognition in those orbs.

'Lamia!' he cried – and no soft-toned reply.
The many heard, and the loud revelry
Grew hush, the stately music no more breathes;
The myrtle sicken'd in a thousand wreaths.
By faint degrees, voice, lute, and pleasure ceased;
A deadly silence step by step increased
Until it seem'd a horrid presence there,
And not a man but felt the terror in his hair.
'Lamia!' he shriek'd; and nothing but the shriek
With its sad echo did the silence break.
'Begone, foul dream!' he cried, gazing again
In the bride's face, where now no azure vein
Wander'd on fair-spaced temples, no soft bloom
Misted the cheek, no passion to illume
The deep-recessed vision: – all was blight;
Lamia, no longer fair, there sat, a deadly white.
'Shut, shut those juggling eyes, thou ruthless man!
Turn them aside, wretch! or the righteous ban
Of all the Gods, whose dreadful images
Here represent their shadowy presences,
May pierce them on the sudden with the thorn
Of painful blindness; leaving thee forlorn,
In trembling dotage to the feeblest fright
Of conscience, for their long-offended might,
For all thine impious proud-heart sophistries,
Unlawful magic, and enticing lies.
Corinthians! look upon that grey-beard wretch.
Mark how, possess'd, his lashless eyelids stretch
Around his demon eyes! Corinthians, see!
My sweet bride withers at their potency.'
'Fool!' said the sophist, in an under-tone,
Gruff with contempt; which a death-nighing moan
From Lycius answer'd, as, heart-struck and lost,
He sank supine beside the aching ghost.

'Fool! Fool!' repeated he, while his eyes still
Relented not, nor mov'd; 'from every ill
Of life have I preserved thee to this day,
And shall I see thee made a serpent's prey?'
Then Lamia breathed death-breath; the sophist's eye,
Like a sharp spear, went through her utterly,
Keen, cruel, perceant, stinging: she, as well
As her weak hand could any meaning tell,
Motion'd him to be silent; vainly so;
He look'd and look'd again a level – No!
'A serpent!' echoed he. No sooner said,
Than with a frightful scream she vanished;
And Lycius' arms were empty of delight,
As were his limbs of life, from that same night.
On the high couch he lay! – his friends came round –
Supported him; no pulse or breath they found,
And in its marriage robe the heavy body wound.

Isabella, or the Pot of Basil

A STORY FROM BOCCACCIO

I

FAIR Isabel, poor simple Isabel!
  Lorenzo, a young palmer in Love's eye!
They could not in the self-same mansion dwell
  Without some stir of heart, some malady;
They could not sit at meals but feel how well
  It soothed each to be the other by;
They could not, sure, beneath the same roof sleep,
But to each other dream, and nightly weep.

II

With every morn their love grew tenderer,
  With every eve deeper and tenderer still;
He might not in house, field, or garden stir,
  But her full shape would all his seeing fill;
And his continual voice was pleasanter
  To her, than noise of trees or hidden rill;
Her lute-string gave an echo of his name,
She spoilt her half-done broidery with the same.

III

He knew whose gentle hand was at the latch,
  Before the door had given her to his eyes;
And from her chamber-window he would catch
  Her beauty farther than the falcon spies;
And constant as her vespers would he watch,
  Because her face was turn'd to the same skies;
And with sick longing all the night outwear,
To hear her morning-step upon the stair.

IV

A whole long month of May in this sad plight
    Made their cheeks paler by the break of June:
'To-morrow will I bow to my delight,
    To-morrow will I ask my lady's boon.' –
'O may I never see another night,
    Lorenzo, if thy lips breathe not love's tune.' –
So spake they to their pillows; but, alas,
Honeyless days and days did he let pass;

V

Until sweet Isabella's untouch'd cheek
    Fell sick within the rose's just domain,
Fell thin as a young mother's, who doth seek
    By every lull to cool her infant's pain:
'How ill she is,' said he, 'I may not speak,
    And yet I will, and tell my love all plain:
If looks speak love-laws, I will drink her tears,
And at the least 'twill startle off her cares.'

VI

So said he one fair morning, and all day
    His heart beat awfully against his side;
And to his heart he inwardly did pray
    For power to speak; but still the ruddy tide
Stifled his voice, and pulsed resolve away –
    Fever'd his high conceit of such a bride,
Yet brought him to the meekness of a child:
Alas! when passion is both meek and wild!

VII

So once more he had wak'd and anguished
    A dreary night of love and misery,
If Isabel's quick eye had not been wed
    To every symbol on his forehead high;

She saw it waxing very pale and dead,
    And straight all flush'd; so, lisped tenderly,
'Lorenzo!' – here she ceased her timid quest,
But in her tone and look he read the rest.

VIII

'O Isabella, I can half perceive
    That I may speak my grief into thine ear;
If thou didst ever anything believe,
    Believe how I love thee, believe how near
My soul is to its doom: I would not grieve
    Thy hand by unwelcome pressing, would not fear
Thine eyes by gazing; but I cannot live
Another night, and not my passion shrive.

IX

'Love! thou art leading me from wintry cold,
    Lady! thou leadest me to summer clime,
And I must taste the blossoms that unfold
    In its ripe warmth this gracious morning time.'
So said, his erewhile timid lips grew bold,
    And poesied with hers in dewy rhyme:
Great bliss was with them, and great happiness
Grew, like a lusty flower in June's caress.

X

Parting they seem'd to tread upon the air,
    Twin roses by the zephyr blown apart
Only to meet again more close, and share
    The inward fragrance of each other's heart.
She, to her chamber gone, a ditty fair
    Sang, of delicious love and honey'd dart;
He with light steps went up a western hill,
And bade the sun farewell, and joy'd his fill.

XI

All close they met again, before the dusk
   Had taken from the stars its pleasant veil,
All close they met, all eves, before the dusk
   Had taken from the stars its pleasant veil,
Close in a bower of hyacinth and musk,
   Unknown of any, free from whispering tale.
Ah! better had it been for ever so,
Than idle ears should pleasure in their woe.

XII

Were they unhappy then? — It cannot be —
   Too many tears for lovers have been shed,
Too many sighs give we to them in fee,
   Too much of pity after they are dead,
Too many doleful stories do we see,
   Whose matter in bright gold were best be read;
Except in such a page where Theseus' spouse
Over the pathless waves towards him bows.

XIII

But, for the general award of love,
   The little sweet doth kill much bitterness;
Though Dido silent is in under-grove,
   And Isabella's was a great distress,
Though young Lorenzo in warm Indian clove
   Was not embalm'd, this truth is not the less —
Even bees, the little almsmen of spring-bowers,
Know there is richest juice in poison-flowers.

XIV

With her two brothers this fair lady dwelt,
   Enriched from ancestral merchandize,
And for them many a weary hand did swelt
   In torched mines and noisy factories,

And many once proud-quiver'd loins did melt
  In blood from stinging whip; with hollow eyes
Many all day in dazzling river stood,
To take the rich-ored driftings of the flood.

XV

For them the Ceylon diver held his breath,
  And went all naked to the hungry shark;
For them his ears gush'd blood; for them in death
  The seal on the cold ice with piteous bark
Lay full of darts; for them alone did seethe
  A thousand men in troubles wide and dark:
Half-ignorant, they turn'd an easy wheel,
That set sharp racks at work, to pinch and peel.

XVI

Why were they proud? Because their marble founts
  Gush'd with more pride than do a wretch's tears? –
Why were they proud? Because fair orange-mounts
  Were of more soft ascent than lazar stairs? –
Why were they proud? Because red-lined accounts
  Were richer than the songs of Grecian years? –
Why were they proud? again we ask aloud,
Why in the name of Glory were they proud?

XVII

Yet were these Florentines as self-retired
  In hungry pride and gainful cowardice,
As two close Hebrews in that land inspired,
  Paled in and vineyarded from beggar-spies;
The hawks of ship-mast forests – the untired
  And pannier'd mules for ducats and old lies –
Quick cat's-paws on the generous stray-away, –
Great wits in Spanish, Tuscan, and Malay.

XVIII

How was it these same ledger-men could spy
    Fair Isabella in her downy nest?
How could they find out in Lorenzo's eye
    A straying from his toil? Hot Egypt's pest
Into their vision covetous and sly!
    How could these money-bags see east and west? –
Yet so they did – and every dealer fair
Must see behind, as doth the hunted hare.

XIX

O eloquent and famed Boccaccio!
    Of thee we now should ask forgiving boon,
And of thy spicy myrtles as they blow,
    And of thy roses amorous of the moon,
And of thy lilies, that do paler grow
    Now they can no more hear thy ghittern's tune,
For venturing syllables that ill beseem
The quiet glooms of such a piteous theme.

XX

Grant thou a pardon here, and then the tale
    Shall move on soberly, as it is meet;
There is no other crime, no mad assail
    To make old prose in modern rhyme more sweet:
But it is done – succeed the verse or fail –
    To honour thee, and thy gone spirit greet;
To stead thee as a verse in English tongue,
An echo of thee in the north-wind sung.

XXI

These brethren having found by many signs
    What love Lorenzo for their sister had,
And how she lov'd him too, each unconfines
    His bitter thoughts to other, well-nigh mad

That he, the servant of their trade designs,
   Should in their sister's love be blithe and glad,
When 'twas their plan to coax her by degrees
To some high noble and his olive-trees.

XXII

And many a jealous conference had they,
 * And many times they bit their lips alone,
Before they fix'd upon a surest way
   To make the youngster for his crime atone;
And at the last, these men of cruel clay
   Cut Mercy with a sharp knife to the bone;
For they resolved in some forest dim
To kill Lorenzo, and there bury him.

XXIII

So on a pleasant morning, as he leant
   Into the sun-rise, o'er the balustrade
Of the garden-terrace, towards him they bent
   Their footing through the dews; and to him said,
'You seem there in the quiet of content,
   Lorenzo, and we are most loth to invade
Calm speculation; but if you are wise,
Bestride your steed while cold is in the skies.

XXIV

'To-day we purpose, ay, this hour we mount
   To spur three leagues towards the Apennine;
Come down, we pray thee, ere the hot sun count
   His dewy rosary on the eglantine.'
Lorenzo, courteously as he was wont,
   Bow'd a fair greeting to these serpents' whine,
And went in haste, to get in readiness,
With belt, and spur, and bracing huntsman's dress.

XXV

And as he to the court-yard pass'd along,
    Each third step did he pause, and listen'd oft
If he could hear his lady's matin-song,
    Or the light whisper of her footstep soft;
And as he thus over his passion hung,
    He heard a laugh full musical aloft;
When, looking up, he saw her features bright
Smile through an in-door lattice all delight.

XXVI

'Love, Isabel!' said he, 'I was in pain
    Lest I should miss to bid thee a good morrow:
Ah! what if I should lose thee, when so fain
    I am to stifle all the heavy sorrow
Of a poor three hours' absence? but we'll gain
    Out of the amorous dark what day doth borrow.
Good bye! I'll soon be back.' – 'Good bye!' said she: –
And as he went she chanted merrily.

XXVII

So the two brothers and their murder'd man
    Rode past fair Florence, to where Arno's stream
Gurgles through straiten'd banks, and still doth fan
    Itself with dancing bulrush, and the bream
Keeps head against the freshets. Sick and wan
    The brothers' faces in the ford did seem,
Lorenzo's flush with love. They pass'd the water
Into a forest quiet for the slaughter.

XXVIII

There was Lorenzo slain and buried in,
    There in that forest did his great love cease;
Ah! when a soul doth thus its freedom win,
    It aches in loneliness – is ill at peace

147

As the break-covert bloodhounds of such sin:
 They dipp'd their swords in the water, and did tease
Their horses homeward, with convulsed spur,
Each richer by his being a murderer.

XXIX

They told their sister how, with sudden speed,
 Lorenzo had ta'en ship for foreign lands,
Because of some great urgency and need
 In their affairs, requiring trusty hands.
Poor girl! put on thy stifling widow's weed,
 And 'scape at once from Hope's accursed bands;
To-day thou wilt not see him, nor to-morrow,
And the next day will be a day of sorrow.

XXX

She weeps alone for pleasures not to be;
 Sorely she wept until the night came on,
And then, instead of love, O misery!
 She brooded o'er the luxury alone:
His image in the dusk she seem'd to see,
 And to the silence made a gentle moan,
Spreading her perfect arms upon the air,
And on her couch low murmuring, 'Where? O where?'

XXXI

But Selfishness, Love's cousin, held not long
 Its fiery vigil in her single breast;
She fretted for the golden hour, and hung
 Upon the time with feverish unrest —
Not long; for soon into her heart a throng
 Of higher occupants, a richer zest,
Came tragic; passion not to be subdued,
And sorrow for her love in travels rude.

XXXII

In the mid days of autumn, on their eves
    The breath of Winter comes from far away,
And the sick west continually bereaves
    Of some gold tinge, and plays a roundelay
Of death among the bushes and the leaves,
    To make all bare before he dares to stray
From his north cavern. So sweet Isabel
By gradual decay from beauty fell,

XXXIII

Because Lorenzo came not. Oftentimes
    She ask'd her brothers, with an eye all pale
Striving to be itself, what dungeon climes
    Could keep him off so long? They spake a tale
Time after time, to quiet her. Their crimes
    Came on them, like a smoke from Hinnom's vale;
And every night in dreams they groan'd aloud,
To see their sister in her snowy shroud.

XXXIV

And she had died in drowsy ignorance,
    But for a thing more deadly dark than all;
It came like a fierce potion, drunk by chance,
    Which saves a sick man from the feather'd pall
For some few grasping moments; like a lance,
    Waking an Indian from his cloudy hall
With cruel pierce, and bringing him again
Sense of the gnawing fire at heart and brain.

XXXV

It was a vision. In the drowsy gloom,
    The dull of midnight, at her couch's foot
Lorenzo stood, and wept: the forest tomb
    Had marr'd his glossy hair which once could shoot

Lustre into the sun, and put cold doom
    Upon his lips, and taken the soft lute
From his lorn voice, and past his loamed ears
Had made a miry channel for his tears.

XXXVI

Strange sound it was, when the pale shadow spake,
    For there was striving, in its piteous tongue,
To speak as when on earth it was awake,
    And Isabella on its music hung:
Languor there was in it, and tremulous shake,
    As in a palsied Druid's harp unstrung;
And through it moan'd a ghostly under-song,
Like hoarse night-gusts sepulchral briars among.

XXXVII

Its eyes, though wild, were still all dewy bright
    With love, and kept all phantom fear aloof
From the poor girl by magic of their light,
    The while it did unthread the horrid woof
Of the late darken'd time – the murderous spite
    Of pride and avarice – the dark pine roof
In the forest – and the sodden turfed dell,
Where, without any word, from stabs he fell.

XXXVIII

Saying moreover, 'Isabel, my sweet!
    Red whortle-berries droop above my head,
And a large flint-stone weighs upon my feet;
    Around me beeches and high chestnuts shed
Their leaves and prickly-nuts; a sheep-fold bleat
    Comes from beyond the river to my bed:
Go, shed one tear upon my heather-bloom,
And it shall comfort me within the tomb.

XXXIX

'I am a shadow now, alas! alas!
  Upon the skirts of human nature dwelling
Alone: I chant alone the holy mass,
  While little sounds of life are round me knelling,
And glossy bees at noon do fieldward pass,
  And many a chapel bell the hour is telling,
Paining me through: those sounds grow strange to me,
And thou art distant in Humanity.

XL

'I know what was, I feel full well what is,
  And I should rage, if spirits could go mad;
Though I forget the taste of earthly bliss,
  That paleness warms my grave, as though I had
A seraph chosen from the bright abyss
  To be my spouse: thy paleness makes me glad:
Thy beauty grows upon me, and I feel
A greater love through all my essence steal.'

XLI

The Spirit mourn'd 'Adieu!' – dissolved, and left
  The atom darkness in a slow turmoil;
As when of healthful midnight sleep bereft,
  Thinking on rugged hours and fruitless toil,
We put our eyes into a pillowy cleft,
  And see the spangly gloom froth up and boil:
It made sad Isabella's eyelids ache,
And in the dawn she started up awake;

XLII

'Ha! ha!' said she, 'I knew not this hard life,
  I thought the worst was simple misery;
I thought some Fate with pleasure or with strife
  Portion'd us – happy days, or else to die;

But there is crime – a brother's bloody knife!
    Sweet Spirit, thou hast school'd my infancy:
I'll visit thee for this, and kiss thine eyes,
And greet thee morn and even in the skies.'

XLIII

When the full morning came, she had devised
    How she might secret to the forest hie;
How she might find the clay, so dearly prized,
    And sing to it one latest lullaby;
How her short absence might be unsurmised,
    While she the inmost of the dream would try.
Resolv'd, she took with her an aged nurse,
And went into that dismal forest-hearse.

XLIV

See, as they creep along the river side,
    How she doth whisper to that aged Dame,
And, after looking round the champaign wide,
    Shows her a knife. – 'What feverous hectic flame
Burns in thee, child? – What good can thee betide
    That thou should'st smile again?' – The evening came,
And they had found Lorenzo's earthy bed;
The flint was there, the berries at his head.

XLV

Who hath not loiter'd in a green church-yard,
    And let his spirit, like a demon mole,
Work through the clayey soil and gravel hard,
    To see skull, coffin'd bones, and funeral stole;
Pitying each form that hungry Death had marr'd,
    And filling it once more with human soul?
Ah! this is holiday to what was felt
When Isabella by Lorenzo knelt.

XLVI

She gaz'd into the fresh-thrown mould, as though
   One glance did fully all its secrets tell;
Clearly she saw, as other eyes would know
   Pale limbs at bottom of a crystal well;
Upon the murderous spot she seem'd to grow,
   Like to a native lily of the dell:
Then with her knife, all sudden she began
To dig more fervently than misers can.

XLVII

Soon she turn'd up a soiled glove, whereon
   Her silk had play'd in purple phantasies;
She kiss'd it with a lip more chill than stone,
   And put it in her bosom, where it dries
And freezes utterly unto the bone
   Those dainties made to still an infant's cries:
Then 'gan she work again; nor stay'd her care,
But to throw back at times her veiling hair.

XLVIII

That old nurse stood beside her wondering,
   Until her heart felt pity to the core
At sight of such a dismal labouring,
   And so she kneeled, with her locks all hoar,
And put her lean hands to the horrid thing:
   Three hours they labour'd at this travail sore;
At last they felt the kernel of the grave,
And Isabella did not stamp and rave.

XLIX

Ah! wherefore all this wormy circumstance?
   Why linger at the yawning tomb so long?
O for the gentleness of old Romance,
   The simple plaining of a minstrel's song!

Fair reader, at the old tale take a glance,
    For here, in truth, it doth not well belong
To speak: — O turn thee to the very tale,
And taste the music of that vision pale.

L

With duller steel than the Perséan sword
    They cut away no formless monster's head,
But one, whose gentleness did well accord
    With death, as life. The ancient harps have said,
Love never dies, but lives, immortal Lord:
    If Love impersonate was ever dead,
Pale Isabella kiss'd it, and low moan'd.
'Twas love; cold, — dead indeed, but not dethroned.

LI

In anxious secrecy they took it home,
    And then the prize was all for Isabel:
She calm'd its wild hair with a golden comb,
    And all around each eye's sepulchral cell
Pointed each fringed lash; the smeared loam
    With tears, as chilly as a dripping well,
She drench'd away: — and still she comb'd and kept
Sighing all day — and still she kiss'd and wept.

LII

Then in a silken scarf, — sweet with the dews
    Of precious flowers pluck'd in Araby,
And divine liquids come with odorous ooze
    Through the cold serpent-pipe refreshfully, —
She wrapp'd it up; and for its tomb did choose
    A garden-pot, wherein she laid it by,
And cover'd it with mould, and o'er it set
Sweet Basil, which her tears kept ever wet.

LIII

And she forgot the stars, the moon, and sun,
  And she forgot the blue above the trees,
And she forgot the dells where waters run,
  And she forgot the chilly autumn breeze;
She had no knowledge when the day was done,
  And the new morn she saw not: but in peace
Hung over her sweet Basil evermore,
And moisten'd it with tears unto the core.

LIV

And so she ever fed it with thin tears,
  Whence thick, and green, and beautiful it grew,
So that it smelt more balmy than its peers
  Of Basil-tufts in Florence; for it drew
Nurture besides, and life, from human fears,
  From the fast mouldering head there shut from view:
So that the jewel, safely casketed,
Came forth, and in perfumed leaflets spread.

LV

O Melancholy, linger here awhile
  O Music, Music, breathe despondingly!
O Echo, Echo, from some sombre isle,
  Unknown, Lethean, sigh to us – Oh sigh!
Spirits in grief, lift up your heads, and smile;
  Lift up your heads, sweet Spirits, heavily,
And make a pale light in your cypress glooms,
Tinting with silver wan your marble tombs.

LVI

Moan hither, all ye syllables of woe,
  From the deep throat of sad Melpomene!
Through bronzed lyre in tragic order go,
  And touch the strings into a mystery;

Sound mournfully upon the winds and low;
   For simple Isabel is soon to be
Among the dead: She withers, like a palm
Cut by an Indian for its juicy balm.

LVII

O leave the palm to wither by itself;
   Let not quick Winter chill its dying hour! –
It may not be – those Baâlites of pelf,
   Her brethren, noted the continual shower
From her dead eyes; and many a curious elf,
   Among her kindred, wonder'd that such dower
Of youth and beauty should be thrown aside
By one mark'd out to be a Noble's bride.

LVIII

And, furthermore, her brethren wonder'd much
   Why she sat drooping by the Basil green,
And why it flourish'd, as by magic touch;
   Greatly they wonder'd what the thing might mean:
They could not surely give belief, that such
   A very nothing would have power to wean
Her from her own fair youth, and pleasures gay,
And even remembrances of her love's delay.

LIX

Therefore they watch'd a time when they might sift
   This hidden whim; and long they watch'd in vain;
For seldom did she go to chapel-shrift,
   And seldom felt she any hunger-pain:
And when she left, she hurried back, as swift
   As bird on wing to breast its eggs again:
And, patient as a hen-bird, sat her there
Beside her Basil, weeping through her hair.

LX

Yet they contrived to steal the Basil-pot,
  And to examine it in secret place:
The thing was vile with green and livid spot,
  And yet they knew it was Lorenzo's face:
The guerdon of their murder they had got,
  And so left Florence in a moment's space,
Never to turn again. – Away they went,
With blood upon their heads, to banishment.

LXI

O Melancholy, turn thine eyes away!
  O Music, Music, breathe despondingly!
O Echo, Echo, on some other day,
  From isles Lethean, sigh to us – O sigh!
Spirits of grief, sing not your 'Well-a-way!'
  For Isabel, sweet Isabel, will die;
Will die a death too lone and incomplete,
Now they have ta'en away her Basil sweet.

LXII

Piteous she look'd on dead and senseless things,
  Asking for her lost Basil amorously:
And with melodious chuckle in the strings
  Of her lorn voice, she oftentimes would cry
After the Pilgrim in his wanderings,
  To ask him where her Basil was; and why
'Twas hid from her: 'For cruel 'tis,' said she,
'To steal my Basil-pot away from me.'

LXIII

And so she pined, and so she died forlorn,
  Imploring for her Basil to the last.
No heart was there in Florence but did mourn
  In pity of her love, so overcast.

And a sad ditty of this story borne
    From mouth to mouth through all the country pass'd:
Still is the burthen sung – 'O cruelty,
To steal my Basil-pot away from me!'

The Eve of St Agnes

I

ST AGNES' EVE – Ah, bitter chill it was!
The owl, for all his feathers, was a-cold;
The hare limp'd trembling through the frozen grass,
And silent was the flock in woolly fold:
Numb were the Beadsman's fingers, while he told
His rosary, and while his frosted breath,
Like pious incense from a censer old,
Seem'd taking flight for heaven, without a death,
Past the sweet Virgin's picture, while his prayer he saith.

II

His prayer he saith, this patient, holy man;
Then takes his lamp, and riseth from his knees,
And back returneth, meagre, barefoot, wan,
Along the chapel aisle by slow degrees:
The sculptur'd dead, on each side, seem to freeze,
Emprison'd in black, purgatorial rails:
Knights, ladies, praying in dumb orat'ries,
He passeth by; and his weak spirit fails
To think how they may ache in icy hoods and mails.

III

Northward he turneth through a little door,
And scarce three steps, ere Music's golden tongue
Flatter'd to tears this aged man and poor;
But no – already had his deathbell rung:
The joys of all his life were said and sung:
His was harsh penance on St Agnes' Eve:
Another way he went, and soon among
Rough ashes sat he for his soul's reprieve,
And all night kept awake, for sinners' sake to grieve.

IV

That ancient Beadsman heard the prelude soft;
And so it chanc'd, for many a door was wide,
From hurry to and fro. Soon, up aloft,
The silver, snarling trumpets 'gan to chide:
The level chambers, ready with their pride,
Were glowing to receive a thousand guests:
The carved angels, ever eager-eyed,
Star'd, where upon their heads the cornice rests,
With hair blown back, and wings put cross-wise on their
    breasts.

V

At length burst in the argent revelry,
With plume, tiara, and all rich array,
Numerous as shadows haunting faerily
The brain, new-stuff'd, in youth, with triumphs gay
Of old romance. These let us wish away,
And turn, sole-thoughted, to one Lady there,
Whose heart had brooded, all that wintry day,
On love, and wing'd St Agnes' saintly care,
As she had heard old dames full many times declare.

VI

They told her how, upon St Agnes' Eve,
Young virgins might have visions of delight,
And soft adorings from their loves receive
Upon the honey'd middle of the night,
If ceremonies due they did aright;
As, supperless to bed they must retire,
And couch supine their beauties, lilly white;
Nor look behind, nor sideways, but require
Of Heaven with upward eyes for all that they desire.

VII

Full of this whim was thoughtful Madeline:
The music, yearning like a God in pain,
She scarcely heard: her maiden eyes divine,
Fix'd on the floor, saw many a sweeping train
Pass by — she heeded not at all: in vain
Came many a tiptoe, amorous cavalier,
And back retir'd; not cool'd by high disdain,
But she saw not: her heart was otherwhere:
She sigh'd for Agnes' dreams, the sweetest of the year.

VIII

She danc'd along with vague, regardless eyes,
Anxious her lips, her breathing quick and short:
The hallow'd hour was near at hand: she sighs
Amid the timbrels, and the throng'd resort
Of whisperers in anger, or in sport;
'Mid looks of love, defiance, hate, and scorn,
Hoodwink'd with faery fancy; all amort,
Save to St Agnes and her lambs unshorn,
And all the bliss to be before to-morrow morn.

IX

So, purposing each moment to retire,
She linger'd still. Meantime, across the moors,
Had come young Porphyro, with heart on fire
For Madeline. Beside the portal doors,
Buttress'd from moonlight, stands he, and implores
All saints to give him sight of Madeline,
But for one moment in the tedious hours,
That he might gaze and worship all unseen;
Perchance speak, kneel, touch, kiss — in sooth such things
. have been.

X

He ventures in: let no buzz'd whisper tell:
All eyes be muffled, or a hundred swords
Will storm his heart, Love's fev'rous citadel:
For him, those chambers held barbarian hordes,
Hyena foemen, and hot-blooded lords,
Whose very dogs would execrations howl
Against his lineage: not one breast affords
Him any mercy, in that mansion foul,
Save one old beldame, weak in body and in soul.

XI

Ah, happy chance! the aged creature came,
Shuffling along with ivory-headed wand,
To where he stood, hid from the torch's flame,
Behind a broad hall-pillar, far beyond
The sound of merriment and chorus bland:
He startled her; but soon she knew his face,
And grasp'd his fingers in her palsied hand,
Saying, 'Mercy, Porphyro! hie thee from this place:
They are all here to-night, the whole blood-thirsty race!

XII

'Get hence! get hence! there's dwarfish Hildebrand;
He had a fever late, and in the fit
He cursed thee and thine, both house and land:
Then there's that old Lord Maurice, not a whit
More tame for his gray hairs – Alas me! flit!
Flit like a ghost away.' – 'Ah, Gossip dear,
We're safe enough; here in this arm-chair sit,
And tell me how' – 'Good saints! not here, not here;
Follow me, child, or else these stones will be thy bier.'

XIII

He follow'd through a lowly arched way,
Brushing the cobwebs with his lofty plume;
And as she mutter'd 'Well-a – well-a-day!'
He found him in a little moonlight room,
Pale, latticed, chill, and silent as a tomb.
'Now tell me where is Madeline,' said he,
'O tell me, Angela, by the holy loom
Which none but secret sisterhood may see,
When they St Agnes' wool are weaving piously.'

XIV

'St Agnes! Ah! it is St Agnes' Eve –
Yet men will murder upon holy days:
Thou must hold water in a witch's sieve,
And be liege-lord of all the Elves and Fays,
To venture so: it fills me with amaze
To see thee, Porphyro! – St Agnes' Eve!
God's help! my lady fair the conjuror plays
This very night: good angels her deceive!
But let me laugh awhile, I've mickle time to grieve.'

XV

Feebly she laugheth in the languid moon,
While Porphyro upon her face doth look,
Like puzzled urchin on an aged crone
Who keepeth clos'd a wond'rous riddle-book,
As spectacled she sits in chimney nook.
But soon his eyes grew brilliant, when she told
His lady's purpose; and he scarce could brook
Tears, at the thought of those enchantments cold,
And Madeline asleep in lap of legends old.

XVI

Sudden a thought came like a full-blown rose,
　Flushing his brow, and in his pained heart
　Made purple riot: then doth he propose
　A stratagem, that makes the beldame start:
　'A cruel man and impious thou art:
　Sweet lady, let her pray, and sleep, and dream
　Alone with her good angels, far apart
　From wicked men like thee. Go, go! — I deem
Thou canst not surely be the same that thou didst seem.'

XVII

'I will not harm her, by all saints I swear,'
　Quoth Porphyro: 'O may I ne'er find grace
　When my weak voice shall whisper its last prayer,
　If one of her soft ringlets I displace,
　Or look with ruffian passion in her face:
　Good Angela, believe me by these tears;
　Or I will, even in a moment's space,
　Awake, with horrid shout, my foemen's ears,
And beard them, though they be more fang'd than wolves and
　　bears.'

XVIII

'Ah! why wilt thou affright a feeble soul?
　A poor, weak, palsy-stricken, churchyard thing,
　Whose passing-bell may ere the midnight toll;
　Whose prayers for thee, each morn and evening,
　Were never miss'd,' — Thus plaining, doth she bring
　A gentler speech from burning Porphyro;
　So woeful, and of such deep sorrowing,
　That Angela gives promise she will do
Whatever he shall wish, betide her weal or woe.

XIX

Which was, to lead him, in close secrecy,
Even to Madeline's chamber, and there hide
Him in a closet, of such privacy
That he might see her beauty unespied,
And win perhaps that night a peerless bride,
While legion'd faeries pac'd the coverlet,
And pale enchantment held her sleepy-eyed.
Never on such a night have lovers met,
Since Merlin paid his Demon all the monstrous debt.

XX

'It shall be as thou wishest,' said the Dame:
'All cates and dainties shall be stored there
Quickly on this feast-night: by the tambour frame
Her own lute thou wilt see: no time to spare,
For I am slow and feeble, and scarce dare
On such a catering trust my dizzy head.
Wait here, my child, with patience, kneel in prayer
The while: Ah! thou must needs the lady wed,
Or may I never leave my grave among the dead.'

XXI

So saying she hobbled off with busy fear.
The lover's endless minutes slowly pass'd;
The dame return'd, and whisper'd in his ear
To follow her; with aged eyes aghast
From fright of dim espial. Safe at last
Through many a dusky gallery, they gain
The maiden's chamber, silken, hush'd, and chaste;
Where Porphyro took covert, pleas'd amain.
His poor guide hurried back with agues in her brain.

XXII

Her faltering hand upon the balustrade,
Old Angela was feeling for the stair,
When Madeline, St Agnes' charmed maid,
Rose, like a mission'd spirit, unaware:
With silver taper's light, and pious care,
She turn'd and down the aged gossip led
To a safe level matting. Now prepare,
Young Porphyro, for gazing on that bed;
She comes, she comes again, like ring-dove fray'd and fled.

XXIII

Out went the taper as she hurried in;
Its little smoke, in pallid moonshine, died:
She closed the door, she panted, all akin
To spirits of the air, and visions wide:
No utter'd syllable, or, woe betide!
But to her heart, her heart was voluble,
Paining with eloquence her balmy side;
As though a tongueless nightingale should swell
Her throat in vain, and die, heart-stifled, in her dell.

XXIV

A casement high and triple-arch'd there was,
All garlanded with carven imag'ries,
Of fruits, and flowers, and bunches of knot-grass,
And diamonded with panes of quaint device,
Innumerable of stains and splendid dyes,
As are the tiger-moth's deep-damask'd wings;
And in the midst, 'mong thousand heraldries,
And twilight saints, and dim emblazonings,
A shielded scutcheon blush'd with blood of queens and kings.

XXV

Full on this casement shone the wintry moon,
  And threw warm gules on Madeline's fair breast,
  As down she knelt for Heaven's grace and boon;
  Rose-bloom fell on her hands, together prest,
  And on her silver cross soft amethyst,
  And on her hair a glory, like a saint:
  She seem'd a splendid angel, newly drest,
  Save wings, for heaven: – Porphyro grew faint:
She knelt, so pure a thing, so free from mortal taint.

XXVI

Anon his heart revives: her vespers done,
  Of all its wreathed pearls her hair she frees;
  Unclasps her warmed jewels one by one;
  Loosens her fragrant boddice; by degrees
  Her rich attire creeps rustling to her knees:
  Half-hidden, like a mermaid in sea-weed,
  Pensive awhile she dreams awake, and sees,
  In fancy, fair St Agnes in her bed,
But dares not look behind, or all the charm is fled.

XXVII

Soon, trembling in her soft and chilly nest,
  In sort of wakeful swoon, perplex'd she lay,
  Until the poppied warmth of sleep oppress'd
  Her soothed limbs, and soul fatigued away;
  Flown, like a thought, until the morrow-day;
  Blissfully haven'd both from joy and pain;
  Clasp'd like a missal where swart Paynims pray;
  Blinded alike from sunshine and from rain,
As though a rose should shut, and be a bud again.

XXVIII

Stol'n to this paradise, and so entranced,
Porphyro gazed upon her empty dress,
And listen'd to her breathing, if it chanced
To wake into a slumberous tenderness;
Which when he heard, that minute did he bless,
And breath'd himself: then from the closet crept,
Noiseless as fear in a wide wilderness,
And over the hush'd carpet, silent, stept,
And 'tween the curtains peep'd, where, lo! – how fast
　　she slept.

XXIX

Then by the bed-side, where the faded moon
Made a dim, silver twilight, soft he set
A table, and, half anguish'd, threw thereon
A cloth of woven crimson, gold, and jet: –
O for some drowsy Morphean amulet!
The boisterous, midnight, festive clarion,
The kettle-drum, and far-heard clarionet,
Affray his ears, though but in dying tone: –
The hall door shuts again, and all the noise is gone.

XXX

And still she slept an azure-lidded sleep,
In blanched linen, smooth, and lavender'd,
While he from forth the closet brought a heap
Of candied apple, quince, and plum, and gourd;
With jellies soother than the creamy curd,
And lucent syrops, tinct with cinnamon;
Manna and dates, in argosy transferr'd
From Fez; and spiced dainties, every one,
From silken Samarcand to cedar'd Lebanon.

XXXI

These delicates he heap'd with glowing hand
On golden dishes and in baskets bright
Of wreathed silver: sumptuous they stand
In the retired quiet of the night,
Filling the chilly room with perfume light. –
'And now, my love, my seraph fair, awake!
Thou art my heaven, and I thine eremite:
Open thine eyes, for meek St Agnes' sake,
Or I shall drowse beside thee, so my soul doth ache.'

XXXII

Thus whispering, his warm, unnerved arm
Sank in her pillow. Shaded was her dream
By the dusk curtains: – 'twas a midnight charm
Impossible to melt as iced stream:
The lustrous salvers in the moonlight gleam;
Broad golden fringe upon the carpet lies:
It seem'd he never, never could redeem
From such a stedfast spell his lady's eyes;
So mus'd, awhile, entoil'd in woofed phantasies.

XXXIII

Awakening up, he took her hollow lute, –
Tumultuous, – and, in chords that tenderest be,
He play'd an ancient ditty, long since mute,
In Provence call'd, 'La belle dame sans mercy':
Close to her ear touching the melody; –
Wherewith disturb'd, she utter'd a soft moan:
He ceased – she panted quick – and suddenly
Her blue affrayed eyes wide open shone:
Upon his knees he sank, pale as smooth-sculptured stone.

XXXIV

Her eyes were open, but she still beheld,
Now wide awake, the vision of her sleep:
There was a painful change, that nigh expell'd
The blisses of her dream so pure and deep
At which fair Madeline began to weep,
And moan forth witless words with many a sigh;
While still her gaze on Porphyro would keep;
Who knelt, with joined hands and piteous eye,
Fearing to move or speak, she look'd so dreamingly.

XXXV

'Ah, Porphyro!' said she, 'but even now
Thy voice was at sweet tremble in mine ear,
Made tunable with every sweetest vow;
And those sad eyes were spiritual and clear:
How changed thou art! how pallid, chill, and drear!
Give me that voice again, my Porphyro,
Those looks immortal, those complainings dear!
Oh leave me not in this eternal woe,
For if thou diest, my Love, I know not where to go.'

XXXVI

Beyond a mortal man impassion'd far
At these voluptuous accents, he arose,
Ethereal, flush'd, and like a throbbing star
Seen 'mid the sapphire heaven's deep repose;
Into her dream he melted, as the rose
Blendeth its odour with the violet, —
Solution sweet: meantime the frost-wind blows
Like Love's alarum, pattering the sharp sleet
Against the window-panes; St Agnes' moon hath set.

XXXVII

'Tis dark: quick pattereth the flaw-blown sleet.
'This is no dream, my bride, my Madeline!'
'Tis dark: the iced gusts still rave and beat:
'No dream, alas! alas! and woe is mine!
Porphyro will leave me here to fade and pine. –
Cruel! what traitor could thee hither bring?
I curse not, for my heart is lost in thine,
Though thou forsakest a deceived thing; –
A dove forlorn and lost with sick unpruned wing.'

XXXVIII

'My Madeline! sweet dreamer! lovely bride!
Say, may I be for aye thy vassal blest?
Thy beauty's shield, heart-shap'd and vermeil dyed?
Ah, silver shrine, here will I take my rest
After so many hours of toil and quest,
A famish'd pilgrim, – sav'd by miracle.
Though I have found, I will not rob thy nest
Saving of thy sweet self; if thou think'st well
To trust, fair Madeline, to no rude infidel.

XXXIX

'Hark! 'tis an elfin-storm from faery land,
Of haggard seeming, but a boon indeed:
Arise – arise! the morning is at hand; –
The bloated wassaillers will never heed: –
Let us away, my love, with happy speed;
There are no ears to hear, or eyes to see, –
Drown'd all in Rhenish and the sleepy mead:
Awake! arise! my love, and fearless be,
For o'er the southern moors I have a home for thee.'

XL

She hurried at his words, beset with fears,
For there were sleeping dragons all around,
At glaring watch, perhaps, with ready spears —
Down the wide stairs a darkling way they found. —
In all the house was heard no human sound.
A chain-droop'd lamp was flickering by each door;
The arras, rich with horseman, hawk, and hound,
Flutter'd in the besieging wind's uproar;
And the long carpets rose along the gusty floor.

XLI

They glide, like phantoms, into the wide hall;
Like phantoms, to the iron porch, they glide;
Where lay the Porter, in uneasy sprawl,
With a huge empty flaggon by his side:
The wakeful bloodhound rose, and shook his hide,
But his sagacious eye an inmate owns:
By one, and one, the bolts full easy slide: —
The chains lie silent on the footworn stones; —
The key turns, and the door upon its hinges groans.

XLII

And they are gone: aye, ages long ago
These lovers fled away into the storm.
That night the Baron dreamt of many a woe,
And all his warrior-guests, with shade and form
Of witch, and demon, and large coffin-worm,
Were long be-nightmar'd. Angela the old
Died palsy-twitch'd, with meagre face deform;
The Beadsman, after thousand aves told,
For aye unsought for slept among his ashes cold.

Ode to a Nightingale

I

MY heart aches, and a drowsy numbness pains
   My sense, as though of hemlock I had drunk,
Or emptied some dull opiate to the drains
   One minute past, and Lethe-wards had sunk:
'Tis not through envy of thy happy lot,
   But being too happy in thy happiness, –
      That thou, light-winged Dryad of the trees,
         In some melodious plot
   Of beechen green, and shadows numberless,
      Singest of summer in full-throated ease.

II

O for a draught of vintage! that hath been
   Cool'd a long age in the deep-delved earth,
Tasting of Flora and the country-green,
   Dance, and Provençal song, and sun-burnt mirth!
O for a beaker full of the warm South,
   Full of the true, the blushful Hippocrene,
      With beaded bubbles winking at the brim,
         And purple-stained mouth;
   That I might drink, and leave the world unseen,
      And with thee fade away into the forest dim:

III

Fade far away, dissolve, and quite forget
   What thou among the leaves hast never known,
The weariness, the fever, and the fret
   Here, where men sit and hear each other groan;
Where palsy shakes a few, sad, last gray hairs,
   Where youth grows pale, and spectre-thin, and dies;
      Where but to think is to be full of sorrow
         And leaden-eyed despairs;
   Where Beauty cannot keep her lustrous eyes,
      Or new Love pine at them beyond to-morrow.

IV

Away! away! for I will fly to thee,
  Not charioted by Bacchus and his pards,
But on the viewless wings of Poesy,
  Though the dull brain perplexes and retards:
Already with thee! tender is the night,
  And haply the Queen-Moon is on her throne,
    Cluster'd around by all her starry Fays;
      But here there is no light,
Save what from heaven is with the breezes blown ,
    Through verdurous glooms and winding mossy ways.

V

I cannot see what flowers are at my feet,
  Nor what soft incense hangs upon the boughs,
But, in embalmed darkness, guess each sweet
  Wherewith the seasonable month endows
The grass, the thicket, and the fruit-tree wild;
  White hawthorn, and the pastoral eglantine;
    Fast-fading violets cover'd up in leaves;
      And mid-May's eldest child,
The coming musk-rose, full of dewy wine,
    The murmurous haunt of flies on summer eves.

VI

Darkling I listen; and for many a time
  I have been half in love with easeful Death,
Call'd him soft names in many a mused rhyme,
  To take into the air my quiet breath;
Now more than ever seems it rich to die,
  To cease upon the midnight with no pain,
    While thou art pouring forth thy soul abroad
      In such an ecstasy!
  Still wouldst thou sing, and I have ears in vain –
    To thy high requiem become a sod.

VII

Thou wast not born for death, immortal Bird!
  No hungry generations tread thee down;
The voice I hear this passing night was heard
  In ancient days by emperor and clown:
Perhaps the self-same song that found a path
    Through the sad heart of Ruth, when, sick for home,
      She stood in tears amid the alien corn;
        The same that oft-times hath
    Charm'd magic casements, opening on the foam
    Of perilous seas, in faery lands forlorn.

VIII

Forlorn! the very word is like a bell
  To toll me back from thee to my sole self!
Adieu! the fancy cannot cheat so well
  As she is fam'd to do, deceiving elf.
Adieu! adieu! thy plaintive anthem fades
  Past the near meadows, over the still stream,
    Up the hill-side; and now 'tis buried deep
      In the next valley-glades:
  Was it a vision, or a waking dream?
    Fled is that music: – Do I wake or sleep?

Ode on a Grecian Urn

I

THOU still unravish'd bride of quietness!
   Thou foster-child of silence and slow time,
Sylvan historian, who canst thus express
   A flowery tale more sweetly than our rhyme:
What leaf-fringed legend haunts about thy shape
   Of deities or mortals, or of both,
      In Tempe or the dales of Arcady?
   What men or gods are these? What maidens loath?
What mad pursuit? What struggle to escape?
      What pipes and timbrels? What wild ecstasy?

II

Heard melodies are sweet, but those unheard
   Are sweeter; therefore, ye soft pipes, play on;
Not to the sensual ear, but, more endear'd,
   Pipe to the spirit ditties of no tone:
Fair youth, beneath the trees, thou canst not leave
   Thy song, nor ever can those trees be bare;
      Bold Lover, never, never canst thou kiss,
   Though winning near the goal — yet, do not grieve;
She cannot fade, though thou hast not thy bliss,
      For ever wilt thou love, and she be fair!

III

Ah, happy, happy boughs! that cannot shed
   Your leaves, nor ever bid the Spring adieu;
And, happy melodist, unwearied,
   For ever piping songs for ever new;
More happy love! more happy, happy love!
   For ever warm and still to be enjoy'd,
      For ever panting and for ever young;
   All breathing human passion far above,
That leaves a heart high sorrowful and cloy'd,
      A burning forehead, and a parching tongue.

176

IV

Who are these coming to the sacrifice?
    To what green altar, O mysterious priest,
Lead'st thou that heifer lowing at the skies,
    And all her silken flanks with garlands drest?
What little town by river or sea-shore,
    Or mountain-built with peaceful citadel,
        Is emptied of its folk, this pious morn?
    And, little town, thy streets for evermore
Will silent be; and not a soul to tell
        Why thou art desolate, can e'er return.

V

O Attic shape! Fair attitude! with brede
    Of marble men and maidens overwrought,
With forest branches and the trodden weed;
    Thou, silent form! dost tease us out of thought
As doth eternity: Cold Pastoral!
    When old age shall this generation waste,
        Thou shalt remain, in midst of other woe
    Than ours, a friend to man, to whom thou say'st,
'Beauty is truth, truth beauty,' – that is all
        Ye know on earth, and all ye need to know.

Ode to Psyche

O GODDESS! hear these tuneless numbers, wrung
   By sweet enforcement and remembrance dear,
And pardon that thy secrets should be sung
   Even into thine own soft-conchèd ear:
Surely I dreamt to-day, or did I see
   The wingèd Psyche with awaken'd eyes?
I wander'd in a forest thoughtlessly,
   And, on the sudden, fainting with surprise,
Saw two fair creatures, couchèd side by side
   In deepest grass, beneath the whisp'ring roof
   Of leaves and trembled blossoms, where there ran
      A brooklet, scarce espied:

'Mid hush'd, cool-rooted flowers, fragrant-eyed,
   Blue, silver-white, and budded Tyrian,
They lay calm-breathing on the bedded grass;
   Their arms embracèd, and their pinions too:
   Their lips touch'd not, but had not bade adieu,
As if disjoinèd by soft-handed slumber,
And ready still past kisses to outnumber
   At tender eye-dawn of aurorean love:
      The wingèd boy I knew;
But who wast thou, O happy, happy dove?
      His Psyche true!

O latest born and loveliest vision far
   Of all Olympus' faded hierarchy!
Fairer than Phoebe's sapphire-region'd star,
Or Vesper, amorous glow-worm of the sky;
Fairer than these, though temple thou hast none,
     Nor altar heap'd with flowers;
Nor virgin-choir to make delicious moan
     Upon the midnight hours;

No voice, no lute, no pipe, no incense sweet
   From chain-swung censer teeming;
No shrine, no grove, no oracle, no heat
   Of pale-mouth'd prophet dreaming.

O brightest! though too late for antique vows,
   Too, too late for the fond believing lyre,
When holy were the haunted forest boughs,
   Holy the air, the water, and the fire;
Yet even in these days so far retir'd
   From happy pieties, thy lucent fans,
   Fluttering among the faint Olympians,
I see, and sing, by my own eyes inspir'd.
So let me be thy choir, and make a moan
      Upon the midnight hours;
Thy voice, thy lute, thy pipe, thy incense sweet
   From swinged censer teeming;
Thy shrine, thy grove, thy oracle, thy heat
   Of pale-mouth'd prophet dreaming.

Yes, I will be thy priest, and build a fane
   In some untrodden region of my mind,
Where branched thoughts, new grown with pleasant pain,
   Instead of pines shall murmur in the wind:
Far, far around shall those dark-cluster'd trees
   Fledge the wild-ridged mountains steep by steep;
And there by zephyrs, streams, and birds, and bees,
   The moss-lain Dryads shall be lull'd to sleep;
And in the midst of this wide quietness
   A rosy sanctuary will I dress
With the wreath'd trellis of a working brain,
   With buds, and bells, and stars without a name.
With all the gardener Fancy e'er could feign,
   Who breeding flowers, will never breed the same:

And there shall be for thee all soft delight
    That shadowy thought can win,
A bright torch, and a casement ope at night,
    To let the warm Love in!

To Fancy

EVER let the fancy roam,
Pleasure never is at home:
At a touch sweet Pleasure melteth,
Like to bubbles when rain pelteth;
Then let winged Fancy wander
Through the thought still spread beyond her:
Open wide the mind's cage-door,
She'll dart forth, and cloudward soar.
O sweet Fancy! let her loose;
Summer's joys are spoilt by use,
And the enjoying of the Spring
Fades as does its blossoming:
Autumn's red-lipp'd fruitage too,
Blushing through the mist and dew,
Cloys with tasting: What do then?
Sit thee by the ingle, when
The sear faggot blazes bright,
Spirit of a winter's night;
When the soundless earth is muffled,
And the caked snow is shuffled
From the ploughboy's heavy shoon;
When the Night doth meet the Noon
In a dark conspiracy
To banish Even from her sky.
Sit thee there, and send abroad,
With a mind self-overaw'd,
Fancy, high-commission'd: – send her:
She has vassals to attend her:
She will bring, in spite of frost,
Beauties that the earth hath lost;
She will bring thee, all together,
All delights of summer weather;

All the buds and bells of May,
From dewy sward or thorny spray;
All the heaped Autumn's wealth,
With a still, mysterious stealth
She will mix these pleasures up
Like three fit wines in a cup,
And thou shalt quaff it: – thou shalt hear
Distant harvest-carols clear;
Rustle of the reaped corn;
Sweet birds antheming the morn:
And, in the same moment – hark!
'Tis the early April lark,
Or the rooks, with busy caw,
Foraging for sticks and straw.
Thou shalt, at one glance, behold
The daisy and the marigold;
White-plum'd lilies, and the first
Hedge-grown primrose that hath burst;
Shaded hyacinth, alway
Sapphire queen of the mid-May;
And every leaf, and every flower
Pearled with the self-same shower.
Thou shalt see the field-mouse peep
Meagre from its celled sleep;
And the snake all winter-thin
Cast on sunny bank its skin!
Freckled nest-eggs thou shalt see
Hatching in the hawthorn-tree,
When the hen-bird's wing doth rest
Quiet on her mossy nest;
Then the hurry and alarm
When the bee-hive casts its swarm;
Acorns ripe down-pattering
While the autumn breezes sing.

Oh, sweet Fancy! let her loose;
Every thing is spoilt by use:
Where's the cheek that doth not fade,
Too much gaz'd at? Where's the maid
Whose lip mature is ever new?
Where's the eye, however blue,
Doth not weary? Where's the face
One would meet in every place?
Where's the voice, however soft,
One would hear so very oft?
At a touch sweet Pleasure melteth
Like to bubbles when rain pelteth.
Let, then, winged Fancy find
Thee a mistress to thy mind:
Dulcet-eyed as Ceres' daughter,
Ere the God of Torment taught her
How to frown and how to chide;
With a waist and with a side
White as Hebe's, when her zone
Slipt its golden clasp, and down
Fell her kirtle to her feet,
While she held the goblet sweet,
And Jove grew languid. – Break the mesh
Of the Fancy's silken leash;
Quickly break her prison-string,
And such joys as these she'll bring. –
Let the winged Fancy roam,
Pleasure never is at home.

[Ode written in a copy of the Works of Beaumont and Fletcher]

BARDS of Passion and of Mirth,
Ye have left your souls on earth!
Have ye souls in heaven too,
Double lived in regions new?
Yes, and those of heaven commune
With the spheres of sun and moon;
With the noise of fountains wond'rous,
And the parle of voices thund'rous;
With the whisper of heaven's trees
And one another, in soft ease
Seated on Elysian lawns
Brows'd by none but Dian's fawns;
Underneath large blue-bells tented,
Where the daisies are rose-scented,
And the rose herself has got
Perfume which on earth is not;
Where the nightingale doth sing
Not a senseless, tranced thing,
But divine melodious truth;
Philosophic numbers smooth;
Tales and golden histories
Of heaven and its mysteries.

Thus ye live on high, and then
On the earth ye live again;
And the souls ye left behind you
Teach us, here, the way to find you,
Where your other souls are joying,
Never slumber'd, never cloying.
Here, your earth-born souls still speak
To mortals, of their little week;

Of their sorrows and delights;
Of their passions and their spites;
Of their glory and their shame;
What doth strengthen, and what maim.
Thus ye teach us, every day,
Wisdom, though fled far away.

Bards of Passion and of Mirth,
Ye have left your souls on earth!
Ye have souls in heaven too,
Double-lived in regions new!

Lines on the Mermaid Tavern

SOULS of poets dead and gone,
What Elysium have ye known,
Happy field or mossy cavern,
Choicer than the Mermaid Tavern?
Have ye tippled drink more fine
Than mine host's Canary wine?
Or are fruits of Paradise
Sweeter than those dainty pies
Of venison? O generous food!
Drest as though bold Robin Hood
Would, with his maid Marian,
Sup and bowse from horn and can.

I have heard that on a day
Mine host's sign-board flew away,
Nobody knew whither, till
An astrologer's old quill
To a sheepskin gave the story,
Said he saw you in your glory,
Underneath a new old sign
Sipping beverage divine,
And pledging with contented smack
The Mermaid in the Zodiac.

Souls of poets dead and gone,
What Elysium have ye known,
Happy field or mossy cavern,
Choicer than the Mermaid Tavern?

Robin Hood
To a Friend *

No! those days are gone away,
And their hours are old and gray,
And their minutes buried all
Under the down-trodden pall
Of the leaves of many years:
Many times have winter's shears,
Frozen North, and chilling East,
Sounded tempests to the feast
Of the forest's whispering fleeces,
Since men knew nor rent nor leases.

No, the bugle sounds no more,
And the twanging bow no more;
Silent is the ivory shrill
Past the heath and up the hill;
There is no mid-forest laugh,
Where lone Echo gives the half
To some wight, amazed to hear
Jesting, deep in forest drear.

On the fairest time of June
You may go, with sun or moon,
Or the seven stars to light you,
Or the polar ray to right you;
But you never may behold
Little John, or Robin bold;
Never one, of all the clan,
Thrumming on an empty can
Some old hunting ditty, while
He doth his green way beguile
To fair hostess Merriment,
Down beside the pasture Trent;

[* J. H. Reynolds, in answer to his Robin Hood Sonnets]

For he left the merry tale
Messenger for spicy ale.

    Gone, the merry morris din;
Gone, the song of Gamelyn;
Gone, the tough-belted outlaw
Idling in the 'grené shawe';
All are gone away and past!
And if Robin should be cast
Sudden from his turfed grave,
And if Marian should have
Once again her forest days,
She would weep, and he would craze;
He would swear, for all his oaks,
Fall'n beneath the dockyard strokes,
Have rotted on the briny seas;
She would weep that her wild bees
Sang not to her – strange! that honey
Can't be got without hard money!

    So it is; yet let us sing
Honour to the old bow-string!
Honour to the bugle-horn!
Honour to the woods unshorn!
Honour to the Lincoln green!
Honour to the archer keen!
Honour to tight Little John,
And the horse he rode upon!
Honour to bold Robin Hood,
Sleeping in the underwood:
Honour to maid Marian,
And to all the Sherwood-clan!
Though their days have hurried by,
Let us two a burden try.

To Autumn

I

SEASON of mists and mellow fruitfulness!
   Close bosom-friend of the maturing sun;
Conspiring with him how to load and bless
   With fruit the vines that round the thatch-eves run;
To bend with apples the moss'd cottage-trees,
     And fill all fruit with ripeness to the core;
       To swell the gourd, and plump the hazel shells
   With a sweet kernel; to set budding more,
And still more, later flowers for the bees,
Until they think warm days will never cease,
       For Summer has o'er-brimm'd their clammy cells.

II

Who hath not seen thee oft amid thy store?
   Sometimes whoever seeks abroad may find
Thee sitting careless on a granary floor,
   Thy hair soft-lifted by the winnowing wind;
Or on a half-reap'd furrow sound asleep,
     Drowsed with the fumes of poppies, while thy hook
      Spares the next swath and all its twined flowers:
And sometime like a gleaner thou dost keep
   Steady thy laden head across a brook;
   Or by a cyder-press, with patient look,
      Thou watchest the last oozings hours by hours.

III

Where are the songs of Spring? Ay, where are they?
   Think not of them, thou hast thy music too, –
While barred clouds bloom the soft-dying day,
   And touch the stubble-plains with rosy hue;

Then in a wailful choir the small gnats mourn
　　Among the river sallows, borne aloft
　　　Or sinking as the light wind lives or dies;
And full-grown lambs loud bleat from hilly bourn;
　　Hedge-crickets sing; and now with treble soft
　　The red-breast whistles from a garden-croft;
　　　And gathering swallows twitter in the skies.

Ode on Melancholy

I

No, no, go not to Lethe, neither twist
   Wolf's-bane, tight-rooted, for its poisonous wine;
Nor suffer thy pale forehead to be kiss'd
   By nightshade, ruby grape of Proserpine;
Make not your rosary of yew-berries,
    Nor let the beetle nor the death-moth be
      Your mournful Psyche, nor the downy owl
A partner in your sorrow's mysteries;
    For shade to shade will come too drowsily,
      And drown the wakeful anguish of the soul.

II

But when the melancholy fit shall fall
   Sudden from heaven like a weeping cloud,
That fosters the droop-headed flowers all,
   And hides the green hill in an April shroud;
Then glut thy sorrow on a morning rose,
    Or on the rainbow of the salt sand-wave,
      Or on the wealth of globed peonies;
Or if thy mistress some rich anger shows,
    Emprison her soft hand, and let her rave,
      And feed deep, deep upon her peerless eyes.

III

She dwells with Beauty – Beauty that must die;
   And Joy, whose hand is ever at his lips
Bidding adieu; and aching Pleasure nigh,
   Turning to Poison while the bee-mouth sips:

Ay, in the very temple of Delight
  Veil'd Melancholy has her sovran shrine,
    Though seen of none save him whose strenuous tongue
  Can burst Joy's grape against his palate fine:
His soul shall taste the sadness of her might,
  And be among her cloudy trophies hung.

HYPERION

A FRAGMENT

Book I

DEEP in the shady sadness of a vale
Far sunken from the healthy breath of morn,
Far from the fiery noon, and eve's one star,
Sat gray-hair'd Saturn, quiet as a stone,
Still as the silence round about his lair;
Forest on forest hung about his head
Like cloud on cloud. No stir of air was there,
Not so much life as on a summer's day
Robs not one light seed from the feather'd grass,
But where the dead leaf fell, there did it rest.
A stream went voiceless by, still deadened more
By reason of his fallen divinity
Spreading a shade: the Naiad 'mid her reeds
Press'd her cold finger closer to her lips.

Along the margin-sand large foot-marks went,
No further than to where his feet had stray'd,
And slept there since. Upon the sodden ground
His old right hand lay nerveless, listless, dead,
Unsceptred; and his realmless eyes were closed;
While his bow'd head seem'd list'ning to the Earth,
His ancient mother, for some comfort yet.

It seem'd no force could wake him from his place:
But there came one, who with a kindred hand
Touch'd his wide shoulders, after bending low
With reverence, though to one who knew it not.
She was a Goddess of the infant world;

By her in stature the tall Amazon
Had stood a pigmy's height: she would have ta'en
Achilles by the hair and bent his neck;
Or with a finger stay'd Ixion's wheel.
Her face was large as that of Memphian sphinx,
Pedestal'd haply in a palace court,
When sages look'd to Egypt for their lore.
But oh! how unlike marble was that face:
How beautiful, if sorrow had not made
Sorrow more beautiful than Beauty's self.
There was a listening fear in her regard,
As if calamity had but begun;
As if the vanward clouds of evil days
Had spent their malice, and the sullen rear
Was with its stored thunder labouring up.
One hand she press'd upon that aching spot
Where beats the human heart, as if just there,
Though an immortal, she felt cruel pain:
The other upon Saturn's bended neck
She laid, and to the level of his ear
Leaning with parted lips, some words she spake
In solemn tenour and deep organ tone:
Some mourning words, which in our feeble tongue
Would come in these like accents; O how frail
To that large utterance of the early Gods!
'Saturn, look up! – though wherefore, poor old King?
I have no comfort for thee, no not one:
I cannot say, "O wherefore sleepest thou?"
For heaven is parted from thee, and the earth
Knows thee not, thus afflicted, for a God;
And ocean too, with all its solemn noise,
Has from thy sceptre pass'd; and all the air
Is emptied of thine hoary majesty.
Thy thunder, conscious of the new command,

Rumbles reluctant o'er our fallen house;
And thy sharp lightning in unpractis'd hands
Scorches and burns our once serene domain.
O aching time! O moments big as years!
All as ye pass swell out the monstrous truth,
And press it so upon our weary griefs
That unbelief has not a space to breathe.
Saturn, sleep on: – O thoughtless, why did I
Thus violate thy slumbrous solitude?
Why should I ope thy melancholy eyes?
Saturn, sleep on! while at thy feet I weep.'

   As when, upon a tranced summer-night,
Those green-rob'd senators of mighty woods,
Tall oaks, branch-charmed by the earnest stars,
Dream, and so dream all night without a stir,
Save from one gradual solitary gust
Which comes upon the silence, and dies off,
As if the ebbing air had but one wave;
So came these words and went; the while in tears
She touch'd her fair large forehead to the ground,
Just where her falling hair might be outspread
A soft and silken mat for Saturn's feet.
One moon, with alterations slow, had shed
Her silver seasons four upon the night,
And still these two were postured motionless,
Like natural sculpture in cathedral cavern;
The frozen God still couchant on the earth,
And the sad Goddess weeping at his feet:
Until at length old Saturn lifted up
His faded eyes, and saw his kingdom gone,
And all the gloom and sorrow of the place,
And that fair kneeling Goddess; and then spake
As with a palsied tongue, and while his beard

Shook horrid with such aspen-malady:
'O tender spouse of gold Hyperion,
Thea, I feel thee ere I see thy face;
Look up, and let me see our doom in it;
Look up, and tell me if this feeble shape
Is Saturn's; tell me, if thou hear'st the voice
Of Saturn; tell me, if this wrinkling brow,
Naked and bare of its great diadem,
Peers like the front of Saturn? Who had power
To make me desolate? whence came the strength?
How was it nurtur'd to such bursting forth,
While Fate seem'd strangled in my nervous grasp?
But it is so; and I am smother'd up,
And buried from all godlike exercise
Of influence benign on planets pale,
Of admonitions to the winds and seas,
Of peaceful sway above man's harvesting,
And all those acts which Deity supreme
Doth ease its heart of love in. — I am gone
Away from my own bosom: I have left
My strong identity, my real self,
Somewhere between the throne, and where I sit
Here on this spot of earth. Search, Thea, search!
Open thine eyes eterne, and sphere them round
Upon all space: space starr'd, and lorn of light;
Space region'd with life-air; and barren void;
Spaces of fire, and all the yawn of hell. —
Search, Thea, search! and tell me, if thou seest
A certain shape or shadow, making way
With wings or chariot fierce to repossess
A heaven he lost erewhile: it must — it must
Be of ripe progress — Saturn must be King.
Yes, there must be a golden victory;
There must be Gods thrown down, and trumpets blown

Of triumph calm, and hymns of festival
Upon the gold clouds metropolitan,
Voices of soft proclaim, and silver stir
Of strings in hollow shells; and there shall be
Beautiful things made new, for the surprise
Of the sky-children; I will give command:
Thea! Thea! Thea! where is Saturn?'

This passion lifted him upon his feet,
And made his hands to struggle in the air,
His Druid locks to shake and ooze with sweat,
His eyes to fever out, his voice to cease.
He stood, and heard not Thea's sobbing deep;
A little time, and then again he snatch'd
Utterance thus. — 'But cannot I create?
Cannot I form? Cannot I fashion forth
Another world, another universe,
To overbear and crumble this to naught?
Where is another chaos? Where?' — That word
Found way unto Olympus, and made quake
The rebel three. — Thea was startled up,
And in her bearing was a sort of hope,
As thus she quick-voiced spake, yet full of awe,
'This cheers our fallen house: come to our friends,
O Saturn! come away, and give them heart;
I know the covert, for thence came I hither.'
Thus brief; then with beseeching eyes she went
With backward footing through the shade a space:
He follow'd, and she turn'd to lead the way
Through aged boughs, that yielded like the mist
Which eagles cleave upmounting from their nest.

Meanwhile in other realms big tears were shed,
More sorrow like to this, and such like woe,

Too huge for mortal tongue or pen of scribe:
The Titans fierce, self-hid, or prison-bound,
Groan'd for the old allegiance once more,
And listen'd in sharp pain for Saturn's voice.
But one of the whole mammoth-brood still kept
His sov'reignty, and rule, and majesty; —
Blazing Hyperion on his orbed fire
Still sat, still snuff'd the incense, teeming up
From man to the sun's God; yet unsecure:
For as among us mortals omen drear
Fright and perplex, so also shudder'd he —
Not at dog's howl, or gloom-bird's hated screech,
Or the familiar visiting of one
Upon the first toll of his passing-bell,
Or prophesyings of the midnight lamp;
But horrors, portion'd to a giant nerve,
Oft made Hyperion ache. His palace bright
Bastion'd with pyramids of glowing gold,
And touch'd with shade of bronzed obelisks,
Glar'd a blood-red through all its thousand courts,
Arches, and domes, and fiery galleries;
And all its curtains of Aurorian clouds
Flush'd angerly: while sometimes eagles' wings,
Unseen before by Gods or wondering men,
Darken'd the place; and neighing steeds were heard,
Not heard before by Gods or wondering men.
Also, when he would taste the spicy wreaths
Of incense, breath'd aloft from sacred hills,
Instead of sweets, his ample palate took
Savour of poisonous brass and metal sick:
And so, when harbour'd in the sleepy west,
After the full completion of fair day, —
For rest divine upon exalted couch
And slumber in the arms of melody,

He pac'd away the pleasant hours of ease
With stride colossal, on from hall to hall;
While far within each aisle and deep recess,
His winged minions in close clusters stood,
Amaz'd and full of fear; like anxious men
Who on wide plains gather in panting troops,
When earthquakes jar their battlements and towers.
Even now, while Saturn, rous'd from icy trance,
Went step for step with Thea through the woods,
Hyperion, leaving twilight in the rear,
Came slope upon the threshold of the west;
Then, as was wont, his palace-door flew ope
In smoothest silence, save what solemn tubes,
Blown by the serious Zephyrs, gave of sweet
And wandering sounds, slow-breathed melodies;
And like a rose in vermeil tint and shape,
In fragrance soft, and coolness to the eye,
That inlet to severe magnificence
Stood full blown, for the God to enter in.

He enter'd, but he enter'd full of wrath;
His flaming robes stream'd out beyond his heels,
And gave a roar, as if of earthly fire,
That scar'd away the meek ethereal Hours
And made their dove-wings tremble. On he flared,
From stately nave to nave, from vault to vault,
Through bowers of fragrant and enwreathed light,
And diamond-paved lustrous long arcades,
Until he reach'd the great main cupola;
There standing fierce beneath, he stamped his foot,
And from the basements deep to the high towers
Jarr'd his own golden region; and before
The quavering thunder thereupon had ceas'd,
His voice leapt out, despite of godlike curb,

To this result: 'O dreams of day and night!
O monstrous forms! O effigies of pain!
O spectres busy in a cold, cold gloom!
O lank-ear'd Phantoms of black-weeded pools!
Why do I know ye? why have I seen ye? why
Is my eternal essence thus distraught
To see and to behold these horrors new?
Saturn is fallen, am I too to fall?
Am I to leave this haven of my rest,
This cradle of my glory, this soft clime,
This calm luxuriance of blissful light,
These crystalline pavilions, and pure fanes,
Of all my lucent empire? It is left
Deserted, void, nor any haunt of mine.
The blaze, the splendour, and the symmetry,
I cannot see – but darkness, death and darkness.
Even here, into my centre of repose,
The shady visions come to domineer,
Insult, and blind, and stifle up my pomp. –
Fall! – No, by Tellus and her briny robes!
Over the fiery frontier of my realms
I will advance a terrible right arm
Shall scare that infant thunderer, rebel Jove,
And bid old Saturn take his throne again.' –
He spake, and ceas'd, the while a heavier threat
Held struggle with his throat but came not forth;
For as in theatres of crowded men
Hubbub increases more they call out 'Hush!'
So at Hyperion's words the Phantoms pale
Bestirr'd themselves, thrice horrible and cold;
And from the mirror'd level where he stood
A mist arose, as from a scummy marsh.
At this, through all his bulk an agony
Crept gradual, from the feet unto the crown,

Like a lithe serpent vast and muscular
Making slow way, with head and neck convuls'd
From over-strained might. Releas'd, he fled
To the eastern gates, and full six dewy hours
Before the dawn in season due should blush,
He breath'd fierce breath against the sleepy portals,
Clear'd them of heavy vapours, burst them wide
Suddenly on the ocean's chilly streams.
The planet orb of fire, whereon he rode
Each day from east to west the heavens through,
Spun round in sable curtaining of clouds;
Not therefore veiled quite, blindfold, and hid,
But ever and anon the glancing spheres,
Circles, and arcs, and broad-belting colure,
Glow'd through, and wrought upon the muffling dark
Sweet-shaped lightnings from the nadir deep
Up to the zenith, – hieroglyphics old,
Which sages and keen-eyed astrologers
Then living on the earth, with labouring thought
Won from the gaze of many centuries:
Now lost, save what we find on remnants huge
Of stone, or marble swart; their import gone,
Their wisdom long since fled. – Two wings this orb
Possess'd for glory, two fair argent wings,
Ever exalted at the God's approach:
And now, from forth the gloom their plumes immense
Rose, one by one, till all outspreaded were;
While still the dazzling globe maintain'd eclipse,
Awaiting for Hyperion's command.
Fain would he have commanded, fain took throne
And bid the day begin, if but for change.
He might not: – No, though a primeval God:
The sacred seasons might not be disturb'd.
Therefore the operations of the dawn

Stay'd in their birth, even as here 'tis told.
Those silver wings expanded sisterly,
Eager to sail their orb; the porches wide
Open'd upon the dusk demesnes of night;
And the bright Titan, frenzied with new woes,
Unus'd to bend, by hard compulsion bent
His spirit to the sorrow of the time;
And all along a dismal rack of clouds,
Upon the boundaries of day and night,
He stretch'd himself in grief and radiance faint.
There as he lay, the Heaven with its stars
Look'd down on him with pity, and the voice
Of Coelus, from the universal space,
Thus whisper'd low and solemn in his ear.
'O brightest of my children dear, earth-born
And sky-engendered, Son of Mysteries
All unrevealed even to the powers
Which met at thy creating; at whose joys
And palpitations sweet, and pleasures soft,
I, Coelus, wonder how they came and whence;
And at the fruits thereof what shapes they be,
Distinct, and visible; symbols divine,
Manifestations of that beauteous life
Diffus'd unseen throughout eternal space:
Of these new-form'd art thou, oh brightest child!
Of these, thy brethren and the Goddesses!
There is sad feud among ye, and rebellion
Of son against his sire. I saw him fall,
I saw my first-born tumbled from his throne!
To me his arms were spread, to me his voice
Found way from forth the thunders round his head!
Pale wox I, and in vapours hid my face.
Art thou, too, near such doom? vague fear there is:
For I have seen my sons most unlike Gods.

Divine ye were created, and divine
In sad demeanour, solemn, undisturb'd,
Unruffled, like high Gods, ye liv'd and ruled:
Now I behold in you fear, hope, and wrath;
Actions of rage and passion; even as
I see them, on the mortal world beneath,
In men who die. – This is the grief, O Son!
Sad sign of ruin, sudden dismay, and fall!
Yet do thou strive; as thou art capable,
As thou canst move about, an evident God;
And canst oppose to each malignant hour
Ethereal presence: – I am but a voice;
My life is but the life of winds and tides,
No more than winds and tides can I avail: –
But thou canst. – Be thou therefore in the van
Of circumstance; yea, seize the arrow's barb
Before the tense string murmur. – To the earth!
For there thou wilt find Saturn, and his woes.
Meantime I will keep watch on thy bright sun,
And of thy seasons be a careful nurse.' –
Ere half this region-whisper had come down,
Hyperion arose, and on the stars
Lifted his curved lids, and kept them wide
Until it ceas'd; and still he kept them wide:
And still they were the same bright, patient stars.
Then with a slow incline of his broad breast,
Like to a diver in the pearly seas,
Forward he stoop'd over the airy shore,
And plung'd all noiseless into the deep night.

Book II

JUST at the self-same beat of Time's wide wings
Hyperion slid into the rustled air,
And Saturn gain'd with Thea that sad place
Where Cybele and the bruised Titans mourn'd.
It was a den where no insulting light
Could glimmer on their tears; where their own groans
They felt, but heard not, for the solid roar
Of thunderous waterfalls and torrents hoarse,
Pouring a constant bulk, uncertain where.
Crag jutting forth to crag, and rocks that seem'd
Ever as if just rising from a sleep,
Forehead to forehead held their monstrous horns;
And thus in thousand hugest phantasies
Made a fit roofing to this nest of woe.
Instead of thrones, hard flint they sat upon,
Couches of rugged stone, and slaty ridge
Stubborn'd with iron. All were not assembled:
Some chain'd in torture, and some wandering.
Coeus, and Gyges, and Briareüs,
Typhon, and Dolor, and Porphyrion,
With many more, the brawniest in assault,
Were pent in regions of laborious breath;
Dungeon'd in opaque element, to keep
Their clenched teeth still clench'd, and all their limbs
Lock'd up like veins of metal, crampt and screw'd;
Without a motion, save of their big hearts
Heaving in pain, and horribly convuls'd
With sanguine, feverous boiling gurge of pulse.
Mnemosyne was straying in the world;
Far from her moon had Phoebe wandered;
And many else were free to roam abroad,
But for the main, here found they covert drear.

Scarce images of life, one here, one there,
Lay vast and edgeways; like a dismal cirque
Of Druid stones, upon a forlorn moor,
When the chill rain begins at shut of eve,
In dull November, and their chancel vault,
The Heaven itself, is blinded throughout night.
Each one kept shroud, nor to his neighbour gave
Or word, or look, or action of despair.
Creüs was one; his ponderous iron mace
Lay by him, and a shatter'd rib of rock
Told of his rage, ere he thus sank and pined.
Iapetus another; in his grasp,
A serpent's plashy neck; its barbed tongue
Squeez'd from the gorge, and all its uncurl'd length
Dead; and because the creature could not spit
Its poison in the eyes of conquering Jove.
Next Cottus: prone he lay, chin uppermost,
As though in pain; for still upon the flint
He ground severe his skull, with open mouth
And eyes at horrid working. Nearest him
Asia, born of most enormous Caf,
Who cost her mother Tellus keener pangs,
Though feminine, than any of her sons:
More thought than woe was in her dusky face,
For she was prophesying of her glory;
And in her wide imagination stood
Palm-shaded temples, and high rival fanes,
By Oxus or in Ganges' sacred isles.
Even as Hope upon her anchor leans,
So leant she, not so fair, upon a tusk
Shed from the broadest of her elephants.
Above her, on a crag's uneasy shelve,
Upon his elbow rais'd, all prostrate else,
Shadow'd Enceladus; once tame and mild

As grazing ox unworried in the meads;
Now tiger-passion'd, lion-thoughted, wroth,
He meditated, plotted, and even now
Was hurling mountains in that second war,
Not long delay'd, that scar'd the younger Gods
To hide themselves in forms of beast and bird.
Nor far hence Atlas; and beside him prone
Phorcus, the sire of Gorgons. Neighbour'd close
Oceanus, and Tethys, in whose lap
Sobb'd Clymene among her tangled hair.
In midst of all lay Themis, at the feet
Of Ops the queen all clouded round from sight;
No shape distinguishable, more than when
Thick night confounds the pine-tops with the clouds:
And many else whose names may not be told.
For when the muse's wings are air-ward spread,
Who shall delay her flight? And she must chaunt
Of Saturn, and his guide, who now had climb'd
With damp and slippery footing from a depth
More horrid still. Above a sombre cliff
Their heads appear'd, and up their stature grew
Till on the level height their steps found ease:
Then Thea spread abroad their trembling arms
Upon the precincts of this nest of pain,
And sidelong fix'd her eye on Saturn's face:
There saw she direst strife; the supreme God
At war with all the frailty of grief,
Of rage, of fear, anxiety, revenge,
Remorse, spleen, hope, but most of all despair.
Against these plagues he strove in vain; for Fate
Had pour'd a mortal oil upon his head,
A disanointing poison: so that Thea,
Affrighted, kept her still, and let him pass
First onwards in, among the fallen tribe.

    As with us mortal men, the laden heart
Is persecuted more, and fever'd more,
When it is nighing to the mournful house
Where other hearts are sick of the same bruise;
So Saturn, as he walk'd into the midst,
Felt faint, and would have sunk among the rest,
But that he met Enceladus's eye,
Whose mightiness, and awe of him, at once
Came like an inspiration; and he shouted,
 'Titans, behold your God!' at which some groan'd;
Some started on their feet; some also shouted,
Some wept, some wail'd, all bow'd with reverence;
And Ops, uplifting her black folded veil,
Show'd her pale cheeks, and all her forehead wan,
Her eye-brows thin and jet, and hollow eyes.
There is a roaring in the bleak-grown pines
When Winter lifts his voice; there is a noise
Among immortals when a God gives sign,
With hushing finger, how he means to load
His tongue with the full weight of utterless thought;
With thunder, and with music, and with pomp:
Such noise is like the roar of bleak-grown pines,
Which, when it ceases in this mountain'd world,
No other sound succeeds; but ceasing here,
Among these fallen, Saturn's voice therefrom
Grew up like organ, that begins anew
Its strain, when other harmonies, stopt short,
Leave the dinn'd air vibrating silverly.
Thus grew it up – 'Not in my own sad breast,
Which is its own great judge and searcher out,
Can I find reason why ye should be thus:
Not in the legends of the first of days,
Studied from that old spirit-leaved book
Which starry Uranus with finger bright

Sav'd from the shores of darkness, when the waves
Low-ebb'd still hid it up in shallow gloom; –
And the which book ye know I ever kept
For my firm-based footstool: – Ah, infirm!
Not there, nor in sign, symbol, or portent
Of element, earth, water, air, and fire, –
At war, at peace, or inter-quarrelling
One against one, or two, or three, or all,
Each several one against the other three,
As fire with air loud warring when rain-floods
Drown both, and press them both against earth's face,
Where, finding sulphur, a quadruple wrath
Unhinges the poor world; – not in that strife,
Wherefrom I take strange lore, and read it deep,
Can I find reason why ye should be thus:
No, no-where can unriddle, though I search,
And pore on Nature's universal scroll
Even to swooning, why ye, Divinities,
The first-born of all shap'd and palpable Gods,
Should cower beneath what, in comparison,
Is untremendous might. Yet ye are here,
O'erwhelm'd, and spurn'd, and batter'd, ye are here!
O Titans, shall I say, 'Arise!' – Ye groan:
Shall I say 'Crouch!' – Ye groan. What can I then?
O Heaven wide! O unseen parent dear!
What can I? Tell me, all ye brethren Gods,
How we can war, how engine our great wrath!
O speak your counsel now, for Saturn's ear
Is all a-hunger'd. Thou, Oceanus,
Ponderest high and deep; and in thy face
I see, astonied, that severe content
Which comes of thought and musing: give us help!'

So ended Saturn; and the God of the Sea,

Sophist and sage, from no Athenian grove,
But cogitation in his watery shades,
Arose, with locks not oozy, and began,
In murmurs, which his first-endeavouring tongue
Caught infant-like from the far-foamed sands.
'O ye, whom wrath consumes! who, passion-stung,
Writhe at defeat, and nurse your agonies!
Shut up your senses, stifle up your ears,
My voice is not a bellows unto ire.
Yet listen, ye who will, whilst I bring proof
How ye, perforce, must be content to stoop:
And in the proof much comfort will I give,
If ye will take that comfort in its truth.
We fall by course of Nature's law, not force
Of thunder, or of Jove. Great Saturn, thou
Hast sifted well the atom-universe;
But for this reason, that thou art the King,
And only blind from sheer supremacy,
One avenue was shaded from thine eyes,
Through which I wander'd to eternal truth.
And first, as thou wast not the first of powers,
So art thou not the last; it cannot be:
Thou art not the beginning nor the end.
From chaos and parental darkness came
Light, the first fruits of that intestine broil,
That sullen ferment, which for wondrous ends
Was ripening in itself. The ripe hour came,
And with it light, and light, engendering
Upon its own producer, forthwith touch'd
The whole enormous matter into life.
Upon that very hour, our parentage,
The Heavens and the Earth, were manifest:
Then thou first-born, and we the giant race,
Found ourselves ruling new and beauteous realms.

Now comes the pain of truth, to whom 'tis pain;
O folly! for to bear all naked truths,
And to envisage circumstance, all calm,
That is the top of sovereignty. Mark well!
As Heaven and Earth are fairer, fairer far
Than Chaos and blank Darkness, though once chiefs;
And as we show beyond that Heaven and Earth
In form and shape compact and beautiful,
In will, in action free, companionship,
And thousand other signs of purer life;
So on our heels a fresh perfection treads,
A power more strong in beauty, born of us
And fated to excel us, as we pass
In glory that old Darkness: nor are we
Thereby more conquer'd, than by us the rule
Of shapeless Chaos. Say, doth the dull soil
Quarrel with the proud forests it hath fed,
And feedeth still more comely than itself?
Can it deny the chiefdom of green groves?
Or shall the tree be envious of the dove
Because it cooeth, and hath snowy wings
To wander wherewithal and find its joys?
We are such forest-trees, and our fair boughs
Have bred forth, not pale solitary doves,
But eagles golden-feather'd, who do tower
Above us in their beauty, and must reign
In right thereof; for 'tis the eternal law
That first in beauty should be first in might;
Yea, by that law, another race may drive
Our conquerors to mourn as we do now.
Have ye beheld the young God of the Seas,
My dispossessor? Have ye seen his face?
Have ye beheld his chariot, foam'd along
By noble winged creatures he hath made?

I saw him on the calmed waters scud,
With such a glow of beauty in his eyes,
That it enforced me to bid sad farewell
To all my empire: farewell sad I took,
And hither came, to see how dolorous fate
Had wrought upon ye; and how I might best
Give consolation in this woe extreme.
Receive the truth, and let it be your balm.'

    Whether through pos'd conviction, or disdain,
They guarded silence, when Oceanus
Left murmuring, what deepest thought can tell?
But so it was, none answer'd for a space,
Save one whom none regarded, Clymene;
And yet she answer'd not, only complain'd,
With hectic lips, and eyes up-looking mild,
Thus wording timidly among the fierce:
'O Father, I am here the simplest voice,
And all my knowledge is that joy is gone,
And this thing woe crept in among our hearts,
There to remain for ever, as I fear:
I would not bode of evil, if I thought
So weak a creature could turn off the help
Which by just right should come of mighty Gods;
Yet let me tell my sorrow, let me tell
Of what I heard, and how it made me weep,
And know that we had parted from all hope.
I stood upon a shore, a pleasant shore,
Where a sweet clime was breathed from a land
Of fragrance, quietness, and trees, and flowers.
Full of calm joy it was, as I of grief;
Too full of joy and soft delicious warmth;
So that I felt a movement in my heart
To chide, and to reproach that solitude

With songs of misery, music of our woes;
And sat me down, and took a mouthed shell
And murmur'd into it, and made melody –
O melody no more! for while I sang,
And with poor skill let pass into the breeze
The dull shell's echo, from a bowery strand
Just opposite, an island of the sea,
There came enchantment with the shifting wind
That did both drown and keep alive my ears.
I threw my shell away upon the sand,
And a wave fill'd it, as my sense was fill'd
With that new blissful golden melody.
A living death was in each gush of sounds,
Each family of rapturous hurried notes,
That fell, one after one, yet all at once,
Like pearl beads dropping sudden from their string:
And then another, then another strain,
Each like a dove leaving its olive perch,
With music wing'd instead of silent plumes,
To hover round my head, and make me sick
Of joy and grief at once. Grief overcame,
And I was stopping up my frantic ears,
When, past all hindrance of my trembling hands,
A voice came, sweeter, sweeter than all tune,
And still it cried, "Apollo! young Apollo!
The morning-bright Apollo! young Apollo!"
I fled, it follow'd me, and cried "Apollo!"
O Father, and O Brethren! had ye felt
Those pains of mine! O Saturn, hadst thou felt,
Ye would not call this too indulged tongue
Presumptuous, in thus venturing to be heard!'

So far her voice flow'd on, like timorous brook
That, lingering along a pebbled coast,

Doth fear to meet the sea: but sea it met,
And shudder'd; for the overwhelming voice
Of huge Enceladus swallow'd it in wrath:
The ponderous syllables, like sullen waves
In the half-glutted hollows of reef-rocks,
Came booming thus, while still upon his arm
He lean'd; not rising, from supreme contempt.
'Or shall we listen to the over-wise,
Or to the over-foolish giant, Gods?
Not thunderbolt on thunderbolt, till all
That rebel Jove's whole armoury were spent,
Not world on world upon these shoulders piled,
Could agonize me more than baby-words
In midst of this dethronement horrible.
Speak! roar! shout! yell! ye sleepy Titans all.
Do ye forget the blows, the buffets vile?
Are ye not smitten by a youngling arm?
Dost thou forget, sham Monarch of the Waves,
Thy scalding in the seas? What! have I roused
Your spleens with so few simple words as these?
O joy! for now I see ye are not lost:
O joy! for now I see a thousand eyes
Wide glaring for revenge!' – As this he said,
He lifted up his stature vast, and stood,
Still without intermission speaking thus:
'Now ye are flames, I'll tell you how to burn,
And purge the ether of our enemies;
How to feed fierce the crooked stings of fire,
And singe away the swollen clouds of Jove,
Stifling that puny essence in its tent.
O let him feel the evil he hath done;
For though I scorn Oceanus's lore,
Much pain have I for more than loss of realms:
The days of peace and slumberous calm are fled;

Those days, all innocent of scathing war,
When all the fair Existences of heaven
Came open-eyed to guess what we would speak: —
That was before our brows were taught to frown,
Before our lips knew else but solemn sounds;
That was before we knew the winged thing,
Victory, might be lost, or might be won.
And be ye mindful that Hyperion,
Our brightest brother, still is undisgraced —
Hyperion, lo! his radiance is here!'

All eyes were on Enceladus's face,
And they beheld, while still Hyperion's name
Flew from his lips up to the vaulted rocks,
A pallid gleam across his features stern:
Not savage, for he saw full many a God
Wroth as himself. He look'd upon them all,
And in each face he saw a gleam of light,
But splendider in Saturn's, whose hoar locks
Shone like the bubbling foam about a keel
When the prow sweeps into a midnight cove.
In pale and silver silence they remain'd,
Till suddenly a splendour, like the morn,
Pervaded all the beetling gloomy steeps,
All the sad spaces of oblivion,
And every gulf, and every chasm old,
And every height, and every sullen depth,
Voiceless, or hoarse with loud tormented streams;
And all the everlasting cataracts,
And all the headlong torrents far and near,
Mantled before in darkness and huge shade,
Now saw the light and made it terrible.
It was Hyperion: — a granite peak
His bright feet touch'd, and there he stay'd to view

The misery his brilliance had betray'd
To the most hateful seeing of itself.
Golden his hair of short Numidian curl,
Regal his shape majestic, a vast shade
In midst of his own brightness, like the bulk
Of Memnon's image at the set of sun
To one who travels from the dusking East:
Sighs, too, as mournful as that Memnon's harp
He utter'd, while his hands, contemplative,
He press'd together, and in silence stood.
Despondence seized again the fallen Gods
At sight of the dejected King of Day,
And many hid their faces from the light:
But fierce Enceladus sent forth his eyes
Among the brotherhood; and, at their glare,
Uprose Iäpetus, and Creüs too,
And Phorcus, sea-born, and together strode
To where he towered on his eminence.
There those four shouted forth old Saturn's name.
Hyperion from the peak loud answer'd, 'Saturn!'
Saturn sat near the Mother of the Gods,
In whose face was no joy, though all the Gods
Gave from their hollow throats the name of 'Saturn!'

Book III

THUS in alternate uproar and sad peace,
Amazed were those Titans utterly.
O leave them, Muse! O leave them to their woes;
For thou art weak to sing such tumults dire:
A solitary sorrow best befits
Thy lips, and antheming a lonely grief.
Leave them, O Muse! for thou anon wilt find
Many a fallen old Divinity
Wandering in vain about bewildered shores.
Meantime touch piously the Delphic harp,
And not a wind of heaven but will breathe
In aid soft warble from the Dorian flute;
For lo! 'tis for the Father of all verse.
Flush everything that hath a vermeil hue,
Let the rose glow intense and warm the air,
And let the clouds of even and of morn
Float in voluptuous fleeces o'er the hills;
Let the red wine within the goblet boil,
Cold as a bubbling well; let faint-lipp'd shells,
On sands or in great deeps, vermilion turn
Through all their labyrinths; and let the maid
Blush keenly, as with some warm kiss surprised.
Chief isle of the embowered Cyclades,
Rejoice, O Delos, with thine olives green,
And poplars, and lawn-shading palms, and beech,
In which the Zephyr breathes the loudest song,
And hazels thick, dark-stemm'd beneath the shade:
Apollo is once more the golden theme!
Where was he, when the Giant of the Sun
Stood bright, amid the sorrow of his peers?
Together had he left his mother fair
And his twin-sister sleeping in their bower,

And in the morning twilight wandered forth
Beside the osiers of a rivulet,
Full ankle-deep in lilies of the vale.
The nightingale had ceas'd, and a few stars
Were lingering in the heavens, while the thrush
Began calm-throated. Throughout all the isle
There was no covert, no retired cave
Unhaunted by the murmurous noise of waves,
Though scarcely heard in many a green recess.
He listen'd, and he wept, and his bright tears
Went trickling down the golden bow he held.
Thus with half-shut suffused eyes he stood,
While from beneath some cumbrous boughs hard by
With solemn step an awful Goddess came,
And there was purport in her looks for him,
Which he with eager guess began to read
Perplex'd, the while melodiously he said:
'How cam'st thou over the unfooted sea?
Or hath that antique mien and robed form
Moved in these vales invisible till now?
Sure I have heard those vestments sweeping o'er
The fallen leaves, when I have sat alone
In cool mid-forest. Surely I have traced
The rustle of those ample skirts about
These grassy solitudes, and seen the flowers
Lift up their heads, as still the whisper pass'd.
Goddess! I have beheld those eyes before,
And their eternal calm, and all that face,
Or I have dream'd.' – 'Yes,' said the supreme shape,
'Thou hast dream'd of me; and awaking up
Didst find a lyre all golden by thy side,
Whose strings touch'd by thy fingers, all the vast
Unwearied ear of the whole universe
Listen'd in pain and pleasure at the birth

Of such new tuneful wonder. Is't not strange
That thou shouldst weep, so gifted? Tell me, youth,
What sorrow thou canst feel; for I am sad
When thou dost shed a tear: explain thy griefs
To one who in this lonely isle hath been
The watcher of thy sleep and hours of life,
From the young day when first thy infant hand
Pluck'd witless the weak flowers, till thine arm
Could bend that bow heroic to all times.
Show thy heart's secret to an ancient Power
Who hath forsaken old and sacred thrones
For prophecies of thee, and for the sake
Of loveliness new born.' – Apollo then,
With sudden scrutiny and gloomless eyes,
Thus answer'd, while his white melodious throat
Throbb'd with the syllables: – 'Mnemosyne!
Thy name is on my tongue, I know not how;
Why should I tell thee what thou so well seest?
Why should I strive to show what from thy lips
Would come no mystery? For me, dark, dark,
And painful vile oblivion seals my eyes:
I strive to search wherefore I am so sad,
Until a melancholy numbs my limbs;
And then upon the grass I sit, and moan,
Like one who once had wings. – Oh why should I
Feel curs'd and thwarted, when the liegeless air
Yields to my step aspirant? why should I
Spurn the green turf as hateful to my feet?
Goddess benign, point forth some unknown thing:
Are there not other regions than this isle?
What are the stars? There is the sun, the sun!
And the most patient brilliance of the moon!
And stars by thousands! Point me out the way

To any one particular beauteous star,
And I will flit into it with my lyre,
And make its silvery splendour pant with bliss.
I have heard the cloudy thunder: where is power?
Whose hand, whose essence, what divinity
Makes this alarum in the elements,
While I here idle listen on the shores
In fearless yet in aching ignorance?
O tell me, lonely Goddess! by thy harp,
That waileth every morn and eventide,
Tell me why thus I rave about these groves!
Mute thou remainest – mute! yet I can read
A wondrous lesson in thy silent face:
Knowledge enormous makes a God of me.
Names, deeds, gray legends, dire events, rebellions,
Majesties, sovran voices, agonies,
Creations and destroyings, all at once
Pour into the wide hollows of my brain,
And deify me, as if some blithe wine
Or bright elixir peerless I had drunk,
And so become immortal.' – Thus the God,
While his enkindled eyes, with level glance
Beneath his white soft temples, stedfast kept
Trembling with light, upon Mnemosyne.
Soon wild commotions shook him, and made flush
All the immortal fairness of his limbs;
Most like the struggle at the gate of death;
Or liker still to one who should take leave
Of pale immortal death, and with a pang
As hot as death's is chill, with fierce convulse
Die into life: so young Apollo anguish'd;
His very hair, his golden tresses famed,
Kept undulation round his eager neck.

During the pain Mnemosyne upheld
Her arms as one who prophesied. At length
Apollo shriek'd; — and lo! from all his limbs
Celestial

*   *   *

SELECTIONS FROM

Posthumous and Fugitive Poems

THE FALL OF HYPERION*

A DREAM

[Canto I]

FANATICS have their dreams, wherewith they weave
A paradise for a sect; the savage, too,
From forth the loftiest fashion of his sleep
Guesses at heaven; pity these have not
Traced upon vellum or wild Indian leaf
The shadows of melodious utterance,
But bare of laurel they live, dream, and die;
For Poesy alone can tell her dreams, –
With the fine spell of words alone can save
Imagination from the sable chain
And dumb enchantment. Who alive can say,
'Thou art no Poet – mayst not tell thy dreams?'
Since every man whose soul is not a clod
Hath visions and would speak, if he had loved,
And been well nurtured in his mother tongue.
Whether the dream now purposed to rehearse
Be poet's or fanatic's will be known
When this warm scribe, my hand, is in the grave.

    Methought I stood where trees of every clime,
Palm, myrtle, oak, and sycamore, and beech,
With plantane and spice-blossoms, made a screen,
In neighbourhood of fountains (by the noise
Soft-showering in mine ears,) and (by the touch
Of scent) not far from roses. Twining round
I saw an arbour with a drooping roof
Of trellis vines, and bells, and larger blooms,
Like floral censers, swinging light in air;
Before its wreathed doorway, on a mound

[* Keats attempted, at the end of 1819, this reconstruction of *Hyperion*.]

Of moss, was spread a feast of summer fruits,
Which, nearer seen, seem'd refuse of a meal
By angel tasted or our Mother Eve;
For empty shells were scatter'd on the grass,
And grapestalks but half-bare, and remnants more
Sweet-smelling, whose pure kinds I could not know.
Still was more plenty than the fabled horn
Thrice emptied could pour forth at banqueting
For Proserpine return'd to her own fields,
Where the white heifers low. And appetite,
More yearning than on earth I ever felt,
Growing within, I ate deliciously, –
And, after not long, thirsted; for thereby
Stood a cool vessel of transparent juice
Sipp'd by the wander'd bee, the which I took,
And pledging all the mortals of the world,
And all the dead whose names are in our lips,
Drank. That full draught is parent of my theme.
No Asian poppy or elixir fine
Of the soon-fading, jealous Caliphat,
No poison gender'd in close monkish cell,
To thin the scarlet conclave of old men,
Could so have rapt unwilling life away.
Among the fragrant husks and berries crush'd
Upon the grass, I struggled hard against
The domineering potion, but in vain.
The cloudy swoon came on, and down I sank,
Like a Silenus on an antique vase.
How long I slumber'd 'tis a chance to guess.
When sense of life return'd, I started up
As if with wings, but the fair trees were gone,
The mossy mound and arbour were no more:
I look'd around upon the curved sides
Of an old sanctuary, with roof august,

Builded so high, it seem'd that filmed clouds
Might spread beneath as o'er the stars of heaven.
So old the place was, I remember'd none
The like upon the earth: what I had seen
Of gray cathedrals, buttress'd walls, rent towers,
The superannuations of sunk realms,
Or Nature's rocks toil'd hard in waves and winds,
Seem'd but the faulture of decrepit things
To that eternal domed monument.
Upon the marble at my feet there lay
Store of strange vessels and large draperies,
Which needs had been of dyed asbestos wove,
Or in that place the moth could not corrupt,
So white the linen, so, in some, distinct
Ran imageries from a sombre loom.
All in a mingled heap confused there lay
Robes, golden tongs, censer and chafing-dish,
Girdles, and chains, and holy jewelries.

    Turning from these with awe, once more I raised
My eyes to fathom the space every way:
The embossed roof, the silent massy range
Of columns north and south, ending in mist
Of nothing; then to eastward, where black gates
Were shut against the sunrise evermore;
Then to the west I look'd, and saw far off
An image, huge of feature as a cloud,
At level of whose feet an altar slept,
To be approach'd on either side by steps
And marble balustrade, and patient travail
To count with toil the innumerable degrees.
Towards the altar sober-paced I went,
Repressing haste as too unholy there;
And, coming nearer, saw beside the shrine
One ministering; and there arose a flame.

When in midday the sickening east-wind
Shifts sudden to the south, the small warm rain
Melts out the frozen incense from all flowers,
And fills the air with so much pleasant health
That even the dying man forgets his shroud; —
Even so that lofty sacrificial fire,
Sending forth Maian incense, spread around
Forgetfulness of everything but bliss,
And clouded all the altar with soft smoke;
From whose white fragrant curtains thus I heard
Language pronounced: 'If thou canst not ascend
These steps, die on that marble where thou art.
Thy flesh, near cousin to the common dust,
Will parch for lack of nutriment; thy bones
Will wither in few years, and vanish so
That not the quickest eye could find a grain
Of what thou now art on that pavement cold.
The sands of thy short life are spent this hour,
And no hand in the universe can turn
Thy hourglass, if these gummed leaves be burnt
Ere thou canst mount up these immortal steps.'
I heard, I look'd: two senses both at once,
So fine, so subtle, felt the tyranny
Of that fierce threat and the hard task proposed.
Prodigious seem'd the toil; the leaves were yet
Burning, when suddenly a palsied chill
Struck from the paved level up my limbs,
And was ascending quick to put cold grasp
Upon those streams that pulse beside the throat.
I shriek'd, and the sharp anguish of my shriek
Stung my own ears; I strove hard to escape
The numbness, strove to gain the lowest step.
Slow, heavy, deadly was my pace: the cold
Grew stifling, suffocating at the heart;

And when I clasp'd my hands I felt them not.
One minute before death my iced foot touch'd
The lowest stair; and, as it touch'd, life seem'd
To pour in at the toes; I mounted up
As once fair angels on a ladder flew
From the green turf to heaven. 'Holy Power,'
Cried I, approaching near the horned shrine,
'What am I that should so be saved from death?
What am I that another death come not
To choke my utterance, sacrilegious, here?'
Then said the veiled shadow: 'Thou hast felt
What 'tis to die and live again before
Thy fated hour; that thou hadst power to do so
Is thine own safety; thou hast dated on
Thy doom.' 'High Prophetess,' said I, 'purge off,
Benign, if so it please thee, my mind's film.'
'None can usurp this height,' returned that shade,
'But those to whom the miseries of the world
Are misery, and will not let them rest.
All else who find a haven in the world,
Where they may thoughtless sleep away their days,
If by a chance into this fane they come,
Rot on the pavement where thou rottedst half.'
'Are there not thousands in the world,' said I,
Encouraged by the sooth voice of the shade,
'Who love their fellows even to the death,
Who feel the giant agony of the world,
And more, like slaves to poor humanity,
Labour for mortal good? I sure should see
Other men here, but I am here alone.'
'Those whom thou spakest of are no visionaries,'
Rejoin'd that voice; 'they are no dreamers weak;
They seek no wonder but the human face,
No music but a happy-noted voice:

They come not here, they have no thought to come;
And thou art here, for thou art less than they.
What benefit canst thou do, or all thy tribe,
To the great world? Thou art a dreaming thing,
A fever of thyself: think of the earth;
What bliss, even in hope, is there for thee?
What haven? every creature hath its home,
Every sole man hath days of joy and pain,
Whether his labours be sublime or low –
The pain alone, the joy alone, distinct:
Only the dreamer venoms all his days,
Bearing more woe than all his sins deserve.
Therefore, that happiness be somewhat shared,
Such things as thou art are admitted oft
Into like gardens thou didst pass erewhile,
And suffer'd in these temples: for that cause
Thou standest safe beneath this statue's knees.'
'That I am favour'd for unworthiness,
By such propitious parley medicined
In sickness not ignoble, I rejoice,
Ay, and could weep for love of such award.'
So answer'd I, continuing, 'If it please,
Majestic shadow, tell me: sure not all
Those melodies sung into the World's ear
Are useless: sure a poet is a sage;
A humanist, physician to all men.
That I am none I feel, as vultures feel
They are no birds when eagles are abroad.
What am I then: Thou spakest of my tribe;
What tribe?' The tall shade veil'd in drooping white
Then spake, so much more earnest, that the breath
Moved the thin linen folds that drooping hung
About a golden censer from the hand
Pendent – 'Art thou not of the dreamer tribe?

The poet and the dreamer are distinct,
Diverse, sheer opposite, antipodes.
The one pours out a balm upon the World,
The other vexes it.' Then shouted I
Spite of myself, and with a Pythia's spleen
'Apollo! faded! O far flown Apollo!
Where is thy misty pestilence to creep
Into the dwellings, through the door crannies
On all mock lyrists, large self worshippers
And careless Hectorers in proud bad verse.
Though I breathe death with them it will be life
To see them sprawl before me into graves.
Majestic shadow, tell me where I am,
Whose altar this, for whom this incense curls;
What image this whose face I cannot see
For the broad marble knees; and who thou art,
Of accent feminine, so courteous?'
      Then the tall shade, in drooping linen veil'd,
Spoke out, so much more earnest, that her breath
Stirr'd the thin folds of gauze that drooping hung
About a golden censer from her hand
Pendent; and by her voice I knew she shed
Long-treasured tears. 'This temple, sad and lone,
Is all spared from the thunder of a war
Foughten long since by giant hierarchy
Against rebellion: this old image here,
Whose carved features wrinkled as he fell,
Is Saturn's; I, Moneta, left supreme,
Sole goddess of this desolation.'
I had no words to answer, for my tongue,
Useless, could find about its roofed home
No syllable of a fit majesty
To make rejoinder to Moneta's mourn:
There was a silence, while the altar's blaze

Was fainting for sweet food. I look'd thereon,
And on the paved floor, where nigh were piled
Faggots of cinnamon, and many heaps
Of other crisped spicewood: then again
I look'd upon the altar, and its horns
Whiten'd with ashes, and its languorous flame,
And then upon the offerings again;
And so, by turns, till sad Moneta cried:
'The sacrifice is done, but not the less
Will I be kind to thee for thy good will.
My power, which to me is still a curse,
Shall be to thee a wonder, for the scenes
Still swooning vivid through my globed brain,
With an electral changing misery,
Thou shalt with these dull mortal eyes behold
Free from all pain, if wonder pain thee not.'
As near as an immortal's sphered words
Could to a mother's soften were these last:
And yet I had a terror of her robes,
And chiefly of the veils that from her brow
Hung pale, and curtain'd her in mysteries,
That made my heart too small to hold its blood.
This saw that Goddess, and with sacred hand
Parted the veils. Then saw I a wan face,
Not pined by human sorrows, but bright-blanch'd
By an immortal sickness which kills not;
It works a constant change, which happy death
Can put no end to; deathwards progressing
To no death was that visage; it had past
The lily and the snow; and beyond these
I must not think now, though I saw that face.
But for her eyes I should have fled away;
They held me back with a benignant light,
Soft, mitigated by divinest lids

Half-closed, and visionless entire they seem'd
Of all external things; they saw me not,
But in blank splendour beam'd, like the mild moon;
Who comforts those she sees not, who knows not
What eyes are upward cast. As I had found
A grain of gold upon a mountain's side,
And, twinged with avarice, strain'd out my eyes
To search its sullen entrails rich with ore,
So, at the view of sad Moneta's brow,
I ask'd to see what things the hollow brow
Behind environ'd: what high tragedy
In the dark secret chambers of her skull
Was acting, that could give so dread a stress
To her cold lips, and fill with such a light
Her planetary eyes, and touch her voice
With such a sorrow? 'Shade of Memory!'
Cried I, with act adorant at her feet,
'By all the gloom hung round thy fallen house,
By this last temple, by the golden age,
By great Apollo, thy dear foster-child,
And by thyself, forlorn divinity,
The pale Omega of a wither'd race,
Let me behold, according as thou saidst,
What in thy brain so ferments to and fro!'
No sooner had this conjuration past
My devout lips, than side by side we stood
(Like a stunt bramble by a solemn pine)
Deep in the shady sadness of a vale
Far sunken from the healthy breath of morn,
Far from the fiery noon and eve's one star.
Onward I look'd beneath the gloomy boughs,
And saw what first I thought an image huge,
Like to the image pedestal'd so high
In Saturn's temple; then Moneta's voice

Came brief upon mine ear. 'So Saturn sat
When he had lost his realms'; whereon there grew
A power within me of enormous ken
To see as a god sees, and take the depth
Of things as nimbly as the outward eye
Can size and shape pervade. The lofty theme
Of those few words hung vast before my mind
With half-unravell'd web. I sat myself
Upon an eagle's watch, that I might see,
And seeing ne'er forget. No stir of life
Was in this shrouded vale, – not so much air
As in the zoning of a summer's day
Robs not one light seed from the feather'd grass;
But where the dead leaf fell there did it rest.
A stream went noiseless by, still deaden'd more
By reason of the fallen divinity
Spreading more shade; the Naiad 'mid her reeds
Prest her cold finger closer to her lips.

    Along the margin-sand large foot-marks went
No further than to where old Saturn's feet
Had rested, and there slept how long a sleep!
Degraded, cold, upon the sodden ground
His old right hand lay nerveless, listless, dead,
Unsceptred, and his realmless eyes were closed;
While his bow'd head seem'd listening to the Earth,
His ancient mother, for some comfort yet.

    It seem'd no force could wake him from his place;
But there came one who, with a kindred hand,
Touch'd his wide shoulders, after bending low
With reverence, though to one who knew it not.
Then came the grieved voice of Mnemosyne,
And grieved I hearken'd. 'That divinity
Whom thou saw'st step from yon forlornest wood,
And with slow pace approach our fallen king,

Is Thea, softest-natured of our brood.'
I mark'd the Goddess, in fair statuary
Surpassing wan Moneta by the head,
And in her sorrow nearer woman's tears.
There was a list'ning fear in her regard,
As if calamity had but begun;
As if the venom'd clouds of evil days
Had spent their malice, and the sullen rear
Was with its stored thunder labouring up.
One hand she press'd upon that aching spot
Where beats the human heart, as if just there,
Though an immortal, she felt cruel pain;
The other upon Saturn's bended neck
She laid, and to the level of his ear
Leaning, with parted lips some words she spoke
In solemn tenour and deep organ-tone;
Some mourning words, which in our feeble tongue
Would come in this like accenting; how frail
To that large utterance of the early gods!
    'Saturn, look up! and for what, poor lost King?
I have no comfort for thee; no, not one;
I cannot say, wherefore thus sleepest thou?
For Heaven is parted from thee, and the Earth
Knows thee not, so afflicted, for a God.
The Ocean, too, with all its solemn noise,
Has from thy sceptre pass'd; and all the air
Is emptied of thy hoary majesty.
Thy thunder, captious at the new command,
Rumbles reluctant o'er our fallen house;
And thy sharp lightning, in unpractised hands,
Scourges and burns our once serene domain.
With such remorseless speed still come new woes,
That unbelief has not a space to breathe.
Saturn! sleep on: me thoughtless, why should I

Thus violate thy slumbrous solitude?
Why should I ope thy melancholy eyes?
Saturn! sleep on, while at thy feet I weep.'
    As when upon a tranced summer-night
Forests, branch-charmed by the earnest stars,
Dream, and so dream all night without a noise,
Save from one gradual solitary gust
Swelling upon the silence, dying off,
As if the ebbing air had but one wave,
So came these words and went; the while in tears
She prest her fair large forehead to the earth,
Just where her fallen hair might spread in curls
A soft and silken net for Saturn's feet.
Long, long these two were postured motionless,
Like sculpture builded-up upon the grave
Of their own power. A long awful time
I look'd upon them: still they were the same;
The frozen God still bending to the earth,
And the sad Goddess weeping at his feet;
Moneta silent. Without stay or prop
But my own weak mortality, I bore
The load of this eternal quietude,
The unchanging gloom and the three fixed shapes
Ponderous upon my senses, a whole moon;
For by my burning brain I measured sure
Her silver seasons shedded on the night,
And every day by day methought I grew
More gaunt and ghostly. Oftentimes I pray'd
Intense, that death would take me from the vale
And all its burthens; gasping with despair
Of change, hour after hour I cursed myself,
Until old Saturn raised his faded eyes,
And look'd around and saw his kingdom gone,
And all the gloom and sorrow of the place,

And that fair kneeling Goddess at his feet.
    As the moist scent of flowers, and grass, and leaves,
Fills forest-dells with a pervading air,
Known to the woodland nostril, so the words
Of Saturn fill'd the mossy glooms around,
Even to the hollows of time-eaten oaks,
And to the windings of the foxes' hole,
With sad, low tones, while thus he spoke, and sent
Strange moanings to the solitary Pan.
'Moan, brethren, moan, for we are swallow'd up
And buried from all godlike exercise
Of influence benign on planets pale,
And peaceful sway upon man's harvesting,
And all those acts which Deity supreme
Doth ease its heart of love in. Moan and wail;
Moan, brethren, moan; for lo, the rebel spheres
Spin round; the stars their ancient courses keep;
Clouds still with shadowy moisture haunt the earth,
Still suck their fill of light from sun and moon;
Still buds the tree, and still the seashores murmur;
There is no death in all the universe,
No smell of death. – There shall be death. Moan, moan;
Moan, Cybele, moan; for thy pernicious babes
Have changed a god into an aching palsy.
Moan, brethren, moan, for I have no strength left;
Weak as the reed, weak, feeble as my voice.
Oh! oh! the pain, the pain of feebleness;
Moan, moan, for still I thaw; or give me help;
Throw down those imps, and give me victory.
Let me hear other groans, [and trumpets blown
Of triumph calm, and hymns of festival,]
From the gold peaks of heaven's high-piled clouds;
Voices of soft proclaim, and silver stir
Of strings in hollow shells; and there shall be

Beautiful things made new, for the surprise
Of the sky-children.' So he feebly ceased,
With such a poor and sickly-sounding pause,
Methought I heard some old man of the earth
Bewailing earthly loss; nor could my eyes
And ears act with that unison of sense
Which marries sweet sound with the grace of form,
And dolorous accent from a tragic harp
With large-limb'd visions. More I scrutinized.
Still fixt he sat beneath the sable trees,
Whose arms spread straggling in wild serpent forms,
With leaves all hush'd; his awful presence there
(Now all was silent) gave a deadly lie
To what I erewhile heard: only his lips
Trembled amid the white curls of his beard;
They told the truth, though round the snowy locks
Hung nobly, as upon the face of heaven
A mid-day fleece of clouds. Thea arose,
And 'stretcht her white arm through the hollow dark,
Pointing some whither: whereat he too rose,
Like a vast giant, seen by men at sea
To grow pale from the waves at dull midnight.
They melted from my sight into the woods;
Ere I could turn, Moneta cried, 'These twain
Are speeding to the families of grief,
Where, rooft in by black rocks, they waste in pain
And darkness, for no hope.' And she spake on,
As ye may read who can unwearied pass
Onward from the antechamber of this dream,
Where, even at the open doors, awhile
I must delay, and glean my memory
Of her high phrase — perhaps no further dare.

END OF CANTO I

'MORTAL, that thou may'st understand aright,
I humanize my sayings to thine ear,
Making comparisons of earthly things;
Or thou mightst better listen to the wind,
Whose language is to thee a barren noise,
Though it blows legend-laden thro' the trees.
In melancholy realms big tears are shed,
More sorrow like to this, and such like woe,
Too huge for mortal tongue or pen of scribe.
The Titans fierce, self-hid or prison-bound,
Groan for the old allegiance once more,
Listening in their doom for Saturn's voice.
But one of the whole eagle-brood still keeps
His sov'reignty, and rule, and majesty:
Blazing Hyperion on his orbed fire
Still sits, still snuffs the incense teeming up
From Man to the Sun's God — yet unsecure,
For as upon the earth dire prodigies
Fright and perplex, so also shudders he;
Not at dog's howl or gloom-bird's hated screech,
Or the familiar visiting of one
Upon the first toll of his passing bell,
Or prophesyings of the midnight lamp;
But horrors, portioned to a giant nerve,
Make great Hyperion ache. His palace bright,
Bastion'd with pyramids of shining gold,
And touch'd with shade of bronzed obelisks,
Glares a blood-red thro' all the thousand courts,
Arches, and domes, and fiery galleries;
And all its curtains of Aurorian clouds
Flash angerly; when he would taste the wreaths
Of incense breathed aloft from sacred hills

Instead of sweets, his ample palate takes
Savour of poisonous brass and metals sick;
Wherefore when harbour'd in the sleepy West,
After the full completion of fair day,
For rest divine upon exalted couch,
And slumber in the arms of melody,
He paces through the pleasant hours of ease,
With strides colossal, on from hall to hall,
While far within each aisle and deep recess
His winged minions in close clusters stand
Amazed, and full of fear; like anxious men
Who on a wide plain gather in sad troops,
When earthquakes jar their battlements and towers
Even now where Saturn, roused from icy trance,
Goes step for step with Thea from yon woods,
Hyperion, leaving twilight in the rear,
Is sloping to the threshold of the West.
Thither we tend.' Now in clear light I stood,
Relieved from the dusk vale. Mnemosyne
Was sitting on a square-edg'd polish'd stone.
That in its lucid depth reflected pure
Her priestess-garments – My quick eyes ran on
From stately nave to nave, from vault to vault,
Through bow'rs of fragrant and enwreathed light
And diamond-paved lustrous long arcades.
Anon rush'd by the bright Hyperion;
His flaming robes stream'd out beyond his heels,
And gave a roar, as if of earthly fire,
That scared away the meek ethereal hours,
And made their dove-wings tremble. On he flared.

*   *   *

UPON a Sabbath-day it fell;
Twice holy was the Sabbath-bell,
That call'd the folk to evening prayer;
The city streets were clean and fair
From wholesome drench of April rains;
And, on the western window panes,
The chilly sunset faintly told
Of unmatur'd green, vallies cold,
Of the green thorny bloomless hedge,
Of rivers new with spring-tide sedge,
Of primroses by shelter'd rills,
And daisies on the aguish hills.
Twice holy was the Sabbath-bell:
The silent streets were crowded well
With staid and pious companies,
Warm from their fire-side orat'ries;
And moving, with demurest air,
To even-song, and vesper prayer.
Each arched porch, and entry low,
Was fill'd with patient folk and slow,
With whispers hush, and shuffling feet,
While play'd the organ loud and sweet.

The bells had ceas'd, the prayers begun,
And Bertha had not yet half done
A curious volume, patch'd and torn,
That all day long, from earliest morn,
Had taken captive her two eyes,
Among its golden broideries;
Perplex'd her with a thousand things, —
The stars of Heaven, and angels' wings,

POEMS OF JOHN KEATS

Martyrs in a fiery blaze,
Azure saints in silver rays,
Moses' breastplate and the seven
Candlesticks John saw in Heaven,
The winged Lion of Saint Mark,
And the Covenantal Ark,
With its many mysteries,
Cherubim and golden mice.

Bertha was a maiden fair,
Dwelling in the old Minster-square;
From her fire-side she could see,
Sidelong, its rich antiquity,
Far as the Bishop's garden-wall;
Where sycamores and elm-trees tall,
Full-leav'd, the forest had outstript,
By no sharp north-wind ever nipt,
So shelter'd by the mighty pile
Bertha arose, and read awhile,
With forehead 'gainst the window-pane
Again she try'd, and then again,
Until the dusk eve left her dark
Upon the legend of St Mark.
From plaited lawn-frill, fine and thin,
She lifted up her soft warm chin,
With aching neck and swimming eyes,
And daz'd with saintly imageries.

All was gloom, and silent all,
Save now and then the still foot-fall
Of one returning homewards late,
Past the echoing minster-gate.

The clamorous daws, that all the day
Above tree-tops and towers play,

Pair by pair had gone to rest,
Each in its ancient belfry-nest,
Where asleep they fall betimes,
To music of the drowsy chimes.

All was silent, all was gloom,
Abroad and in the homely room;
Down she sat, poor cheated soul!
And struck a lamp from the dismal coal;
Lean'd forward, with bright drooping hair
And slant book, full against the glare.
Her shadow, in uneasy guise,
Hover'd about, a giant size,
On ceiling-beam and old oak chair,
The parrot's cage, and panel square;
And the warm angled winter screen,
On which were many monsters seen,
Call'd doves of Siam, Lima mice,
And legless birds of Paradise,
Macaw, and tender Avadavat,
And silken-furr'd Angora cat.
Untir'd she read, her shadow still
Glower'd about, as it would fill
The room with wildest forms and shades,
As though some ghostly queen of spades
Had come to mock behind her back,
And dance, and ruffle her garments black.

Untir'd she read the legend page,
Of holy Mark, from youth to age,
On land, on sea, in pagan chains,
Rejoicing for his many pains.
Sometimes the learned eremite,
With golden star, or dagger bright,

POEMS OF JOHN KEATS

Referr'd to pious poesies
Written in smallest crow-quill size
Beneath the text; and thus the rhyme
Was parcell'd out from time to time:
—'Als writith he of swevenis,
Men han beforne they wake in bliss,
Whanne that hir friendes thinke hem bound
In crimped shroude farre under grounde;
And how a litling child mote be
A saint er its nativitie,
Gif that the modre (God her blesse!)
Kepen in solitarinesse.
And kissen devoute the holy croce.
Of Goddes love, and Sathan's force, --
He writith; and thinges many mo:
Of swiche thinges I may not shew.
Bot I must tellen verilie
Somdel of Saintè Cicilie,
And chieflie what he auctorethe
Of Saintè Markis life and dethe:'

At length her constant eyelids come
Upon the fervent martyrdom;
Then lastly to his holy shrine,
Exalt amid the tapers' shine
At Venice, –

A Prophecy: To George Keats in America

'Tɪs the witching hour of night,
Orbed is the moon and bright,
And the stars they glisten, glisten,
Seeming with bright eyes to listen –
      For what listen they?
For a song and for a charm,
See they glisten in alarm,
And the moon is waxing warm
        To hear what I shall say.
Moon! keep wide thy golden ears –
Hearken, stars! and hearken, spheres! –
Hearken, thou eternal sky!
I sing an Infant's lullaby,
      A pretty lullaby.
Listen, listen, listen, listen,
Glisten, glisten, glisten, glisten,
      And hear my lullaby!
Though the rushes that will make
Its cradle still are in the lake –
Though the linen that will be
Its swathe, is on the cotton tree –
Though the woollen that will keep
It warm, is on the silly sheep –
Listen, starlight, listen, listen,
Glisten, glisten, glisten, glisten,
      And hear my lullaby!
Child, I see thee! Child, I've found thee
Midst of the quiet all around thee!
Child, I see thee! Child, I spy thee!
And thy mother sweet is nigh thee!
Child, I know thee! Child no more,
But a Poet evermore!

See, see, the lyre, the lyre,
In a flame of fire,
Upon the little cradle's top
Flaring, flaring, flaring,
Past the eysight's bearing.
Awake it from its sleep,
And see if it can keep
Its eyes upon the blaze —
      Amaze, amaze!
It stares, it stares, it stares,
It dares what no one dares!
It lifts its little hand into the flame
Unharm'd, and on the strings
Paddles a little tune, and sings,
With dumb endeavour sweetly —
Bard art thou completely!
      Little child
        O' th' western wild,
Bard art thou completely!
Sweetly with dumb endeavour,
A Poet now or never,
      Little child
        O' th' western wild,
A Poet now or never!

Epistle to J. H. Reynolds

DEAR Reynolds! as last night I lay in bed,
There came before my eyes that wonted thread
Of shapes, and shadows, and remembrances,
That every other minute vex and please:
Things all disjointed come from north and south, –
Two Witch's eyes above a Cherub's mouth,
Voltaire with casque and shield and habergeon,
And Alexander with his nightcap on;
Old Socrates a-tying his cravat,
And Hazlitt playing with Miss Edgeworth's cat;
And Junius Brutus, pretty well, so so,
Making the best of 's way towards Soho.

Few are there who escape these visitings, –
Perhaps one or two whose lives have patent wings,
And thro' whose curtains peeps no hellish nose,
No wild-boar tushes, and no Mermaid's toes;
But flowers bursting out with lusty pride,
And young Aeolian harps personified;
Some Titian colours touch'd into real life, –
The sacrifice goes on; the pontiff knife
Gleams in the Sun, the milk-white heifer lows,
The pipes go shrilly, the libation flows:
A white sail shows above the green-head cliff,
Moves round the point, and throws her anchor stiff;
The mariners join hymn with those on land.

You know the Enchanted Castle, – it doth stand
Upon a rock, on the border of a Lake,
Nested in trees, which all do seem to shake
From some old magic-like Urganda's Sword.
O Phoebus! that I had thy sacred word

To show this Castle, in fair dreaming wise,
Unto my friend, while sick and ill he lies!

   You know it well enough, where it doth seem
A mossy place, a Merlin's Hall, a dream;
You know the clear Lake, and the little Isles,
The mountains blue, and cold near neighbour rills,
All which elsewhere are but half animate;
There do they look alive to love and hate,
To smiles and frowns; they seem a lifted mound
Above some giant, pulsing underground.

   Part of the Building was a chosen See,
Built by a banished Santon of Chaldee;
The other part, two thousand years from him,
Was built by Cuthbert de Saint Aldebrim;
Then there's a little wing, far from the Sun,
Built by a Lapland Witch turn'd maudlin Nun;
And many other juts of aged stone
Founded with many a mason-devil's groan.

   The doors all look as if they oped themselves,
The windows as if latch'd by Fays and Elves,
And from them comes a silver flash of light,
As from the westward of a Summer's night;
Or like a beauteous woman's large blue eyes
Gone mad thro' olden songs and poesies.

   See! what is coming from the distance dim!
A golden Galley all in silken trim!
Three rows of oars are lightening, moment whiles,
Into the verd'rous bosoms of those isles;
Towards the shade, under the Castle wall,
It comes in silence, – now 'tis hidden all.

The Clarion sounds, and from a Postern-gate
An echo of sweet music doth create
A fear in the poor Herdsman, who doth bring
His beasts to trouble the enchanted spring, –
He tells of the sweet music, and the spot,
To all his friends, and they believe him not.

O that our dreamings all, of sleep or wake,
Would all their colours from the sunset take:
From something of material sublime,
Rather than shadow our own soul's day-time
In the dark void of night. For in the world
We jostle, – but my flag is not unfurl'd
On the Admiral-staff, – and to philosophize
I dare not yet! Oh, never will the prize,
High reason, and the love of good and ill,
Be my award! Things cannot to the will
Be settled, but they tease us out of thought;
Or is it that imagination brought
Beyond its proper bound, yet still confin'd,
Lost in a sort of Purgatory blind,
Cannot refer to any standard law
Of either earth or heaven? It is a flaw
In happiness, to see beyond our bourn, –
It forces us in summer skies to mourn,
It spoils the singing of the Nightingale.

Dear Reynolds! I have a mysterious tale,
And cannot speak it: the first page I read
Upon a Lampit rock of green sea-weed
Among the breakers; 'twas a quiet eve,
The rocks were silent, the wide sea did weave
An untumultuous fringe of silver foam
Along the flat brown sand; I was at home

And should have been most happy, – but I saw
Too far into the sea, where every maw
The greater on the less feeds evermore. –
But I saw too distinct into the core
Of an eternal fierce destruction,
And so from happiness I far was gone.
Still am I sick of it, and though, to-day,
I've gather'd young spring-leaves, and flowers gay
Of periwinkle and wild strawberry,
Still do I that most fierce destruction see, –
The Shark at savage prey, – the Hawk at pounce, –
The gentle Robin, like a Pard or Ounce,
Ravening a Worm, – Away, ye horrid moods!
Moods of one's mind! You know I hate them well.
You know I'd sooner be a clapping Bell
To some Kamschatkan Missionary Church,
Than with these horrid moods be left i' the lurch.

La Belle Dame Sans Merci

I

O WHAT can ail thee, knight-at-arms,
　　Alone and palely loitering?
The sedge is wither'd from the lake,
　　And no birds sing.

II

O what can ail thee, knight-at-arms,
　　So haggard and so woe-begone?
The squirrel's granary is full,
　　And the harvest's done.

III

I see a lily on thy brow
　　With anguish moist and fever dew;
And on thy cheek a fading rose
　　Fast withereth too.

IV

I met a lady in the meads,
　　Full beautiful – a faery's child,
Her hair was long, her foot was light,
　　And her eyes were wild.

V

I made a garland for her head,
　　And bracelets too, and fragrant zone;
She look'd at me as she did love,
　　And made sweet moan.

VI

I set her on my pacing steed,
   And nothing else saw all day long,
For sideways would she lean, and sing
   A faery's song.

VII

She found me roots of relish sweet,
   And honey wild, and manna dew;
And sure in language strange she said –
   'I love thee true!'

VIII

She took me to her elfin grot,
   And there she gazed and sigh'd full sore,
And there I shut her wild wild eyes
   With kisses four.

IX

And there she lulled me asleep,
   And there I dream'd – ah! woe betide!
The latest dream I ever dream'd
   On the cold hill side.

X

I saw pale kings and princes too,
   Pale warriors, death-pale were they all;
Who cried – 'La Belle Dame sans merci
   Hath thee in thrall!'

XI

I saw their starv'd lips in the gloam,
   With horrid warning gaped wide,
And I awoke, and found me here,
   On the cold hill side.

XII

And this is why I sojourn here,
    Alone and palely loitering,
Though the sedge is wither'd from the lake,
    And no birds sing.

Meg Merrilies

I

OLD MEG she was a Gipsy,
   And lived upon the Moors:
Her bed it was the brown heath turf,
   And her house was out of doors.

II

Her apples were swart blackberries,
   Her currants pods o' broom;
Her wine was dew of the wild white rose,
   Her book a churchyard tomb.

III

Her Brothers were the craggy hills,
   Her Sisters larchen trees –
Alone with her great family
   She lived as she did please.

IV

No breakfast had she many a morn,
   No dinner many a noon,
And 'stead of supper she would stare
   Full hard against the Moon.

V

But every morn of woodbine fresh
   She made her garlanding,
And every night the dark glen Yew
   She wove, and she would sing.

VI

And with her fingers old and brown
   She plaited Mats of Rushes,
And gave them to the Cottagers
   She met among the Bushes.

VII

Old Meg was brave as Margaret Queen
   And tall as Amazon:
An old red blanket cloak she wore;
   A chip-hat had she on.
God rest her aged bones somewhere –
   She died full long agone!

[*Lines supposed to have been addressed to Fanny Brawne*]

THIS living hand, now warm and capable
Of earnest grasping, would, if it were cold
And in the icy silence of the tomb,
So haunt thy days and chill thy dreaming nights
That thou would[st] wish thine own heart dry of blood
So in my veins red life might stream again,
And thou be conscience-calm'd – see here it is –
I hold it towards you.

Lines to Fanny

WHAT can I do to drive away
Remembrance from my eyes? for they have seen,
Aye, [but] an hour ago, my brilliant Queen!
Touch has a memory. O say, love, say,
What can I do to kill it and be free
In my old liberty?
When every fair one that I saw was fair
Enough to catch me in but half a snare,
Not keep me there:
When, howe'er poor or particolour'd things,
My muse had wings,
And ever ready was to take her course
Whither I bent her force,
Unintellectual, yet divine to me; —
Divine, I say! — What sea-bird o'er the sea
Is a philosopher the while he goes
Winging along where the great water throes?

How shall I do
To get anew
Those moulted feathers, and so mount once more
Above, above
The reach of fluttering Love,
And make him cower lowly while I soar?
Shall I gulp wine? No, that is vulgarism,
A heresy and schism,
Foisted into the canon-law of love; —
No, — wine is only sweet to happy men;
More dismal cares
Seize on me unawares, —
Where shall I learn to get my peace again?

To banish thoughts of that most hateful land,
Dungeoner of my friends, that wicked strand
Where they were wreck'd and live a wrecked life;
That monstrous region, whose dull rivers pour,
Ever from their sordid urns unto the shore,
Unown'd of any weedy-haired gods;
Whose winds, all zephyrless, hold scourging rods,
Iced in the great lakes, to afflict mankind;
Whose rank-grown forests, frosted, black, and blind,
Would fright a Dryad; whose harsh herbag'd meads
Make lean and lank the starv'd ox while he feeds;
There [bad?] flowers have no scent, birds no sweet song,
And great unerring Nature once seems wrong.

O, for some sunny spell
To dissipate the shadows of this hell!
Say they are gone, – with the new dawning light
Steps forth my lady bright!
O, let me once more rest
My soul upon that dazzling breast!
Let once again these aching arms be plac'd,
The tender gaolers of thy waist!
And let me feel that warm breath here and there
To spread a rapture in my very hair, –
O, the sweetness of the pain!
Give me those lips again!
Enough! Enough! it is enough for me
To dream of thee!

Ode to Fanny

I

PHYSICIAN Nature! let my spirit blood!
  O ease my heart of verse and let me rest;
Throw me upon thy Tripod, till the flood
    Of stifling numbers ebbs from my full breast.
A theme! a theme! great nature! give a theme;
      Let me begin my dream.
I come – I see thee, as thou standest there,
Beckon me [out] into the wintry air.

II

Ah! dearest love, sweet home of all my fears,
  And hopes, and joys, and panting miseries, –
To-night, if I may guess, thy beauty wears
      A smile of such delight,
      As brilliant and as bright,
  As when with ravished, aching, vassal eyes,
      Lost in soft amaze,
      I gaze, I gaze!

III

Who now, with greedy looks, eat up my feast?
  What stare outfaces now my silver moon!
Ah! keep that hand unravished at the least;
      Let, let, the amorous burn –
      But, pr'ythee, do not turn
  The current of your heart from me so soon.
      O! save, in charity,
      The quickest pulse for me.

IV

Save it for me, sweet love! though music breathe
  Voluptuous visions into the warm air;
Though swimming through the dance's dangerous wreath,

Be like an April day,
Smiling and cold and gay,
A temperate lilly, temperate as fair;
Then, Heaven! there will be
A warmer June for me.

v

Why, this – you'll say, my Fanny! is not true:
Put your soft hand upon your snowy side,
Where the heart beats: confess – 'tis nothing new –
Must not a woman be
A feather on the sea,
Sway'd to and fro by every wind and tide?
Of as uncertain speed
As blow-ball from the mead?

vi

I know it – and to know it is despair
To one who loves you as I love, sweet Fanny!
Whose heart goes fluttering for you every where,
Nor, when away you roam,
Dare keep its wretched home,
Love, love alone, his pains severe and many:
Then, loveliest! keep me free,
From torturing jealousy.

vii

Ah! if you prize my subdued soul above
The poor, the fading, brief, pride of an hour;
Let not profane my Holy See of love,
Or with a rude hand break
The sacramental cake:
Let none else touch the just new-budded flower;
If not – may my eyes close,
Love! on their lost repose.

Ode on Indolence

'They toil not, neither do they spin.'

I

ONE morn before me were three figures seen,
    With bowed necks, and joined hands, side-faced;
And one behind the other stepp'd serene,
    In placid sandals, and in white robes graced;
        They pass'd, like figures on a marble urn,
    When shifted round to see the other side;
They came again; as when the urn once more
        Is shifted round, the first seen shades return;
    And they were strange to me, as may betide
With vases, to one deep in Phidian lore.

II

How is it, Shadows! that I knew ye not?
    How came ye muffled in so hush a mask?
Was it a silent deep-disguised plot
    To steal away, and leave without a task
        My idle days? Ripe was the drowsy hour;
    The blissful cloud of summer-indolence
Benumb'd my eyes; my pulse grew less and less;
        Pain had no sting, and pleasure's wreath no flower:
    Oh, why did ye not melt, and leave my sense
Unhaunted quite of all but – nothingness?

III

A third time pass'd they by, and, passing, turn'd
    Each one the face a moment whiles to me;
Then faded, and to follow them I burn'd
    And ach'd for wings, because I knew the three;
        The first was a fair Maid, and Love her name;

The second was Ambition, pale of cheek,
And ever watchful with fatigued eye;
    The last, whom I love more, the more of blame
  Is heap'd upon her, maiden most unmeek, –
I knew to be my demon Poesy.

IV

They faded, and, forsooth! I wanted wings:
  O folly! What is Love? and where is it?
And for that poor Ambition! it springs
  From a man's little heart's short fever-fit;
    For Poesy! – no, – she has not a joy, –
  At least for me, – so sweet as drowsy noons,
And evenings steep'd in honied indolence;
    O, for an age so shelter'd from annoy,
  That I may never know how change the moons,
Or hear the voice of busy common-sense!

V

And once more came they by; – alas! wherefore?
  My sleep had been embroider'd with dim dreams;
My soul had been a lawn besprinkled o'er
  With flowers, and stirring shades, and baffled beams:
    The morn was clouded, but no shower fell,
  Tho' in her lids hung the sweet tears of May;
The open casement press'd a new-leav'd vine,
  Let in the budding warmth and throstle's lay;
    O Shadows! 'twas a time to bid farewell!
Upon your skirts had fallen no tears of mine.

VI

So, ye three Ghosts, adieu! Ye cannot raise
  My head cool-bedded in the flowery grass;
For I would not be dieted with praise,
  A pet-lamb in a sentimental farce!

Fade softly from my eyes, and be once more
In masque-like figures on the dreamy urn;
Farewell! I yet have visions for the night,
And for the day faint visions there is store;
Vanish, ye Phantoms! from my idle spright,
Into the clouds, and never more return!

Fragment of an Ode to Maia, written on May Day, 1818

MOTHER of Hermes! and still youthful Maia!
        May I sing to thee
As thou wast hymned on the shores of Baiae?
        Or may I woo thee
In earlier Sicilian? or thy smiles
Seek as they once were sought, in Grecian isles,
By bards who died content on pleasant sward,
   Leaving great verse unto a little clan?
O, give me their old vigour, and unheard
   Save of the quiet Primrose, and the span
      Of heaven and few ears,
Rounded by thee, my song should die away
      Content as theirs,
   Rich in the simple worship of a day.

'Under the flag
Of each his faction, they to battle bring
Their embryo atoms.'—MILTON.

WELCOME joy, and welcome sorrow,
    Lethe's weed and Hermes' feather;
Come to-day and come to-morrow,
    I do love you both together!
    I love to mark sad faces in fair weather;
And hear a merry laugh amid the thunder;
    Fair and foul I love together:
Meadows sweet where flames are under,
And a giggle at a wonder;
Visage sage at pantomime;
Funeral, and steeple-chime;
Infant playing with a skull;
Morning fair, and shipwreck'd hull;
Nightshade with the woodbine kissing;
Serpents in red roses hissing;
Cleopatra regal-dress'd
With the aspic at her breast;
Dancing music, music sad,
Both together, sane and mad;
Muses bright and muses pale;
Sombre Saturn, Momus hale; –
Laugh and sigh, and laugh again;
Oh the sweetness of the pain!
Muses bright and muses pale,
Bare your faces of the veil;
Let me see; and let me write
Of the day and of the night –
Both together: – let me slake
All my thirst for sweet heart-ache;

Let my bower be of yew,
Interwreath'd with myrtles new;
Pines and lime-trees full in bloom
And my couch a low grass-tomb.

CHIEF of organic numbers!
Old Scholar of the Spheres!
Thy spirit never slumbers,
But rolls about our ears,
For ever, and for ever!
O what a mad endeavour
       Worketh he,
Who to thy sacred and ennobled hearse
Would offer a burnt sacrifice of verse
       And melody.

How heavenward thou soundest,
Live Temple of sweet noise,
And Discord unconfoundest,
Giving Delight new joys,
And Pleasure nobler pinions!
O, where are thy dominions?
       Lend thine ear
To a young Delian oath, – ay, by thy soul,
By all that from thy mortal lips did roll,
And by the kernel of thine earthly love,
Beauty, in things on earth, and things above
       I swear!

     When every childish fancy
     Has vanish'd from my rhyme,
     Will I, grey-gone in passion,
     Leave to an after-time,
     Hymning and Harmony
Of thee, and of thy works, and of thy life;
But vain is now the burning and the strife,

Pangs are in vain, until I grow high-rife
      With old Philosophy,
And mad with glimpses of futurity!

For many years my offering must be hush'd;
When I do speak, I'll think upon this hour,
Because I feel my forehead hot and flush'd,
Even at the simplest vassal of thy power, –
      A lock of thy bright hair, –
      Sudden it came,
And I was startled, when I caught thy name
      Coupled so unaware;
Yet, at the moment, temperate was my blood.
I thought I had beheld it from the flood.

Lines written in the Highlands after a visit to Burns's country

THERE is a charm in footing slow across a silent plain,
Where patriot battle has been fought, where glory had the gain;
There is a pleasure on the heath where Druids old have been,
Where mantles grey have rustled by and swept the nettled green;
There is a joy in every spot made known by times of old,
New to the feet, although each tale a hundred times be told;
There is a deeper joy than all, more solemn in the heart,
More parching to the tongue than all, of more divine a smart,
When weary steps forget themselves upon a pleasant turf,
Upon hot sand, or flinty road, or sea-shore iron surf,
Toward the castle or the cot, where long ago was born
One who was great through mortal days, and died of fame
    unshorn,
Light heather-bells may tremble then, – but they are far away;
Wood-lark may sing from sandy fern, – the Sun may hear his
    lay;
Runnels may kiss the grass on shelves and shallows clear,
But their low voices are not heard, though come on travels
    drear;
Blood-red the sun may set behind black mountain peaks,
Blue tides may sluice and drench their time in caves and weedy
    creeks,
Eagles may seem to sleep wing-wide upon the air;
Ring-doves may fly convuls'd across to some high-cedared
    lair,
But the forgotten eye is still fast lidded to the ground,
As Palmer's, that with weariness, mid-desert shrine hath found.
At such a time the soul's a child, in childhood is the brain;
Forgotten is the worldly heart – alone, it beats in vain: –
Aye, if a madman could have leave to pass a healthful day
To tell his forehead's swoon and faint when first began decay,

He might make tremble many a one whose spirit had gone forth
To find a Bard's low cradle-place about the silent North!
Scanty the hour and few the steps beyond the bourn of care,
Beyond the sweet and bitter world, – beyond it unaware!
Scanty the hour and few the steps, because a longer stay
Would bar return, and make a man forget his mortal way:
O horrible! to lose the sight of well remember'd face,
Of Brother's eyes, of Sister's brow – constant to every place;
Filling the air, as on we move, with portraiture intense;
More warm than those heroic tints that pain a painter's sense,
When shapes of old come striding by, and visages of old,
Locks shining black, hair scanty grey, and passions manifold.
No, no, that horror cannot be, for at the cable's length
Man feels the gentle anchor pull and gladdens in its strength: –
One hour, half-idiot, he stands by mossy waterfall,
But in the very next he reads his soul's memorial: –
He reads it on the mountain's height, where chance he may sit
    down
Upon rough marble diadem – that hill's eternal crown.
Yet be his anchor e'er so fast, room is there for a prayer
That man may never lose his mind on mountains black and bare;
That he may stray league after league, some great birthplace to
    find
And keep his vision clear from speck, his inward sight unblind.

Song

[Written in a copy of the *Works* of Beaumont and Fletcher]

I

SPIRIT here that reignest!
Spirit here that painest!
Spirit here that turnest!
Spirit here that mournest!
    Spirit, I bow
    My forehead low,
  Enshaded with thy pinions.
    Spirit, I look
    All passion-struck
  Into thy pale dominions.

II

Spirit here that laughest!
Spirit here that quaffest!
Spirit here that dancest!
Noble soul that prancest!
    Spirit, with thee
    I join in the glee
  A-nudging the elbow of Momus.
    Spirit, I flush
    With a Bacchanal blush
  Just fresh from the Banquet of Comus.

Stanzas

I

In a drear-nighted December,
Too happy, happy tree,
Thy branches ne'er remember
Their green felicity:
The north cannot undo them,
With a sleety whistle through them;
Nor frozen thawings glue them
From budding at the prime.

II

In a drear-nighted December,
Too happy, happy brook,
Thy bubblings ne'er remember
Apollo's summer look;
But with a sweet forgetting,
They stay their crystal fretting,
Never, never petting
About the frozen time.

III

Ah! would 'twere so with many
A gentle girl and boy!
But were there ever any
Writhed not at passed joy?
To know the change and feel it,
When there is none to heal it,
Nor numbed sense to steel it,
Was never said in rhyme.

You Say You Love

I

You say you love; but with a voice
    Chaster than a nun's, who singeth
The soft Vespers to herself
    While the chime-bell ringeth –
      O love me truly!

II

You say you love; but with a smile
    Cold as sunrise in September,
As you were Saint Cupid's nun,
    And kept his weeks of Ember.
      O love me truly!

III

You say you love – but then your lips
    Coral tinted teach no blisses,
More than coral in the sea –
    They never pout for kisses –
      O love me truly!

IV

You say you love; but then your hand
    No soft squeeze for squeeze returneth,
It is like a statue's dead –
    While mine to passion burneth –
      O love me truly!

V

O breathe a word or two of fire!
    Smile, as if those words should burn me,
Squeeze as lovers should – O kiss
    And in thy heart inurn me!
      O love me truly!

Modern Love

AND what is Love? It is a doll dress'd up
For idleness to cosset, nurse, and dandle;
A thing of soft misnomers, so divine
That silly youth doth think to make itself
Divine by loving, and so goes on
Yawning and doting a whole summer long,
Till Miss's comb is made a pearl tiara,
And common Wellingtons turn Romeo boots;
Then Cleopatra lives at number seven,
And Antony resides in Brunswick Square.
Fools! if some passions high have warm'd the world,
If Queens and Soldiers have play'd deep for hearts,
It is no reason why such agonies
Should be more common than the growth of weeds.
Fools! make me whole again that weighty pearl
The Queen of Egypt melted, and I'll say
That ye may love in spite of beaver hats.

I

SHED no tear – O shed no tear!
The flower will bloom another year.
Weep no more – O weep no more!
Young buds sleep in the root's white core.
Dry your eyes – O dry your eyes,
For I was taught in Paradise
To ease my breast of melodies –
              Shed no tear.

Overhead – look overhead
'Mong the blossoms white and red –
Look up, look up – I flutter now
On this flush pomegranate bough –
See me – 'tis this silvery bill
Ever cures the good man's ill –
Shed no tear – O shed no tear!
The flower will bloom another year.
Adieu – Adieu – I fly, adieu,
I vanish in the heaven's blue –
              Adieu, Adieu!

II

AH! woe is me! poor silver-wing!
  That I must chant thy lady's dirge,
And death to this fair haunt of spring,
Of melody, and streams of flowery verge, –
    Poor silver-wing! ah! woe is me!
      That I must see
These blossoms snow upon thy lady's pall!
  Go, pretty page! and in her ear
  Whisper that the hour is near!

Softly tell her not to fear
Such calm favonian burial!
   Go, pretty page! and soothly tell, –
   The blossoms hang by a melting spell,
And fall they must, ere a star wink thrice,
            Upon her closed eyes,
That now in vain are weeping their last tears
   At sweet life leaving, and these arbours green, –
Rich dowry from the Spirit of the Spheres, –
            Alas! poor Queen!

Song

I HAD a dove, and the sweet dove died;
    And I have thought it died of grieving:
O, what could it grieve for? its feet were tied
    With a single thread of my own hand's weaving;
Sweet little red feet, why should you die –
Why should you leave me, sweet bird, why?
You lived alone in the forest tree,
Why, pretty thing! would you not live with me?
I kiss'd you oft and gave you white peas;
Why not live sweetly, as in the green trees?

On Death

I

CAN death be sleep, when life is but a dream,
 And scenes of bliss pass as a phantom by?
The transient pleasures as a vision seem,
 And yet we think the greatest pain's to die.

II

How strange it is that man on earth should roam,
 And lead a life of woe, but not forsake
His rugged path; nor dare he view alone
 His future doom which is but to awake.

Women, Wine, and Snuff

GIVE me women, wine, and snuff
Until I cry out 'hold, enough!'
You may do so sans objection
Till the day of resurrection;
For bless my beard they aye shall be
My beloved Trinity.

Sharing Eve's Apple

I

O BLUSH not so! O blush not so!
  Or I shall think you knowing;
And if you smile the blushing while,
  Then maidenheads are going.

II

There's a blush for won't, and a blush for shan't,
  And a blush for having done it:
There's a blush for thought and a blush for naught,
  And a blush for just begun it.

III

O sigh not so! O sigh not so!
  For it sounds of Eve's sweet pippin;
By these loosen'd lips you have tasted the pips
  And fought in an amorous nipping.

IV

Will you play once more at nice-cut-core,
  For it will only last your youth out,
And we have the prime of the kissing time,
  We have not one sweet tooth out.

V

There's a sigh for yes, and a sigh for no,
  And a sigh for I can't bear it!
O what can be done, shall we stay or run?
  O cut the sweet apple and share it!

A Song about Myself

[From a Letter to Fanny Keats]

I

THERE was a naughty Boy,
   A naughty boy was he,
He would not stop at home,
   He could not quiet be –
      He took
      In his Knapsack
      A Book
      Full of vowels
      And a shirt
      With some towels –
      A slight cap
      For night cap –
      A hair brush,
      Comb ditto,
      New Stockings
      For old ones
      Would split O!
      This Knapsack
      Tight at's back
      He rivetted close
And followed his Nose
   To the North,
   To the North,
And follow'd his nose
   To the North.

II

There was a naughty boy
   And a naughty boy was he,

For nothing would he do
   But scribble poetry –
      He took
      An ink stand
      In his hand
      And a pen
      Big as ten
      In the other.
      And away
      In a Pother
      He ran
      To the mountains
      And fountains
      And ghostes
      And Postes
      And witches
      And ditches
      And wrote
      In his coat
      When the weather
      Was cool,
      Fear of gout,
      And without
      When the weather
      Was warm –
      Och the charm
      When we choose
   To follow one's nose
      To the north,
      To the north,
   To follow one's nose
      To the north!

III

There was a naughty boy
  And a naughty boy was he,
He kept little fishes
  In washing tubs three
    In spite
    Of the might
    Of the Maid
    Nor afraid
    Of his Granny-good —
    He often would
    Hurly burly
    Get up early
    And go
    By hook or crook
    To the brook
    And bring home
    Miller's thumb
    Tittlebat
    Not over fat,
    Minnows small
    As the stall
    Of a glove,
    Not above
    The size
    Of a nice
    Little Baby's
    Little fingers —
    O he made
    'Twas his trade
  Of Fish a pretty Kettle
    A Kettle —

281

A Kettle
Of Fish a pretty Kettle
A Kettle!

IV

There was a naughty Boy,
    And a naughty Boy was he,
He ran away to Scotland
    The people for to see –
        Then he found
        That the ground
        Was as hard,
        That a yard
        Was as long,
        That a song
        Was as merry,
        That a cherry
        Was as red –
        That lead
        Was as weighty,
        That fourscore
        Was as eighty,
        That a door
        Was as wooden
        As in England –
So he stood in his shoes
    And he wonder'd
    He wonder'd,
He stood in his shoes
    And he wonder'd.

Devon Maid

[Stanzas sent in a Letter to Benjamin Haydon]

I

WHERE be ye going, you Devon Maid?
  And what have ye there in the Basket?
Ye tight little fairy just fresh from the dairy,
  Will ye give me some cream if I ask it?

II

I love your Meads, and I love your flowers,
  And I love your junkets mainly,
But 'hind the door I love kissing more,
  O look not so disdainly.

III

I love your hills, and I love your dales,
  And I love your flocks a-bleating –
But O, on the heather to lie together,
  With both our hearts a-beating!

IV

I'll put your Basket all safe in a nook,
  Your shawl I hang up on the willow,
And we will sigh in the daisy's eye
  And kiss on a grass green pillow.

Dawlish Fair

OVER the Hill and over the Dale,
   And over the Bourne to Dawlish,
Where ginger-bread wives have a scanty sale,
   And ginger-bread nuts are smallish.

Teignmouth

['Some Doggerel' Sent in a Letter to B. R. Haydon]

I

HERE all the summer could I stay,
   For there's Bishop's teign
   And King's teign
And Coomb at the clear teign head –
   Where close by the stream
   You may have your cream
All spread upon barley bread.

II

   There's arch Brook
   And there's larch Brook
Both turning many a mill;
   And cooling the drouth
   Of the salmon's mouth,
And fattening his silver gill.

III

   There is Wild wood,
   A Mild hood
To the sheep on the lea o' the down,
   Where the golden furze,
   With its green, thin spurs,
Doth catch at the maiden's gown.

IV

   There is Newton marsh
   With its spear grass harsh –
A pleasant summer level
   Where the maidens sweet
   Of the Market Street,
Do meet in the dusk to revel.

V

There's the Barton rich
With dyke and ditch
And hedge for the thrush to live in
And the hollow tree
For the buzzing bee
And a bank for the wasp to hive in.

VI

And O, and O
The daisies blow
And the primroses are waken'd,
And violets white
Sit in silver plight,
And the green bud's as long as the spike end.

VII

Then who would go
Into dark Soho,
And chatter with dack'd hair'd critics,
When he can stay
For the new-mown hay,
And startle the dappled Prickets?

On Oxford

A PARODY

I

The Gothic looks solemn,
The plain Doric column
Supports an old Bishop and Crosier;
The mouldering arch,
Shaded o'er by a larch
Stands next door to Wislon the Hosier.

II

Vicè – that is, by turns, –
O'er pale faces mourns
The black tassell'd trencher and common hat;
The Chantry boy sings,
The Steeple-bell rings,
Ard as for the Chancellor – *dominat*.

III

There are plenty of trees,
And plenty of ease,
And plenty of fat deer for Parsons;
And when it is venison,
Short is the benison, –
Then each on a leg or thigh fastens.

Two or Three

[From a Letter to his Sister]

Two or three Posies
With two or three simples –
Two or three Noses
With two or three pimples –
Two or three wise men
And two or three ninny's –
Two or three purses
And two or three guineas –
Two or three raps
At two or three doors –
Two or three naps
Of two or three hours –
Two or three Cats
And two or three mice –
Two or three sprats –
At a very great price –
Two or three sandies
And two or three tabbies –
Two or three dandies
And two Mrs [Abbeys]   mum!
Two or three Smiles
And two or three frowns –
Two or three Miles
To two or three towns –
Two or three pegs
For two or three bonnets –
Two or three dove eggs
To hatch into sonnets.

A GROUP OF SONNETS

On the Sonnet

If by dull rhymes our English must be chain'd,
And, like Andromeda, the Sonnet sweet
Fetter'd, in spite of pained loveliness,
Let us find out, if we must be constrain'd,
   Sandals more interwoven and complete
To fit the naked foot of Poesy.
Let us inspect the Lyre, and weigh the stress
Of every chord, and see what may be gain'd
   By ear industrious, and attention meet;
Misers of sound and syllable, no less
Than Midas of his coinage, let us be
   Jealous of dead leaves in the bay wreath crown;
So, if we may not let the Muse be free,
   She will be bound with garlands of her own.

On Peace

O Peace! and dost thou with thy presence bless
   The dwellings of this war-surrounded Isle;
Soothing with placid brow our late distress,
   Making the triple kingdom brightly smile?
Joyful I hail thy presence; and I hail
   The sweet companions that await on thee;
Complete my joy – let not my first wish fail,
   Let the sweet mountain nymph thy favourite be,
With England's happiness proclaim Europa's Liberty.
O Europe! let not sceptred tyrants see
   That thou must shelter in thy former state;
Keep thy chains burst, and boldly say thou art free;
   Give thy kings law – leave not uncurbed the great;
   So with the horrors past thou'lt win thy happier fate!

To Byron

BYRON! how sweetly sad thy melody!
  Attuning still the soul to tenderness,
  As if soft Pity, with unusual stress,
Had touch'd her plaintive lute, and thou, being by,
Hadst caught the tones, nor suffer'd them to die.
  O'ershadowing sorrow doth not make thee less
  Delightful: thou thy griefs dost dress
With a bright halo, shining beamily,
As when a cloud the golden moon doth veil,
  Its sides are ting'd with a resplendent glow,
Through the dark robe oft amber rays prevail,
  And like fair veins in sable marble flow;
Still warble, dying swan! still tell the tale,
  The enchanting tale, the tale of pleasing woe.

To Chatterton

O CHATTERTON! how very sad thy fate!
  Dear child of sorrow – son of misery!
  How soon the film of death obscur'd that eye,
Whence Genius mildly flash'd, and high debate.
How soon that voice, majestic and elate,
  Melted in dying numbers! Oh! how nigh
  Was night to thy fair morning. Thou didst die
A half-blown flow'ret which cold blasts amate.
But this is past: thou art among the stars
  Of highest heaven: to the rolling spheres
Thou sweetly singest: naught thy hymning mars,
  Above the ingrate world and human fears.
On earth the good man base detraction bars
  From thy fair name, and waters it with tears.

To Spenser

SPENSER! a jealous honourer of thine,
    A forester deep in thy midmost trees,
Did last eve, ask my promise to refine
    Some English that might strive thine ear to please.
    But Elfin Poet 'tis impossible
For an inhabitant of wintry earth
    To rise like Phoebus with a golden quill,
Fire-wing'd and make a morning in his mirth.
    It is impossible to escape from toil
O' the sudden and receive thy spiriting:
    The flower must drink the nature of the soil
Before it can put forth its blossoming:
    Be with me in the summer days and I
    Will for thine honour and his pleasure try.

To a Young Lady who sent me a Laurel Crown

FRESH morning gusts have blown away all fear
    From my glad bosom, – now from gloominess
    I mount for ever – not an atom less
Than the proud laurel shall content my bier.
No! by the eternal stars! or why sit here
    In the Sun's eye, and 'gainst my temples press
    Apollo's very leaves, woven to bless
By thy white fingers and thy spirit clear.
Lo! who dares say, 'Do this'? Who dares call down
    My will from its high purpose? Who say, 'Stand',
Or 'Go'? This mighty moment I would frown
    On abject Caesars – not the stoutest band
Of mailed heroes should tear off my crown:
    Yet would I kneel and kiss thy gentle hand.

[On the death of his grandmother]

As from the darkening gloom a silver dove
   Upsoars, and darts into the Eastern light,
   On pinions that naught moves but pure delight,
So fled thy soul into the realms above,
Regions of peace and everlasting love;
   Where happy spirits, crown'd with circlets bright
Of starry beam, and gloriously bedight,
   Taste the high joy none but the blest can prove.
There thou or joinest the immortal quire
   In melodies that even Heaven fair
Fill with superior bliss, or, at desire
   Of the omnipotent Father, cleavest the air
   On holy message sent. – What pleasure's higher?
Wherefore does any grief our joy impair?

★

Oh! how I love, on a fair summer's eve,
   When streams of light pour down the golden west,
   And on the balmy zephyrs tranquil rest
The silver clouds, far – far away to leave
All meaner thoughts, and take a sweet reprieve
   From little cares; to find, with easy quest,
   A fragrant wild, with Nature's beauty drest,
And there into delight my soul deceive.
There warm my breast with patriotic lore,
   Musing on Milton's fate – on Sydney's bier –
Till their stern forms before my mind arise:
Perhaps on wing of Poesy upsoar,
   Full often dropping a delicious tear,
When some melodious sorrow spells mine eyes.

Written in Disgust of Vulgar Superstition

THE church bells toll a melancholy round,
   Calling the people to some other prayers,
   Some other gloominess, more dreadful cares,
More hearkening to the sermon's horrid sound.
Surely the mind of man is closely bound
   In some black spell; seeing that each one tears
   Himself from fireside joys, and Lydian airs,
And converse high of those with glory crown'd.
Still, still they toll, and I should feel a damp, –
   A chill as from the tomb, did I not know
That they are dying like an outburnt lamp;
   That t' is their sighing, wailing ere they go
   Into oblivion; – that fresh flowers will grow,
And many glories of immortal stamp.

*

AFTER dark vapors have oppress'd our plains
   For a long dreary season, comes a day
   Born of the gentle South, and clears away
From the sick heavens all unseemly stains.
The anxious month, relieved of its pains,
   Takes as a long-lost right the feel of May;
   The eyelids with the passing coolness play
Like rose leaves with the drip of Summer rains.
The calmest thoughts come round us; as of leaves
   Budding – fruit ripening in stillness – Autumn suns
Smiling at eve upon the quiet sheaves –
Sweet Sappho's cheek – a smiling infant's breath –
   The gradual sand that through an hour-glass runs –
A woodland rivulet – a Poet's death.

[Written at the end of Chaucer's 'The Floure and The Lefe']

THIS pleasant tale is like a little copse:
    The honied lines do freshly interlace
    To keep the reader in so sweet a place,
So that he here and there full-hearted stops;
And oftentimes he feels the dewy drops
    Come cool and suddenly against his face,
    And, by the wandering melody, may trace
Which way the tender-legged linnet hops.
Oh! what a power hath white Simplicity!
    What mighty power has this gentle story!
    I that for ever feel athirst for glory
Could at this moment be content to lie
    Meekly upon the grass, as those whose sobbings
    Were heard of none beside the mournful robins.

[To Haydon with a sonnet written on seeing the Elgin Marbles]

HAYDON! forgive me that I cannot speak
    Definitively on these mighty things;
    Forgive me that I have not Eagle's wings –
That what I want I know not where to seek:
And think that I would not be overmeek
    In rolling out upfollow'd thunderings,
    Even to the steep of Heliconian springs,
Were I of ample strength for such a freak –
Think too, that all these numbers should be thine;
    Whose else? In this who touch thy vesture's hem?
For when men star'd at what was most divine
    With browless idiotism – o'erwise phlegm –
Thou hadst beheld the Hesperian shine
    Of their star in the East, and gone to worship them.

On Seeing the Elgin Marbles

MY spirit is too weak – mortality
    Weighs heavily on me like unwilling sleep,
    And each imagin'd pinnacle and steep
Of godlike hardship, tells me I must die
Like a sick Eagle looking at the sky.
    Yet 'tis a gentle luxury to weep,
    That I have not the cloudy winds to keep,
Fresh for the opening of the morning's eye.
Such dim-conceived glories of the brain
    Bring round the heart an indescribable feud;
So do these wonders a most dizzy pain,
    That mingles Grecian grandeur with the rude
Wasting of old Time – with a billowy main –
    A sun – a shadow of a magnitude.

On the Sea

IT keeps eternal whisperings around
    Desolate shores, and with its mighty swell
    Gluts twice ten thousand Caverns, till the spell
Of Hecate leaves them their old shadowy sound.
Often 'tis in such gentle temper found,
    That scarcely will the very smallest shell
    Be mov'd for days from where it sometimes fell,
When last the winds of Heaven were unbound.
Oh ye! who have your eye-balls vex'd and tir'd,
    Feast them upon the wideness of the Sea;
      Oh ye! whose ears are dinn'd with uproar rude,
    Or fed too much with cloying melody –
      Sit ye near some old Cavern's Mouth, and brood
Until ye start, as if the sea-nymphs quir'd!

On Leigh Hunt's Poem, the 'Story of Rimini'

WHO loves to peer up at the morning sun,
    With half-shut eyes and comfortable cheek,
    Let him, with this sweet tale, full often seek
For meadows where the little rivers run;
Who loves to linger with that brightest one
    Of heaven – Hesperus – let him lowly speak
    These numbers to the night, and starlight meek,
Or moon, if that her hunting be begun.
He who knows these delights, and too is prone
    To moralize upon a smile or tear,
    Will find at once a region of his own,
    A bower for his spirit, and will steer
To alleys where the fir-tree drops its cone,
    Where robins hop, and fallen leaves are sear.

To a Cat

CAT! who has pass'd thy grand climacteric,
    How many mice and rats hast in thy days
    Destroy'd? – How many tit bits stolen? Gaze
With those bright languid segments green, and prick
Those velvet ears – but pr'ythee do not stick
    Thy latent talons in me – and upraise
    Thy gentle mew – and tell me all thy frays
Of fish and mice, and rats and tender chick.
Nay, look not down, nor lick thy dainty wrists –
    For all the wheezy asthma, – and for all
Thy tail's tip is nick'd off – and though the fists
    Of many a maid have given thee many a maul,
Still is that fur as soft as when the lists
    In youth thou enter'dst on glass bottled wall.

296

On *Sitting down to read* King Lear *once again*

O GOLDEN TONGUED Romance with serene lute!
  Fair plumed Syren! Queen of far-away!
  Leave melodizing on this wintry day,
Shut up thine olden volume, and be mute:
Adieu! for, once again, the fierce dispute
  Betwixt damnation and impassion'd clay
  Must I burn through; once more humbly assay
The bitter-sweet of this Shakespearian fruit:
Chief Poet! and ye clouds of Albion,
  Begetters of our deep eternal theme,
When through the old oak Forest I am gone,
  Let me not wander in a barren dream,
But, when I am consumed in the fire,
Give me new Phoenix-wings to fly at my desire.

*

WHEN I have fears that I may cease to be
  Before my pen has glean'd my teeming brain,
Before high-piled books, in charactery,
  Hold like full garners the full-ripen'd grain;
When I behold, upon the night's starr'd face,
  Huge cloudy symbols of a high romance,
And feel that I may never live to trace
  Their shadows, with the magic hand of chance;
And when I feel, fair creature of an hour,
  That I shall never look upon thee more,
Never have relish in the faery power
  Of unreflecting love; – then on the shore
Of the wide world I stand alone, and think,
Till Love and Fame to nothingness do sink.

To the Nile

SON of the old moon-mountains African!
Chief of the Pyramid and Crocodile!
We call thee fruitful, and, that very while,
A desert fills our seeing's inward span;
Nurst of swart nations since the world began,
Art thou so fruitful? or dost thou beguile
Such men to honour thee, who, worn with toil,
Rest for a space 'twist Cairo and Decan?
O may dark fancies err! They surely do;
'Tis ignorance that makes a barren waste
Of all beyond itself, thou dost bedew
Green rushes like our rivers, and dost taste
The pleasant sun-rise, green isles hast thou too,
And to the sea as happily dost haste.

To a Lady Seen for a few Moments at Vauxhall

TIME's sea hath been five years at its slow ebb,
   Long hours have to and fro let creep the sand,
Since I was tangled in thy beauty's web,
   And snared by the ungloving of thine hand.
And yet I never look on midnight sky,
   But I behold thine eyes' well memory'd light;
I cannot look upon the rose's dye,
   But to thy cheek my soul doth take its flight.
I cannot look on any budding flower,
   But my fond ear, in fancy at thy lips
And hearkening for a love-sound, doth devour
   Its sweets in the wrong sense: – Thou dost eclipse
Every delight with sweet remembering,
And grief unto my darling joys dost bring.

To J. H. Reynolds

O THAT a week could be an age, and we
    Felt parting and warm meeting every week,
Then one poor year a thousand years would be,
    The flush of welcome ever on the cheek:
So could we live long life in little space,
    So time itself would be annihilate,
So a day's journey in oblivious haze
    To serve our joys would lengthen and dilate.
O to arrive each Monday morn from Ind!
    To land each Tuesday from the rich Levant!
In little time a host of joys to bind,
    And keep our souls in one eternal pant!
This morn, my friend, and yester-evening taught
Me how to harbour such a happy thought.

The Human Seasons

FOUR seasons fill the measure of the year;
    There are four seasons in the mind of man:
He has his lusty Spring, when fancy clear
    Takes in all beauty with an easy span:
He has his Summer, when luxuriously
    Spring's honied cud of youthful thought he loves
To ruminate, and by such dreaming nigh
    His nearest unto heaven: quiet coves
His soul has in its Autumn, when his wings
    He furleth close; contented so to look
On mists in idleness – to let fair things
    Pass by unheeded as a threshold brook.
He has his Winter too of pale misfeature,
Or else he would forego his mortal nature.

To Homer

STANDING aloof in giant ignorance,
  Of thee I hear and of the Cyclades,
As one who sits ashore and longs perchance
  To visit dolphin-coral in deep seas.
So thou wast blind; – but then the veil was rent;
  For Jove uncurtain'd Heaven to let thee live,
And Neptune made for thee a spumy tent,
  And Pan made sing for thee his forest-hive;
Ay, on the shores of darkness there is light,
  And precipices show untrodden green,
There is a budding morrow in midnight,
  There is a triple sight in blindness keen;
Such seeing hadst thou, as it once befel
To Dian, Queen of Earth, and Heaven, and Hell.

Written in the Cottage where Burns was Born

THIS mortal body of a thousand days
Now fills, O Burns, a space in thine own room,
Where thou didst dream alone on budded bays,
Happy and thoughtless of thy day of doom!
My pulse is warm with thine own Barley-bree,
My head is light with pledging a great soul,
My eyes are wandering, and I cannot see,
Fancy is dead and drunken at its goal;
Yet can I stamp my foot upon thy floor,
Yet can I ope thy window-sash to find
The meadow thou hast tramped o'er and o'er, –
Yet can I think of thee till thought is blind, –
Yet can I gulp a bumper to thy name, –
O smile among the shades, for this is fame!

On Visiting the Tomb of Burns

The town, the churchyard, and the setting sun,
The clouds, the trees, the rounded hills all seem,
Though beautiful, cold – strange – as in a dream,
I dreamed long ago, now new begun.
The short-liv'd paly Summer is but won
From Winter's ague, for one hour's gleam;
Though sapphire-warm, their stars do never beam:
All is cold Beauty; pain is never done:
For who has mind to relish, Minos-wise,
The Real of Beauty, free from that dead hue
Sickly imagination and sick pride
Cast wan upon it! Burns! with honour due
I oft have honour'd thee. Great shadow, hide
Thy face; I sin against thy native skies.

To Ailsa Rock

Hearken, thou craggy ocean-pyramid!
    Give answer from thy voice, the sea-fowl's screams!
    When were thy shoulders mantled in huge streams?
When, from the sun, was thy broad forehead hid?
How long is't since the mighty power bid
    Thee heave to airy sleep from fathom dreams?
    Sleep in the lap of thunder or sunbeams,
Or when grey clouds are thy cold coverlid.
Thou answer'st not; for thou art dead asleep.
    Thy life is but two dead eternities –
The last in air, the former in the deep;
    First with the whales, last with the eagle-skies –
Drown'd wast thou till an earthquake made thee steep,
    Another cannot wake thy giant size.

Written upon the Top of Ben Nevis

READ me a lesson, Muse, and speak it loud
Upon the top of Nevis, blind in mist!
I look into the chasms, and a shroud
Vaporous doth hide them, – just so much I wist
Mankind do know of hell; I look o'erhead,
And there is sullen mist, – even so much
Mankind can tell of heaven; mist is spread
Before the earth, beneath me, – even such,
Even so vague is man's sight of himself!
Here are the craggy stones beneath my feet, –
Thus much I know that, a poor witless elf,
I tread on them, – that all my eye doth meet
Is mist and crag, not only on this height,
But in the world of thought and mental might!

To Sleep

O SOFT embalmer of the still midnight,
   Shutting, with careful fingers and benign,
Our gloom-pleas'd eyes, embower'd from the light,
   Enshaded in forgetfulness divine:
O soothest Sleep! if so it please thee, close
   In midst of this thine hymn my willing eyes,
Or wait the 'Amen.', ere thy poppy throws
   Around my bed its lulling charities.
   Then save me, or the passed day will shine
Upon my pillow, breeding many woes, –
   Save me from curious Conscience, that still lords
Its strength for darkness, burrowing like a mole;
   Turn the key deftly in the oiled wards,
And seal the hushed Casket of my soul.

I

FAME, like a wayward Girl, will still be coy
   To those who woo her with too slavish knees,
But makes surrender to some thoughtless Boy,
   And dotes the more upon a heart at ease;
She is a Gipsy, will not speak to those
   Who have not learnt to be content without her;
A Jilt, whose ear was never whisper'd close,
   Who thinks they scandal her who talk about her;
A very Gipsy is she, Nilus-born,
   Sister-in-law to jealous Potiphar;
Ye love-sick Bards! repay her scorn for scorn,
   Ye Artists lovelorn! madmen that ye are!
Make your best bow to her and bid adieu,
Then, if she likes it, she will follow you.

II

   'You cannot eat your cake and have it too.' – *Proverb*

How fever'd is the man, who cannot look
   Upon his mortal days with temperate blood,
Who vexes all the leaves of his life's book,
   And robs his fair name of its maidenhood;
It is as if the rose should pluck herself,
   Or the ripe plum finger its misty bloom,
As if a Naiad, like a meddling elf,
   Should darken her pure grot with muddy gloom,
But the rose leaves herself upon the briar,
   For winds to kiss and grateful bees to feed,
And the ripe plum still wears its dim attire;
   The undisturbed lake has crystal space;
   When then should man, teasing the world for grace,
Spoil his salvation for a fierce miscreed?

WHY did I laugh to-night? No voice will tell:
    No God, no Demon of severe response,
Deigns to reply from Heaven or from Hell.
    Then to my human heart I turn at once.
Heart! Thou and I are here, sad and alone;
    I say, why did I laugh! O mortal pain!
O Darkness! Darkness! ever must I moan,
    To question Heaven and Hell and Heart in vain.
Why did I laugh? I know this Being's lease,
    My fancy to its utmost blisses spreads;
Yet would I on this very midnight cease,
    And the world's gaudy ensigns see in shreds;
Verse, Fame, and Beauty are intense indeed,
But Death intenser – Death is Life's high meed.

*

THE day is gone, and all its sweets are gone!
    Sweet voice, sweet lips, soft hand, and softer breast,
Warm breath, light whisper, tender semi-tone,
    Bright eyes, accomplish'd shape, and lang'rous waist!
Faded the flower and all its budded charms,
    Faded the sight of beauty from my eyes,
Faded the shape of beauty from my arms,
    Faded the voice, warmth, whiteness, paradise –
Vanish'd unseasonably at shut of eve,
    When the dusk holiday – or holinight
Of fragrant-curtain'd love begins to weave
    The woof of darkness thick, for hid delight;
But, as I've read love's missal through to-day,
He'll let me sleep, seeing I fast and pray.

To Fanny

I CRY your mercy – pity – love! – aye, love!
    Merciful love that tantalizes not,
One-thoughted, never-wandering, guileless love,
    Unmask'd, and being seen – without a blot!
O! let me have thee whole, – all – all – be mine!
    That shape, that fairness, that sweet minor zest
Of love, your kiss, – those hands, those eyes divine,
    That warm, white, lucent, million-pleasured breast, –
Yourself – your soul – in pity give me all,
    Withhold no atom's atom or I die,
Or living on perhaps, your wretched thrall,
    Forget, in the midst of idle misery,
    Life's purposes, – the palate of my mind
Losing its gust, and my ambition blind!

[Written on a blank page in Shakespeare's *Poems*]

BRIGHT star, would I were stedfast as thou art –
    Not in lone splendour hung aloft the night
And watching, with eternal lids apart,
    Like Nature's patient, sleepless Eremite,
The moving waters at their priestlike task
    Of pure ablution round earth's human shores,
Or gazing on the new soft-fallen mask
    Of snow upon the mountains and the moors –
No – yet still stedfast, still unchangeable,
    Pillow'd upon my fair love's ripening breast,
To feel for ever its soft fall and swell,
    Awake for ever in a sweet unrest,
Still, still to hear her tender-taken breath,
And so live ever – or else swoon to death.

INDEX OF FIRST LINES

MORE ABOUT PENGUINS, PELICANS
AND PUFFINS

For further information about books available from Penguins please write to Dept EP, Penguin Books Ltd, Harmondsworth, Middlesex UB7 0DA.

In the U.S.A.: For a complete list of books available from Penguins in the United States write to Dept DG, Penguin Books, 299 Murray Hill Parkway, East Rutherford, New Jersey 07073.

In Canada: For a complete list of books available from Penguins in Canada write to Penguin Books Canada Ltd, 2801 John Street, Markham, Ontario L3R 1B4.

In Australia: For a complete list of books available from Penguins in Australia write to the Marketing Department, Penguin Books Australia Ltd, P.O. Box 257, Ringwood, Victoria 3134.

In New Zealand: For a complete list of books available from Penguins in New Zealand write to the Marketing Department, Penguin Books (N.Z.) Ltd, Private Bag, Takapuna, Auckland 9.

In India: For a complete list of books available from Penguins in India write to Penguin Overseas Ltd, 706 Eros Apartments, 56 Nehru Place, New Delhi 110019.

JOHN KEATS
THE COMPLETE POEMS
Edited by John Barnard

Keats survives as the archetypal Romantic genius who suffered
a tragically early death. He was, wrote Matthew Arnold, 'a great
spirit'. But his poetry has proved equally durable, withstanding
all revaluation of the Romantics, and few would now dispute
his right to be regarded as one of the foremost English poets.

This revised second edition contains all the poems and plays
known to have been written by Keats, as well as two poems and
a fragment of a play which are of doubtful attribution. There are
extensive notes, including long extracts from the letters, and a
dictionary of classical names based largely on the work of
Lemprière, with which Keats himself was familiar. In addition,
Keats's annotations to *Paradise Lost* and his review of Edmund
Kean's acting, both difficult for the modern reader to get hold of,
are printed as Appendices.

JOHN KEATS

Robert Gittings

Winner of the W. H. Smith Literary Award, Robert Gittings's *John Keats* is a sensitive and brilliant study of a great poet whose life 'was a living illustration of his own summing-up – "That which is creative must create itself."'

'A glowing, generous rewarding and extremely enjoyable exercise' – Dennis Potter in *The Times*

'Robert Gittings's *John Keats* is a splendid work, impressive both in its scholarship and in its critical perception and deeply moving. The Keats it gives us is of a quite extraordinary – sometimes startling – actuality' – Lionel Trilling

CLASSICS IN TRANSLATION
IN PENGUINS

☐ *Remembrance of Things Past* Marcel Proust
☐ Volume One: *Swann's Way, Within a Budding Grove* £7.50
☐ Volume Two: *The Guermantes Way, Cities of the Plain* £7.50
☐ Volume Three: *The Captive, The Fugitive, Time Regained* £7.50

Terence Kilmartin's acclaimed revised version of C. K. Scott Moncrieff's original translation, published in paperback for the first time.

☐ *The Canterbury Tales* Geoffrey Chaucer £2.50

'Every age is a Canterbury Pilgrimage . . . nor can a child be born who is not one of these characters of Chaucer' – William Blake

☐ *Gargantua & Pantagruel* Rabelais £3.95

The fantastic adventures of two giants through which Rabelais (1495–1553) caricatured his life and times in a masterpiece of exuberance and glorious exaggeration.

☐ *The Brothers Karamazov* Fyodor Dostoevsky £3.95

A detective story on many levels, profoundly involving the question of the existence of God, Dostoevsky's great drama of parricide and fraternal jealousy triumphantly fulfilled his aim: 'to find the man in man . . . [to] depict all the depths of the human soul.'

☐ *Fables of Aesop* £1.95

This translation recovers all the old magic of fables in which, too often, the fox steps forward as the cynical hero and a lamb is an ass to lie down with a lion.

☐ *The Three Theban Plays* Sophocles £2.95

A new translation, by Robert Fagles, of *Antigone, Oedipus the King* and *Oedipus at Colonus*, plays all based on the legend of the royal house of Thebes.

ENGLISH AND AMERICAN
LITERATURE IN PENGUINS

☐ *Emma* **Jane Austen**   £1.10

'I am going to take a heroine whom no one but myself will much like,'
declared Jane Austen of Emma, her most spirited and controversial
heroine in a comedy of self-deceit and self-discovery.

☐ *Tender is the Night* **F. Scott Fitzgerald**   £2.95

Fitzgerald worked on seventeen different versions of this novel, and
its obsessions – idealism, beauty, dissipation, alcohol and insanity –
were those that consumed his own marriage and his life.

☐ *The Life of Johnson* **James Boswell**   £2.25

Full of gusto, imagination, conversation and wit, Boswell's immortal
portrait of Johnson is as near a novel as a true biography can be, and
still regarded by many as the finest 'life' ever written. This shortened
version is based on the 1799 edition.

☐ *A House and its Head* **Ivy Compton-Burnett**   £3.95

In a novel 'as trim and tidy as a hand-grenade' (as Pamela Hansford
Johnson put it), Ivy Compton-Burnett penetrates the facade of a
conventional, upper-class Victorian family to uncover a chasm of
violent emotions – jealousy, pain, frustration and sexual passion.

☐ *The Trumpet Major* **Thomas Hardy**   £1.25

Although a vein of unhappy unrequited love runs through this novel,
Hardy also draws on his warmest sense of humour to portray
Wessex village life at the time of the Napoleonic wars.

☐ *The Complete Poems of Hugh MacDiarmid*

☐ Volume One   £8.95
☐ Volume Two   £8.95

The definitive edition of work by the greatest Scottish poet since
Robert Burns, edited by his son Michael Grieve, and W. R. Aitken.

KING PENGUIN

☐ **Selected Poems** Tony Harrison £3.95

Poetry Book Society Recommendation. 'One of the few modern poets who actually has the gift of composing poetry' – James Fenton in the *Sunday Times*

☐ **The Book of Laughter and Forgetting**
Milan Kundera £3.95

'A whirling dance of a book . . . a masterpiece full of angels, terror, ostriches and love . . . No question about it. The most important novel published in Britain this year' – Salman Rushdie in the *Sunday Times*

☐ **The Sea of Fertility** Yukio Mishima £9.95

Containing *Spring Snow, Runaway Horses, The Temple of Dawn* and *The Decay of the Angel*: 'These four remarkable novels are the most complete vision we have of Japan in the twentieth century' – Paul Theroux

☐ **The Hawthorne Goddess** Glyn Hughes £2.95

Set in eighteenth century Yorkshire where 'the heroine, Anne Wylde, represents the doom of nature and the land . . . Hughes has an arresting style, both rich and abrupt' – *The Times*

☐ **A Confederacy of Dunces** John Kennedy Toole £3.95

In this Pulitzer Prize-winning novel, in the bulky figure of Ignatius J. Reilly an immortal comic character is born. 'I succumbed, stunned and seduced . . . it is a masterwork of comedy' – *The New York Times*

☐ **The Last of the Just** André Schwartz-Bart £3.50

The story of Ernie Levy, the last of the just, who was killed at Auschwitz in 1943: 'An outstanding achievement, of an altogether different order from even the best of earlier novels which have attempted this theme' – John Gross in the *Sunday Telegraph*

PLAYS IN PENGUINS

PENGUIN BOOKS OF POETRY

THE PENGUIN POETRY LIBRARY

These books should be available at all good bookshops or news-agents, but if you live in the UK or the Republic of Ireland and have difficulty in getting to a bookshop, they can be ordered by post. Please indicate the titles required and fill in the form below.

NAME _____ BLOCK CAPITALS

ADDRESS _____

_____

_____

Enclose a cheque or postal order payable to The Penguin Bookshop to cover the total price of books ordered, plus 50p for postage. Readers in the Republic of Ireland should send £IR equivalent to the sterling prices, plus 67p for postage. Send to: The Penguin Bookshop, 54/56 Bridlesmith Gate, Nottingham, NG1 2GP.

You can also order by phoning (0602) 599295, and quoting your Barclaycard or Access number.

Every effort is made to ensure the accuracy of the price and availability of books at the time of going to press, but it is sometimes necessary to increase prices and in these circumstances retail prices may be shown on the covers of books which may differ from the prices shown in this list or elsewhere. This list is not an offer to supply any book.

This order service is only available to residents in the UK and the Republic of Ireland.

● ● ●